Best Wishes from
Joan Wallace
20/11/87

TWO OF CLUBS
by
Joan Wallace

Published by Gowan Publishing Ltd.,
Nottingham

First edition 1985

©Joan Wallace 1985

ISBN 0 947790 02 0

Typeset by Spectrum Graphics (Nottm.) Ltd., Nottingham
Printed by Cempress Ltd., Carlton, Nottingham
Cover design by Hilary Evans

Acknowledgements

The author gratefully acknowledges the help and advice of:-

Pat and George Waite, Briddocks, Parliament Street, Nottingham.
Tracy Bent (formerly Maureen Kent of the Kent Sisters).

The paperback section staffs of:-

Hudsons, Milton Street and Wheeler Gate, Nottingham.
W. H. Smiths, Victoria Centre and Lister Gate, Nottingham.

Also by JOAN WALLACE

Independent Street (published in 1984)

About the Author

Joan Wallace has lived in Nottingham all her life and was educated at the Bentinck Road Secondary and William Crane schools.

She has written over one hundred short stories — many of these have been published in the London Evening News, Nottingham Evening Post, Woman's Own and various other magazines. Her regional stories have been broadcast on radios Nottingham, Derby and Trent. She has won the Silver Jubilee Cup presented by the Nottingham Writers' Club for the best radio story and has twice been awarded their Writer of the Year award.

The author was a singer in the pubs and clubs in and around Nottingham for twenty five years and so the book is well authenticated.

To Alan

FOREWORD

Helen is a barmaid in a nightclub and bored with her work. She forms a singing duo with Rita, an effervescent blonde. After lots of hard work and practice the Dumonte Sisters act is on its way.

The book gives a marvellous insight into how it was for artistes working in the pubs and clubs in the fifties and sixties. Noisy audiences, sex-starved entertainment secretaries, scheming agents, useless microphones and archaic dressing-room facilities.

Helen and Rita work with comedians and magicians — colourful characters sparkling with personality and humour — but now, thirty years on, a dying breed being tucked away into the folds of showbusiness history.

Strippers reveal their innermost thoughts, confess what they really think about when taking off their clothes in front of an audience.

We gasp at the outrageous behaviour of the strippers, cringe at the corny jokes of the comedians, suffer the agonies of stage-fright with Helen and Rita and applaud their tenacity and success.

Jealousy, passion, love and heartache thread their way through the story but, most important of all, there is plenty of laughter. As Helen says, "When you're young and healthy and doing the kind of work you enjoy, there's plenty to laugh about."

The characters in the book are all fictionalised and bear no similarity whatsoever to anyone living or dead, with the exception of the late Jack Sargent who was a personal friend of the author and who told her many times that he would dearly love a mention in her book about showbusiness.

"TWO OF CLUBS"
by
JOAN WALLACE

An April morning in the late fifties

I shuffled reluctantly towards the end of the bus queue and thought about the boring day ahead of me. Serving food to people, clearing away crockery, then putting it all back on the tables again.

I need more excitement in my life, I thought to myself, although friends keep telling me I'm never satisfied. Divorced at twenty-four, they say, you can't get anything much more exciting than that. But getting divorced is not exciting — it is horrible. I'd rather clean the insides of a hundred gas-ovens than go through that little lot again.

Why couldn't I have been born into a theatrical family? A dad who juggled with balls and made budgies disappear up his trouser-leg? I could have been his assistant - sung a few songs in between his fire-eating and sword-swallowing.

The bus lumbered down the road and the queue, which had been individual blobs of humanity, fused like mercury into a large cluster and rolled itself onto the bus.

I looked for a vacant seat but they had all been taken. I smiled femininely at the older men but they had all been glued to the green plastic seats. I glared menacingly at a few schoolboys who were chewing on gobstoppers and other kinds of disgusting rubbish, but they chewed with mouths wide open and stared back at me defiantly.

The schoolboys were only travelling three stops — why didn't children walk to school anymore? In a few thousand years everyone will have great fat behinds and legs wasting away through lack of use, I thought. I smiled to myself at the idea of such a population and thought how lucky it was I had a zany sense of humour. And stuck inside Carlin and Priestley's restaurant five and a half days a week I needed to have a sense of the ridiculous, it was torture working there for a living.

Oh dear, my waitresses' legs were already beginning to ache. I was dying for a seat, funny how the things we can't get always seem so much more desirable!

Just like getting married — all my friends were doing it — I couldn't be left out of the fun, I had thought. But like the proverbial monkey with its hand in the sweet-jar, once you had grabbed at the sweets you couldn't get out of the jar again.

I leaned against a seat and took the weight off my left leg. Only a few more stops to go now.

What was it someone had once told me! Ah yes, I remember now. Waitresses develop great big varicose veins and thick swollen ankles. I looked down at my legs and could have sworn I saw a vein looking a bit suspect.

The bus pulled up at the stop facing the school entrance. The boys streamed from the bus with a tremendous roar, like a descant on choir practice day gone wrong. I flopped down into a seat and worried about varicose veins again.

The bus cruised into the terminus and the rest of the passengers and I were churned out of the platform of the bus like slabs of fudge on an assembly line — we scattered in all directions. I headed for Carlin & Priestley, a high-class store established in 1896. The staff were trained to look superior and look down their noses at the customers, that way they frightened you into buying things you couldn't afford. And the girls on the make-up and perfume counters all looked like painted dolls.

I hung my coat on a nail and hurried to my position in the restaurant to check if anyone had pinched my cutlery.

Oh, what a life! The morning dragged on and on and so did my poor feet. I began to feel really miserable and could not concentrate. I served toasted teacake and coffee instead of crumpets and tea, and Mrs. Dodsley, a regular misery-guts, was furious to find a man with a long beard sitting in her favourite seat by the window, she of course took it out on me.

I ushered Mrs. Dodsley to another seat and decided I must do something positive about my boring life. A new job might help? Yes, that was the answer — I would find new faces and different surroundings. I would buy a midday newspaper and have a look through the situations vacant.

I began to feel better and gave Mrs. Dodsley a friendly smile although she didn't deserve it. She had a face like a bad tempered parrot and had the most atrocious dress-sense. She always wore tons of jewellery. Today she displayed large diamond ear-rings, a sapphire and diamond brooch, rings on five of her fingers and rows and rows of pearls round her neck. Oh, and three gold teeth in her upper dentures. I bet she slept in a safe at night or at least I'll bet her dentures did!

At lunchtime I bribed the chef with a bottle of his favourite brown ale and he packed some chicken sandwiches for me which I sneaked out in my handbag. I bought a newspaper and set off for the Castle grounds which were ideal for a leisurely lunch and a quiet perusal of the situations vacant.

Secretary wanted ... telephonist ... pastry shop manageress ... dry-cleaners assistant. No, I didn't fancy any of those. Ah-ha, here was something more like it! 'Attractive cocktail barmaids wanted for new exclusive nightclub on the outskirts of the city. Experience not necessary, will train. Aged 18-30. Six nights a week with meals provided and late night transport home. Very good wages to right applicants'.

I dialled the number of the club. "Hello ... I'm ringing about the vacancy ... er, cocktail-barmaid." The receptionist told me to wait a moment. Now a man's voice asked the questions. I replied in a husky voice which I hoped sounded sexy.

"Yes ... all right. Friday at eight then. Oh yes, I know where the club is ... I can get a bus in the city centre, bring me almost to the door. Pardon? Oh yes, I'm sorry ... my name's Helen ... Helen Linsey."

CHAPTER ONE

I arrived at the Cresta club ten minutes before the arranged time. The doorman told me to wait near the bar and I stood with one leg in front of the other posing and hoping I looked like the sophisticated, cocktail-bar type of woman.

The Cresta club had obviously only recently been refurbished and smelled deliciously of fresh wood, paint and leather. There was a tiny dance floor and at the back of this a stage. Three musicians played with sensitivity, I liked the feel of the place immediately.

A tall blonde was also waiting, but at the other end of the bar. She must have come for an interview as well. She had on lots of make-up and a large cocktail-barmaid bust thrusting out from underneath a very tight fitting sweater. I felt very plain at the side of her and wished I hadn't bothered to turn up for the interview. I should have realised they would only want lots of glamorous types behind the bar. Oh well, I was here now — may as well go through with it.

The door marked 'Private' opened and a well-made confident looking man, in his early fifties I guessed, beckoned to the blonde. He looked in my direction and called out, "Be with you in a few minutes, love".

I smiled at him and tried to look worldly and glamorous but felt stupid and plain.

Ten minutes ticked themselves away into history and then the door opened once more. The blonde walked towards me smiling and said, "Mr. Bowler will see you now. He says go on in".

The big man pointed towards a chair and I sat down gratefully because my legs felt trembly. We then went through a kind of one act play for two.

"How old are you then, Helen?"

"I'm twenty four."

"Have you done this sort of work before?"

"No ... not this sort exactly ... but I'm used to serving people."

"Can you add up? ... I don't want girls who can't add up."

"Oh yes ... I can add up very well. I do it all the time at Carlin and Priestley's."

"No family commitments of any sort? No husband complaining about the late hours you'd have to keep?"

"No ... I'm ... er ... divorced." The stigma always there.

"No children needing babysitters? You'd need one six nights a week."

"No ... no children." I felt myself blushing. "No children."

On and on we went. I sensed he liked me and realised it was all a game to him. An unfair game because experience or none, if a man liked the look of you then it was ninety nine per cent certain you would get the job — especially if he had an eye for the women and was on the wrong side of forty.

9

He rubbed his hands together and asked, "Well then, Helen ... when can you start?"

I tried to swallow but no saliva came. I tried again but my mouth felt as though it was filled with dry toast. I coughed and cleared my throat.

"I can start anytime, Mr. Bowler ... anytime convenient to you. I'll have to serve a week's notice at the restaurant but I can start here as soon as you want me ... it won't affect my daytime job." It was done — I was in.

"Right you are then, Helen ... we'll see you next Monday at eight." He put his hand on my shoulder and stroked it in a fatherly way. "You'll like working here, Helen ... we're all one big happy family."

"Oh, I'm sure I will, Mr. Bowler."

"You just call me, Ray." His hand pressed my shoulder more firmly. "Everybody calls me, Ray."

He opened the door for me and led me towards the cocktail-bar.

"You'll soon get the hang of it, Helen. Nice little job ... plenty of tips for the right girl." He winked at me. "Know what I mean, love? Butter the men up a bit ... get them to spend their money."

He opened the door at the entrance of the club for me and I stepped out into the warm April night.

The moon was almost full and smiled down at me from the middle of a star glistening backcloth of deep blue. It was the kind of night you wanted to store away forever in a secret corner of your mind. I was so happy I wanted to cry. I had not felt this way since I had been in love.

I walked down the main street and window-gazed for a while then I caught a bus back into the city centre.

My mind was brimming over with excitement. And to think that at the beginning of the week I had been terribly depressed because of the lack of excitement in my life. No more of that nonsense, I told myself, life itself is exciting — you never know what's waiting round the corner. The world was full of Cresta clubs — you just had to go out and find them.

10

CHAPTER TWO

Monday evening I made my way down the tiny side street, which was tucked away at the back of rows of shops, and arrived at the entrance to the Cresta club once more. I opened the door and the doorman beamed a welcome. His cheeky grin heightened my confidence and I thought if the men didn't like the looks of me tonight they never would.

My make-up had taken ages to apply and I had treated my hair to a new colour-rinse. It was blue-black, the colour of Victoria plums and the conditioner in the rinse had given my hair a lovely sheen. I had suffered the discomfort of sleeping in about fifty hair-grips and this had given my hair lots of natural looking waves and curls.

I had chosen to wear my cream woollen dress which was high at the neck and snug fitting. I was proud of my tiny waist and liked to accentuate it whenever possible. I had stuffed my bra with cottonwool so I went in-and-out at all the right places.

The doorman pointed to a door at the far end of the room and said, "You can hang your coat up in there, love. Take your handbag behind the bar with you."

I sat on a stool in front of the staff-room mirror and patted at my hair. I applied more lipstick although there was no need as my mouth was already daubed with extra layers of bright red. I always pat my hair and plonk more lipstick on my lips when I'm nervous.

I took a deep breath and walked across to the bar. The blonde was already there — I might have known he wouldn't be able to resist her charms.

"Hello ... I'm Rita." She smiled at me and rubbed vigorously at a whisky glass with a tea towel.

"Oh, hello ... I'm Helen." I tucked my handbag behind two bottles of lime-juice and took up my position behind the bar.

The trio started to play 'I Remember April' which pleased and relaxed me as it was one of my favourites.

Rita proved to be a great help. She had worked as a barmaid in quite a few pubs and clubs she told me and also didn't mind showing me how to go on.

"You'll soon get to know 'what's what'," she polished another glass and held it up to the light. "You can earn damned good money if you know 'what's what'."

I picked up a beer glass and emulated her and wondered what the devil she meant by 'what's what'. Perhaps she was an alcoholic?

Customers started to drift in at about ten o'clock. They were mainly representatives and leaned against the bar or sat at the tables in small groups. Rita and I had one or two drinks bought for us but the men didn't seem to want to throw their money about.

"They're on expenses," Rita explained, "it'll be better at the week-end when everybody's been paid."

Rita and I took turns to go for our free meal. The staff did not have much of a choice — no posh à la carte or prawn cocktails for starters, but what we did get was well cooked and very appetising.

In between serving the customers Rita and I chatted together and by the end of the evening were getting along splendidly. She seemed more worldly than I but her dry sense of humour and endless hilarious anecdotes soon broke down the barriers of shyness.

The bar closed at two o'clock and by two fifteen we had checked the two tills and tidied up the bar. A taxi arrived at two thirty to take us both home.

Rita lived nearest the club so we dropped her off first then continued on up to Malperry where I had been living since my divorce.

I prepared myself for bed and was soon snuggling down into the comfort and warmth. I pulled the top sheet over my face — just my nose and mouth sticking out — I felt safe in the womb of bedclothes.

I thought about Ray Bowler. He seemed very nice, a good sort to work for. He had put his arm around my waist and given me a squeeze when I had poured a bottle of beer too quickly, half the contents frothing all over the bar counter. A bit different to the restaurant manageress at Carlin and Priestley's who was always moaning and took it out of her waitresses whenever she had a hangover — which was frequently.

★ ★ ★ ★ ★ ★ ★ ★ ★ ★ ★ ★ ★ ★ ★ ★ ★

The days catapulted themselves into weeks and Rita and I became very good friends. When the weather permitted we went along to the lido in the afternoons and lazed about on the grass lawns getting gorgeous suntans. On rainy or cold afternoons we went to the cinema or did shopping. The mornings of course were spent in bed as we were usually late getting off to sleep.

Not much time for dating but nevertheless Rita found herself a boyfriend.

"He's got a smashing house up at Bradcote ... the driveways are all full of Jaguars and Mercs." She popped a handful of nuts into her mouth and continued, "His parents died and left him pots of money. He owns loads of newsagents shops. He's very generous ... always buys me doubles when he takes me out anywhere."

Rita was always impressed if a man bought her doubles. I pulled her leg a bit.

"I should hope he does treat you to doubles. He only takes you out on Sundays ... oh and sometimes for a quick one before you come on duty."

"I'll soon be seeing much more of him," she answered, "he's applied for membership here ... says he wants to keep an eye on me." She looked very pleased with herself. "He's ever so jealous of me. I daren't chat anybody up ... not when he's looking." She reached for two glasses and looked round the room. "Where's old Bow-legs?" Her name for Ray Bowler. "I'll pour us a drink while the coast's clear. Fancy a drop of gin, kid?"

I looked round nervously. This was part of the 'what's what' Rita had told me about. Free drinks whenever we could pinch a few. Everybody in the trade did it, Rita had informed me, the bosses knew it went on and turned a blind-eye. But it still made me nervous until she had actually poured the drink into the glasses. Then we just had to say a customer had treated us to the drinks. If we had been asked which customer, then all we had to say was he's just left.

We were just having a good guzzle of our free drinks when the door marked 'Private' opened and Ray walked across to the bar. He looked immaculate, as usual. Beautifully hand tailored pale grey suit. White freshly laundered shirt and dark grey tie with a faint silver stripe. Black highly polished real leather shoes and a handkerchief neatly folded into his breast pocket.

Rita held her glass in the air and looking over to the dance floor said to nobody in particular, "Happy birthday ... cheers, love ... all the best." I was too nervous to say anything so I gulped down a mouthful of gin-and-orange and quickly found a glass that needed polishing.

"Bit busier tonight, girls." Ray rubbed his hands together and his large diamond ring sent out sparks of technicolor. It could have passed for an imitation ring from Woolworths, but everything about Ray Bowler shouted rich — the diamond must have been real all right.

Ray carried on rubbing his hands together and said, "We've got some first class entertainment on tonight, girls. Makes a big difference when you get a good artist. Very nice singer they tell me. She'd better be ... her agent charged me five quid over the top. He says she's been on the radio ... and done a bit round the halls. I don't mind paying for something good. You've got to speculate to accumulate ... as the vicar said to the pregnant members of his mothers' union. Now how did the rest of that joke go?"

"Would you like your usual, Ray?" I asked him.

"Yes please, Helen. A nice large one with just a trace of soda for my digestion. Ha-ha-ha."

I poured the drink and handed it to him with a smile, hoping that he hadn't cottoned on about our free drinks. He didn't appear to be concerned about what we were drinking but leaned against the bar and continued, "Been on the television as well, you know. Sings songs from the shows ... none of this pop rubbish. Pop stuff wouldn't go down here anyway ... we've got a good class of clientele."

Rita looked at me and I raised my eyebrows ever so slightly.

"We've got the law in tonight, darlings." Ray nodded towards a table at the front of the stage. "Mind how you go. Close the bar dead on two. That's him over there look, talking to Jim, make a fuss of him, girls. He's a nice enough bloke, even though he is with the law. He's got to do his job, hasn't he? If he picks a woman up and she's," he winked at us, "you know what ... he'll bogger off early. I'll just go and have a word ... like to keep friendly ... never know when you're going to need them."

Ray walked over to where the young detective was sitting and sat down at the table. Ray smiled an over friendly smile and looked like an advertisement in a dentist's waiting-room.

The club filled up — the noise got louder and the smoke got denser. Men from the surrounding pubs hurried into the club after having their other beer supply cut off. One or two of them had already had enough to drink but as long as they behaved reasonably and kept flashing money around that was all right with Ray Bowler.

The girl singer arrived. Her first performance was to be at eleven and the next spot at one o'clock. She was carrying a large battered suitcase and a red patent leather handbag. Tall and blonde with a figure like Jane Russell she looked stunning. An out of the ordinary looking girl — the way I always thought artists should try to look — a real stagey type.

Ray was by her side quicker than a popped champagne cork. He took a hold on her

13

suitcase and ushered her past the bar into his private room.

We listened hard as they passed by the front of the bar and heard him say, "You come and get changed in my office, love. You'll be nice and warm in there. Turns a bit chilly in the evenings, doesn't it!"

"She'll be red hot when he gets cracking," said Rita and promptly poured two more gins into our glasses.

A little before eleven the musicians went across to Ray's office for a quick look through the singer's music. A few minutes later they returned to the stage followed by Ray. He took hold of the microphone then blew into it, checking to see if it was working correctly. He had another blow then said loudly, "Ladies and gentlemen! May I have your attention, please! It is cabaret time once again at the Cresta. We have for your entertainment ... a beautiful young lady of television and radio fame who will delight you with her lovely singing voice. Ladies and gentlemen ... may I present ... Adele."

Adele tottered across the room on gold shoes, which had two and a half inch heels, and climbed onto the stage. She was dressed in a dark blue sequin covered gown which was cut very low at the front and exposed almost all of her thirty eight 'C' cup bosom. She bent forwards as she took the microphone from Ray and her breasts wobbled like jellies in a gale.

"Good evening, everyone," she spoke in a half whisper, "how very nice it is to be here at the fabulous Cresta club. I would like to open my first spot with a selection from that wonderful show ... Oklahoma."

The pianist gave her a few opening bars and she was away with her first number, 'I'm just a girl who can't say no'. The band played enthusiastically and Adele's voice boomed out from every loudspeaker in the room.

"With a figure like hers, who needs a voice?" Rita giggled and added, "the song's much too high for her."

I agreed and whispered back, "I think she'd be a lot better singing some of the pop stuff. Still, she's getting paid good money for her efforts ... and Ray seems to be enjoying her." I nodded towards Ray. "Look at the expression on his face ... he thinks her singing's terrific by the looks of him."

"It's not her voice, you dope," Rita whispered back, "she'd better look out later on."

Adele received mild applause from the audience at the end of her first song but it didn't seem to bother her. She bowed and smiled as though receiving a standing ovation and wobbled her breasts as much as she could.

The applause died down and she spoke into the microphone once more.

"And now ... ladies and gentlemen ... I would like to give you ... Out of my Dreams." She giggled and looked at Ray. "I would like to tell you about one or two things from out of my dreams ... but you'd only be shocked."

She giggled again and turned towards the boys in the trio. "O.K. ... let's go, boys."

The boys played her introduction and she commenced warbling again. After she had sung the opening verse Adele stepped down from the stage, swung the microphone flex behind her very professionally, and bent low over Ray. Everyone in the room was watching them now. Ray chewed on the end of his cigar furiously — it went up and down like a miniature see-saw.

Rita turned to me and said, "It's enough to turn sane people to drink." Two more free gins found their way into our glasses.

After Adele had finished the final song of her first spot Ray led her by the arm over to the bar.

"Large brandy and soda please, Rita." Ray smiled at Adele and added, "What would you like to drink, love? A nice drop of mother's ruin, eh?" Adele looked into his eyes, eyelashes fluttering like a Japanese maiden's fan.

"Oh, I'd love the same as you, Mr. Bowler please ... a nice drop of brandy with just a touch of soda. It's ever so good for the voice you know."

"Should hear a slight improvement then," Rita whispered to me after turning her back to reach for the soda syphon. I tried hard not to laugh.

"A nice large brandy for our little canary," Ray gushed, because it was obvious that every man in the room was watching him and the voluptuous lady singer.

Peculiar thing that, I thought, most artists seemed to have a special attraction - a charisma that they all seemed to be born with.

Rita handed the drink to Adele and asked, "Have you had your voice trained then, love?"

"Oh no," Adele was thrilled and flattered with the question. "Never ... ! it just seems to flow out of me quite naturally. I've always had an ear for music though, so that helps tremendously. You have to have a sensitive ear for music." Her bosom heaved up and down as she sipped at her drink.

"Oh, anybody can see you're ever so sensitive," Ray agreed.

"I read somewhere." Adele liked to talk a lot as well as sing, I noted. "Now where did I read it? Oh yes, in the Daily Telegraph I think it was." Now she was showing off her reading habits too.

"I read in the Daily Telegraph that Frank Sinatra or somebody famous like him didn't have his voice trained either ... and look where he got." Adele perched herself on a stool.

"Yes," Ray puffed at his cigar, "and he hasn't got a pair of lungs like you, love. You should go far with a pair of lungs like you've got." Ray goggled at the place where her lungs were.

Adele laughed loud and rather too long which made her sound far too common for a Daily Telegraph reader, I thought. I could not imagine somehow, Adele scrutinising all the comings and goings of the royal family in the Court and Social columns.

Ray put his arm around Adele's waist and gave her one of his fatherly squeezes. Adele responded, not quite like a daughter, and pressed her right thigh against his left thigh. The end of Ray's cigar had burnt itself out, but the end of something else was probably glowing to make up for it, I thought.

Ray ordered two more large brandies and ushered Adele towards his office.

"Now she's got to earn her return booking," said Rita. The customers came up to the bar for refills and we were kept busy for a while. I forgot all about Ray and Adele until I saw the boys in the trio making their way to Ray's office once more for another quick look at Adele's music.

The bass player knocked on the office door and it was quite a while before the door finally opened and Ray let them inside.

Adele followed the musicians across to the stage once more and again took hold of the microphone and announced her first song, "Ladies and gentlemen ... I would now like to give you ... The Nuns' Chorus."

Rita and I stood mesmerised. Nobody on earth could have looked less like a nun.

15

Her dress was bright orange jersey silk. It looked as though it had been sewn onto her skin. Her breasts looked as though they would flop out of the boned platform they were resting on at any moment. Her ears were adorned with long swaying diamante ear-rings and they caught the beams of light from the spotlight making her look like an orange Christmas tree.

"Holy maid ... lend your aid ... let the convent save me."

"Oh dear ... it would take more than a convent to save her," Rita started to giggle. "I don't know about holy maid! ... the Pope would have his work cut out saving her."

The audience had had two more hours in which to consume more alcohol and when Adele had finished her song they applauded loudly. Adele bowed low - her breasts wavering precariously on the brink of disaster. The applause went even louder than before.

"Thank you everyone, so much." Adele blew a kiss to the boys in the trio. "And now the boys and I will give you a lovely medley of songs written by that fine composer ... Ivor Novello."

The trio played a few opening bars and Adele began to sing her first number. 'My dearest dear.' The audience stopped chattering. She stepped down from the stage. The main lights had been turned off, only the table lights were switched on and these gave a nice intimate glow from beneath the red brocade lamp-shades.

Adele rubbed her fingers through a grinning fat man's hair and sang as though for him alone. The fat man's female companion was smiling but the smile was the sort that makes your face ache when posing for a photograph to be taken. When Adele moved away from their table the woman gave her companion a drop-dead look but he just grinned and gulped down his gin-and-tonic.

Adele now selected a young man in his early twenties. She sat on his knee and put an arm around his neck. He looked embarrassed and his friends looked envious. The young man tried to look at her face but I think he had difficulty because her breasts were in the way.

Adele released the young man from his ordeal and selected a man with a shiny bald head. She sat on the man's knee and kissed his head, leaving the bright red imprint of her lips on his shiny dome.

"Oh ... I don't think I'd fancy kissing bald heads," I pulled a face at Rita, "not strange ones anyway."

"I'll bet she's not fussy what she kisses ... just look at her performing with that old bloke." Rita stood with arms folded across her chest. "If she doesn't get off his knee quick ... we'll be 'phoning for an ambulance ... he'll have a heart attack!" We stifled laughter and continued to watch the performance and the antics of the audience - I had an idea about the whole set-up, but decided to keep it to myself because the more I thought about it the more preposterous it seemed.

After her final song Adele walked slowly across to Ray's office to get changed once more. Ray allowed her a few minutes then he too went into his office.

The customers had been quite generous and the glass holding our tips was almost full. Nearly two o'clock - the customers fluttered round the bar anxious to have just 'one more' before leaving.

We closed the bar and the customers started to drift away. A few men lingered, the men who lived by themselves perhaps, I thought, men who were desperately lonely or unhappy - men who were afraid of their own company, and a few women also who felt the same way. They were searching for something special out of life, I guessed, but probably wouldn't recognise it if they found it. Clubs could be very depressing places at two o'clock in the morning I decided. I counted change for tomorrow's float and tried not to think too much about it.

At half-past two Ray and Adele came out of the office - I noticed that this time Adele carried her own suitcase.

"Bye for now then, love ... see you soon." Ray perched himself on a bar stool. "And don't forget to confirm the booking, either in writing, or you can give me a ring a week before."

"Bye bye, Ray ... and thank you for a lovely evening. I've really enjoyed working here." Adele sounded weary. She looked like a child does when hurrying away after a duty visit to an aged relative - eager to escape yet anxious to do so without seeming impolite.

"Bye bye, girls," she glanced towards us, "see you again." Only the faint aroma of her perfume remained. Our star of radio and television fame stepped into her waiting taxi and was whisked away.

"I'll have a large brandy please, Helen," Ray smiled at me, "just to round a very pleasant evening off." He lit a cigar and leaned with elbows on the bar. "Have a drink on me, girls. Takings should be good tonight. Lovely singer, that Adele ... bit of class about her. That's what this club needs ... good class artists. You can bring 'em in when you put a good show on." He blew cigar smoke into the air and watched the spiralling mistiness - then he finished his drink and took the bar takings through to the safe in his office.

"Goodnight, Ray."

"Oh ... goodnight, girls."

"What do you think they got up to?" I asked Rita as we put on our coats.

"Your guess is as good as mine," Rita yawned. "I wonder if he's made arrangements to take her out?"

"Don't know ... she didn't seem very bothered about him when she was leaving."

"No need ... not once she'd got a return booking."

"Not a bad life is it, Rita? Good money ... plenty of free drinks ... and lots of attention from men."

"Sounds like our jobs," Rita waved to the taxi-driver. "Only we don't have to kiss bald heads."

"Hey-up, ladies," the taxi-driver leaned over and opened the door for us. "You two are always laughing about summat. Had a good night, have you then?" I expect he hoped we had because then he would get a good tip.

I thought about what the taxi-driver had said. Yes, we were always laughing. Well, I thought, if you don't get fun out of life when you're twenty four, when do you start.

I snuggled down in the car seat contented and ready for sleep.

CHAPTER THREE

The idea I'd had the night Adele had appeared at the Cresta would not leave my mind. I decided to see what Rita thought and asked, "What do you think to the standard ... of the singers we get at the club?"

"All right, I suppose," Rita nibbled on a few salted nuts. "Some of the comedians are a bit pathetic, but the singers aren't too bad."

"I used to do a bit of singing," I helped myself to some salt and vinegar crisps. "I belonged to a drama group ... we used to do concerts to raise money for scenery. Everybody said they liked my singing."

"Oh ... are you going to give us a song tonight then?" Rita laughed. I ignored her remark and continued, "And you're not a bad singer either. I've heard you singing along to the trio ... you've got a nice voice."

"You haven't heard the concerts I give in my bathroom."

"Listen, Rita ... I'm being serious. How about you and me teaming up? I'll have a go at the harmony and you sing straight. We could do as well as some of the artists that appear here ... if not better."

"You're having me on!" Rita chewed on more salted nuts. "I wouldn't dare! I've never done anything like that,"

"Everybody has to learn." I could see she was interested.

"But how would we go about it?"

"We'd learn songs from records ... buy sheet music and learn the words and practice the harmony as we went along."

"But we're stuck here at the club every night!" Rita put obstacles in the way of stardom. "It wouldn't be any use going to all that trouble ... not while we're working here at the Cresta."

"We get Sundays off." I would not let go of the idea. "That's when all the clubs and pubs want artists. I don't mean nightclubs ... I was thinking more of the miners' welfares and the working mens' clubs, that sort of place."

"But say we learnt a few songs ... then how would we go about getting bookings?" Rita still held back.

"An agent of course ... let an agent do all the work. Then all we'd have to do is turn up at the clubs and pubs he sorts out for us."

"You're nuts!" Rita poured two large gins and handed one to me. "Stark raving mad. We can't just ... er ... well we can't!" She was wavering. A couple more gins and she would be ready to sing a song at the Cresta, I thought. I was confident we could get an act together. I would plan everything and Rita would not be able to resist.

"When we've practised a few songs, we could get your cousin Vera to make some lovely evening gowns. All we'd need are some glamorous gowns ... the same style,

18

because we'd be a sister act. All sister acts dress the same. We could have beautiful satins and velvets ... get the material from the stall on the market ... the one owned by those two brothers Mad Mike and Honest Harry."

"Yes, we could have black velvet gowns with great big slits up each side." Rita downed the rest of her gin. "The men would love that ... plenty of thigh on show."

"It would look terrific, Rita. Black velvet with some sparkling jewellery."

"And we could balance our busts on boned platforms, like Adele."

."And we could wear black fishnet stockings and have the dresses made really tight ... that tight we wouldn't be able to wear any knickers."

We polished glasses, poured drinks, smiled at the customers and planned. Our fantastic dream was shattered for a while by the appearance of a crowd of young and not so young, smartly dressed men who walked across to the bar and commenced joking and larking about.

"Oh no!" Rita pulled a face. "Here's that bunch of dynamic crisp salesmen again! The last of the bigtime tippers ... I don't think."

"Good evening, gentlemen." I smiled my barmaid's welcoming smile. "This sure is our lucky night. Eight hunks of gorgeous manhood all under one roof. I don't know where to look first."

"The door marked exit," whispered Rita, "here we go ... eyes down, look in, kid."

"Well hello there, darlings." A gorgeous hunk of manhood who looked like an owl with a moustache eyed us up-and-down. "Have you missed me, you little darlings?"

"Missed you ... I'll say I've missed you, handsome. Since you promised me your body last week I haven't been able to sleep properly. And look at the weight I've lost. I've been living on liquid refreshment."

"Oh yeah ... liquid gin was it? You need one of my meat injections, darlin' ... that'd soon put some weight on you." He twiddled his moustache and his eyes looked as though they were going to pop out of his head.

How boring and predictable men were, I thought, they must all share the same joke book. Men had been offering me their meat injections for years now, even the schoolboys were on to that one.

"By the way," Owl-face continued, "talking about weight reminds me of a joke. There was this priest you see ... regular kind like ... boozer, womaniser and in on the Bingo fiddles at the church-hall. Well this priest went visiting all the young widows and there was this nice young piece who hadn't had a bit of ... "

"Come on now, boys," Rita interrupted the joke, "let's have your order please. You must all be very thirsty after eating all those salty crisps." She pulled down her sweater and her breasts jutted out temptingly.

"Er ... right you are then, love. Eight halves of your best bitter."

"Blimey," Rita looked cheeky, "don't go mad with your expenses. There'll be a steward's enquiry at your next board meeting if you carry on like that. I tell you what though, boys." She lowered her voice to conspiratorial level. "We've had some lovely bottles of champagne delivered this morning. It's ever so cheap as well ... Mr. Bowler got a special cheap consignment because he ordered extra."

"Oooh ... hark at her," Owl-face helped himself to nuts, "you must think we're loaded."

"No, listen," Rita continued, "the beer's like water here and it'll only make you feel bloated. The champagne's only two quid a bottle. Have a bottle each and you won't

19

have a bad head in the morning either. And it'll draw the women like a magnet. Women can't resist champagne ... nor the men who are buying it."

The men went into a huddle like a refined rugby scrum.

"Two quid a bottle." A podgy salesman who was wearing a toupèe which had a parting down the side, like Hitler used to wear his hair, chimed in the conversation. "Can't be much cop for two quid. What's in it ... maid's water?" He roared with laughter at his own superlative wit and his three chins joined in the frivolity. "Bottle it yourselves, did you?"

"Those wigs stay on your head in a wind tunnel with the wind blowing at a hundred miles an hour." Rita whispered as she straightened a beer-mat on the counter. "I saw an advert once in a hair-clinic's window."

"Yes, I know," I replied, "the wigs stay on your head ... but your flesh blows off your body."

"Attention please, girls." Owl-face made his decision. "I'd like a bottle of champers, please. I feel like going mad tonight." He opened his wallet and took out two pound notes. As far as I could see that was all he had in his wallet. His friends agreed to champagne and soon the corks were popping. This drew attention from the rest of the customers and one or two unattached women moved in - invisible free drink antennas quivering in anticipation.

Ray, who had been chatting up a bored looking blonde excused himself and came over to the bar. Something about Ray which I admired tremendously - he looked the part - always in control - talked and moved with ease, and tonight as usual, immaculately dressed. His dark brown silk jacket and cream coloured trousers looked casual but elegant. He had style this man and he knew it.

"Eight bottles of that special vintage champagne gone, Ray." Rita sounded businesslike but her eyes sparkled with devilment. "We'll probably need a few more bottles later on."

Yes, I thought, when the women start guzzling it. Not very often the Cresta hostesses got a chance to drink champagne As soon as they had latched themselves on to a man they usually ordered lager or a bottle of beer. They had to wait until the man was well-oiled before they had spirits and then there was the free meal of course, if they picked the right mug.

"My word," Ray rubbed his hands together, "some very discerning gentlemen drinkers in the club this evening. Would you just like to nip down the cellar with me, Helen ... help me carry some bottles up to the bar?"

The cellar was dimly lit and smelled musty like the old caves you find underneath castles. I held onto the piece of rope which ran down one side of the cellar steps and tried not to stumble in my high-heeled shoes.

"Didn't think we'd get rid of that rubbish as quickly as this, Helen." Ray's voice echoed round the racks of cobwebbed bottles - the bottles looked like rows of monstrous spiders sleeping in their home spun shrouds.

"It smells very musty down here, Ray," I wrinkled my nose, "just like a dog's fur when it's been out in the rain."

Ray laughed and replied, "I'll bet some of these bottles are older than you, love. You have to keep them nice and cool ... handle them with care. Not like a woman ey, Helen!" He put an arm around my waist and gave me a squeeze. Keep a woman nice and hot and treat her rough."

I wriggled from his grasp and said, "We'd better get that champagne."

He reached out for a bottle but instead of selecting champagne took hold of a bottle of red wine. He handled the wine gently— cradled it in his hands as though it were a delicate baby.

"Fetch us two glasses and a corkscrew. I want to try this one ... you can see what you think as well."

I did as he asked and hurried back into the cellar. Ray opened the red wine and sniffed at the contents then he poured some into the two glasses. He handed a glass to me.

"It's my birthday today, Helen. Wish me happy birthday."

"Oh ... very many happy returns, Ray." I held out my glass.

Ray stepped towards me and said, "Don't I get a kiss then?" I backed away thinking how on earth do I get out of this situation. I thought quickly and decided to laugh it off. Men were always put off when you laughed at their advances. I laughed and it sounded peculiar— echoey laughter reverberating round the cold cellar.

But Ray was persistent and got me in a clinch. I let him kiss me and his moustache tickled the end of my nose.

"How about that then?" Ray still held me in his arms. "Can't beat kissing a man with a moustache. Kiss a man without a moustache and it's like eating strawberries without the cream." He slid his hand over my left breast so I wriggled free and pushed him away. Birthday or no birthday, I thought, he was not going to have me as one of his presents! I finished my wine and asked, "Shall I carry some champagne up for you then?"

"You can carry this for me." Ray rubbed at the front of his trousers. "You're a lovely looking girl you know, Helen ... bloody lovely."

I grabbed two bottles of champagne and rushed up the cellar steps as fast as I could without tripping.

"I'm only normal," Ray shouted after me, "I'm only normal, Helen!" I placed the bottles on the counter and said to Rita, "You can help Ray with the rest of the bottles." To my surprise Rita began to laugh.

"What's the matter, Helen ... is Ray having another one of his birthdays?"

"Oh ... I see." So that was it, I thought, Rita had experienced a similar groping session. Nevertheless, it was all very embarrassing.

The salesmen were nearly all dancing now. If you can call pressing up close to someone and moving your feet up and down dancing! Owl was dancing with a tall brunette, a lovely looking woman who knew how to extract the goodies from the meanest of men. Marian had worked at the club in the old days— before Ray had taken over— she was a professional eater but had still managed to retain her gorgeous figure. Owl started to kiss Marian's neck but she remained impassive and stared into fresh air.

"He's wasting his time," Rita nodded in their direction, "wait till she finds out he's only a crisp salesman."

"Yes ... old Marian goes more for the director type ... or a rich bookie like Sam. By the way, I haven't seen old Sam for ages. What's happened to him, do you know, Rita? I like Sam ... he always buys me a gin."

"Oh ... Sam's wife found out about him and Marian. Sam made Marian a non-runner after his wife had threatened divorce. He used to take Marian all over the place you know. Lots of race-meetings and week-ends in Brighton. Still ... you know what they say ... all good things must come to an end."

"Yes," I giggled, "and I think I know what sort of end you're talking about. Marian will want more than a tin of crisps if she performs tonight."

The music stopped— the dancers returned to seats or leaning positions against the bar. Toupèe ordered another bottle of champagne and smiled at Lorraine, another club-hostess, with an outsize appetite for food and an unquenchable thirst for whisky and orange.

"Lorraine's just hooked herself another fish." I whispered to Rita.

"What will it be?" Rita smiled at them.

"Oh ... I think I'll try a whisky and orange, please." Lorraine held on to Toupèe's arm and radiated a smile at him straight between the eyes.

"But I've ordered champagne, darling." Toupèe looked anxious.

"Oh ... you can manage to drink another bottle," Lorraine would not budge from her decision. "And I'm feeling a bit hungry, aren't you? Should we have a teensie bite to eat?"

What a saleswoman, I thought, wait till she starts to order her planned teensie meal, he'll have a fit when he gets the bill. I hoped he'd brought his cheque-book because his wallet had looked empty.

Lorraine got her way and they sat down at a table, Toupèe studying his wallet and Lorraine studying the menu.

"You know, he's quite an attractive man." Rita nodded towards Toupèe. I like big, jolly men. I don't know why men like that have to wear wigs. They'd look much better if they accepted their baldness. To tell you the truth ... if a man's got a good personality I never notice his hair much. I tend to look at his face all the time. I look to see if a man's got a kind mouth and nice eyes. If he's lost his hair doesn't matter at all. And anyway," she laughed, "they say it's a sign of a man's vigorous sexual powers. Bald-headed men are all supposed to be ever so sexy."

"They're bound to feel awful though." I hadn't thought about the subject very much before. "Think how we'd feel if our hair suddenly started falling out."

"It's a wonder mine hasn't ... all the rinses and stuff I put on it." Rita rubbed her fingers through her platinum blonde curls. "I think I might be a redhead next month. I love wearing green and green goes lovely with red hair."

Lorraine and Marian were now both tucking into fillet steaks. They smiled at us in between mouthfuls of mushrooms, braised asparagus, creamed potatoes and carrots.

"I'm glad I'm not those two." Rita nodded in their direction. "All that bouncing about later on. It's ever so bad for your digestion! Here you are, a nice gin before I call time," she poured the drinks and added, "I couldn't eat a large meal at this time in the morning if you paid me."

We sipped at our drinks and commenced washing the glasses. The night ebbed gently away but nobody seemed to notice— they were all working hard at enjoying themselves. But eventually, the last tune was played, the last drink was swallowed down and the last behind was stroked.

Rita and I emptied the tills and tidied the bar. We talked once more about our plans and I lost my feeling of tiredness which was always there at the end of every evening. Rita checked to see if Ray was looking then poured two more gins. "To celebrate our future success as singing stars," she clinked my glass with hers, "here's mud in your eye,

22

kid."

"Oh ... I've got stars in mine," I answered her, "good health and lots of laughs." I felt it was important to laugh a lot, it was good for your soul.

CHAPTER FOUR

Saturday morning Rita and I met outside Carlin and Priestley's as arranged then we set off for the music store. At the store we thumbed through the top-twenty list. We didn't fancy anything in the top-twenty so we then looked through the ballads, standards and songs from the shows.

"I like this one." Rita held up a book with a photograph of a relaxed looking Frank Sinatra on the cover. The contents included 'Blue Moon', 'The Lady is a Tramp' and 'All the Way'.

"How about some of these?" I thumbed through a selection from Oklahoma. The songs included 'Out of my Dreams', 'Oh What a Beautiful Morning' and 'Many a New Day' which were all very popular songs of the moment.

As long as I live I will never forget that first morning in the music shop. I already felt like a real artiste. My imagination went zooming off again - I imagined we were selecting music for our debut at the Talk of the Town. I could see Rita and me flying off in a 'plane to record a programme for American television.

It was very important that we had a good opening number - something people would always associate with our act. I thought and thought and at last had a brain-wave. We would open our act with 'Sisters'. It would be ideal. I knew other sister acts used the song but it wouldn't matter. I asked the shop assistant if he had a copy in stock. Just one left, there it was waiting in the bottom drawer for us. The assistant rolled the copy up and popped it in the bag with the rest of our selections.

I took hold of Rita's arm when we got outside the shop and told her, "We have now got to learn every word ... we have got to practice like mad until we are word perfect. We must go over the songs again and again until we're sick to death of hearing them."

Rita nodded agreement then added, "Well, now we're fixed up with the songs, how about going down the market to have a look at some material?"

"O.K." I agreed, "but let's nip into Carlin and Priestley's first for a snack. I could just fancy a nice cup of coffee with real cream."

We walked back to Carlin and Priestley's and took the lift up to the fifth floor. We ordered coffee, spaghetti on toast and chocolate éclairs. I had a quick word with one or two of the waitresses and told them about my job at the Cresta. They were very interested in my cocktail barmaid's job but when I casually mentioned that Rita and I were going into showbusiness they stood with their mouths open. I piled on the agony, loving all the attention we were getting. "And of course," I sipped at my coffee, "we're going to get ourselves an agent."

"Oooh! ... you lairy pair of boggers!" Nancy, the oldest waitress at the restaurant, looked impressed. "Will yer be on the television or 'owt like that then?"

"Probably ... later on when we've established our act," said Rita.

"Will yer be on at any of the Welfares?"

"Our pub has acts on at the week-ends, come to our pub."

"Blimey, Helen ... you've got cracking since yer left here. Ey up ... yer want to watch them there club secretaries 'an all. They'll have hold of yer if yer don't watch out."

"Give 'em a smack round the kisser if they try 'owt on, Helen."

Rita and I left an extra large tip for our waitress. Poor thing, I thought, fancy having to work at Carlin and Priestley's for a living. Now going on the stage was what you called living. I thought about what one of the older waitresses had said about the club secretaries and felt excited for some strange reason. All of a sudden I felt very desirable - I longed to get in there and tempt the men with everything I'd got.

★ ★ ★ ★ ★ ★ ★ ★ ★ ★ ★ ★ ★ ★ ★ ★ ★

We arrived at the market and made our way to the material stall. Women bustled round the front of the stall. The women were mostly middle-aged, plain and drab looking in shapeless felt hats or head scarves. One or two had hair curlers sticking out from underneath the scarves. They grabbed at the materials and rubbed and stroked with fingers and thumbs. The stall owners were two good looking brothers in their mid-thirties I guessed. One of the brothers started flirting like mad with us.

"Here yer are, me darlin's ... how about this nice piece of velvet then? Make yourselves two lovely frocks out of this." He stroked the length of cloth and added, "Oh, I love to feel a nice bit of velvet. You can't beat having a nice stroke."

"Oooh, you cheeky bogger you." A large lady grabbed at the material the brother was holding out to us. "How much yer want fer it then?"

"To you, me darlin' ... half a nicker a yard. Cheapest stall in the country we are."

"Ten bob?" Large lady let go of the material. "You can get it for that at Jesslers ... and it 'ent got no faults in it."

Rita took hold of the black velvet remnant and gently pulled it towards her. "It'll make two smashing frocks," she whispered to me, "let's see if we can knock them down a bit."

"Oh ... go on then," said brother number two, "let them have it for seven-and-six a yard ... we'll be bleddy bankrupt soon but I don't care ... me missis has just run off with the breadman so I'm in a good mood today."

"Oh ... there's nowt' like running yer hands over a nice bit of velvet," repeated brother number one.

"Ah ... 'specially when there's a body inside it," laughed his brother.

The women customers joined in the fun and pushed nearer the front of the stall.

"I'd better have some of that there velvet," said a coarse faced woman in hair curlers and head scarf, "my husband en't felt my body for years."

"Come round here, me darlin' ... let's show you what you've been missing." Mad Mike's dark brown eyes twinkled with mischief. "I'm like that there King Solomon, I am ... I could cope with a thousand wives given the chance."

"He hasn't heard that there song has he, missis?" His brother joined in.

"King Solomon had a thousand wives
He serenaded them daily
But what's the use of a thousand wives
When you've only got one ukalele."

25

We left the brothers to their appreciative and laughing customers and carried on to the Singer Sewing-machine stall where we selected two long zips. We were going to have the dresses made skin tight so they would be very hard work getting in to without extra long zips.

Rita chose a pattern for the dresses and said, "We can use this pattern for lots of the dresses. Vera can use it as a basic but with slight variations here and there. We can buy lots of different materials ... stick a big artificial flower down the front of one dress and have extra lace or net on another." She put her arm in mine and hugged me. "Oh, Helen ... do you think it will work? I mean, do you really think anybody'll book us to sing at their club?"

"I'm certain they will. If people like Adele can get away with it, we should go down a treat."

I had never felt so enthusiastic about anything in my life. The songs — dresses — everything about it was thrilling. I could not think of anything else. I was burning to step out on to my first stage although, parodoxically, the idea terrified hell out of me. But that was the part I liked best — the terror — because it made me feel as though I was at last going to live my life at full pelt.

We caught a bus back to Rita's flat and got down to some really hard work. We put a record on the turn-table and listened carefully. We had bought four records to start off with and of course 'Sisters' was the most important one.

Rita kept quiet for a while and I sang along with the record — listening for the pauses, practising the harmony. We played the record over and over and then Rita joined in. It sounded very good, I thought, and so did Rita. We sang it again and this time with more confidence. The harmony began to blend in just right, I had got it spot on almost straight away.

"We must do exactly the same movements." Rita put her right leg in front of her and pointed her toes slightly outwards. " Now, Helen ... you do the same with your left leg ... and put your arm out like this."

I did as she instructed.

"When we come to this bit here," she held out the sheet music and continued, "point at your eye and then at me. Then at the next line ... stick out your hip and shake it three times."

We pointed our toes and wiggled our hips again and again. We decided to sing the last line three times then slow up and repeat the last line again, holding on to the very last note and singing very loudly to give a good ending to the song. We sang the song ten times more then Rita selected another record — it was 'The Lady is a Tramp'. Rita seemed to be taking control. "Look, Helen ... we'll alter the words slightly here. Away we went, feet tapping, hips swaying. We rubbed our fingers through our hair and tried to look sultry.

"Let's turn the record player up as loud as we can," Rita had another idea, "then we can go through to the bedroom and stand in front of the wardrobe mirror. Then we can see what we look like when we're doing the actions."

We rehearsed some more and it was very hard work seeing as neither of us could read a word of music. We played the records and learned the words from the sheet music. Rita marked in pencil on the sheet music the parts where we had decided to go back to a verse or sing a particular line twice or three times.

The time went quicker than a school playtime — we were so engrossed in our work we nearly missed the bus back into town. We had to carry on with our work at the Cresta. It was our bread and butter job. The singing would be our sherry trifle - for the time being that is!

★ ★ ★ ★ ★ ★ ★ ★ ★ ★ ★ ★ ★ ★ ★ ★

We practised every afternoon and on the following Thursday travelled to Rutledge to see Rita's cousin Vera. She was one of the nicest people I had ever met. Lovely smiling faced woman of thirty six. She had five children and a house which brimmed over with chaos and happiness.

Vera took our measurements and wrote them down on a crumpled paper bag. A fat baby gurgled at us from a seen-better-days sofa. Vera absent-mindedly put the paper bag down on the sofa, baby grinned and promptly chomped on our measurements with wet toothless gums. Vera snatched the bag away and asked, "Do yer want a cuppa, gels? I'm allus ready for one meself."

I wondered how long it would take Vera to make our dresses, she seemed to be a bit slap-happy. Still, I thought, they would probably be well worth waiting for — she had made some lovely clothes for Rita.

"Do you want any more measurements, Vera?" I asked.

"Don't think so, love." Vera reached for the tea-caddy. "I'll see when you try them on where you want the hems to come to. I'd say just covering the ankles. You don't want them any longer else you'll fall and break yer bleddy necks. 'Specially when our Rita's been supping her gin."

We told Vera of our plans, she listened as she mashed the tea.

"And we're going to get ourselves an agent." Rita moved a pile of clothes from a chair and beckoned me to sit down.

"Fancy you going on the stage, our Rita!" Vera plonked a bottle of milk on the middle of the table. I'll have the frocks done by Sunday. All but the zips ... you'll have to have a try on for me ... but I can soon whip the zips in. Come after Sunday dinner, the old man'll be snoring his ale off in bed then. And the kid's will have boggered off to Sunday-school."

We sipped our tea and ate two of Vera's home-made scones. The scones melted in the mouth, crumbs shot everywhere.

"How much do you want for making the frocks, Vera?" Rita tickled the baby underneath its chin.

"Oh ... you can buy me some nice scent. I don't want any money. You can buy me some scent ... I haven't had any nice scent for donkey's years. The only nice smell in this house is from the baby when I put talcum powder on his bum."

I smiled at her and thought what a lovely woman she was. If we get famous and earn lots of money, I thought, we'll buy you the largest bottle of Chanel No. 5 we can find.

Rita made her agree to a realistic price for making our clothes and she beamed with pleasure and insisted we try one of her home-made biscuits shaped like a pixie.

The baby gurgled at us and kicked his legs not in the least impressed that we were going to be famous one day.

★ ★ ★ ★ ★ ★ ★ ★ ★ ★ ★ ★ ★ ★ ★ ★

Rita and I rehearsed for two whole weeks and then, one Friday afternoon, I rang the local information bureau. I asked if they knew of any theatrical agencies we could contact. The helpful girl gave us the address and telephone number of an agency called the 'Top Liners'.

Rita and I squeezed into a telephone box and rang the number. A man answered and told us that he would be willing to audition us at his studio the following Saturday afternoon. He asked if we had our own pianist and, when we said we hadn't, offered to hire one for us for two pounds. He told us to be at his studio at three o'clock and to bring a good selection of music.

Rita replaced the telephone and said, "Oh, Helen ... I can't go and sing in front of an agent. Just the thought of it makes me feel sick."

"Of course you can ... after all the rehearsing we've done! ... we can sing in front of anybody." I scoffed at her nerves but the insides of my stomach jangled up and down as though on the end of a piece of elastic.

We were still inside the telephone box when there was a loud tapping on the window-panes. A woman in a Bow-street-runner hat grinned at us from the other side of the glass. We stepped outside the box.

"Hurry up, gels ... I've got to ring the doctor's surgery," she told us from somewhere underneath the comical hat.

"Sorry, love ... is it an emergency?" I asked.

"I'll say it is, love. They're going to let me know the results of me pregnancy test."

"Oh ... there's far worse things than having a baby," I laughed at her, "we've all got our problems." I thought about our audition.

"Maybe so," she laughed back before putting her finger in the dial, "but I haven't had a bit with my old man for over a year now. Get out of that problem if you can."

Rita and I laughed all the way down the street — all tension gone — released with the laughter.

CHAPTER FIVE

The next day Rita and I sat picking at our lunches. We had no appetites but plenty of nerves. I could feel the food going into my mouth but there didn't seem to be any sort of taste - my stomach felt like a block of concrete had formed inside.

"Come on then," Rita made the first move, "let's start putting our faces on. We'll feel tons better when we've got our war-paint on."

We did a good decorating job on our faces then changed our clothes. We had decided to wear identical, tight fitting, pale blue jersey wool dresses we had bought from C. and A.'s. The colour was flattering to both blondes and brunettes. The dresses were cut very low at the front and the skirts were swathed to one side, falling in two soft pleats. Rita looked terrific in her dress and her breasts protruded triumphantly.

"I'll need some padding in my bust." I turned sideways and looked in the mirror. "I've got to have a good cleavage." I folded a scarf into two halves and stuffed them down the front of my bra. The result was amazing - up popped an instant cleavage.

We were almost ready. We put on our coats and these were also identical. Dark brown rabbit fur. I would never wear musquash or mink or anything like that, poor things, but rabbit doesn't seem so bad because people eat them, we are only using the bit that's left over.

The coats had been bought from a man that Rita knew. He had let us pay a deposit of five pounds and a pound a week.

"Come on then, Lita Roza," I picked up our sheet music. "Let's go and get it over with."

Rita gave me a pound note towards the pianist's fee and we were on our way.

At ten minutes to three we walked slowly up the High Street and entered Cranmer Road. The buildings were five stories high and covered in grime from the traffic fumes and chimney factories. We arrived at number twenty five and walked up the steps. The notice board gave a list of the different offices. 'Top Liners' agency - second floor. I pushed Rita in front of me and said, "Go on ... after you."

Rita knocked on the office door.

"Come in." A man's voice summoned us inside.

The studio was smaller than I had expected. Not a bit like the ones you see on the pictures or television. There was a desk and this was covered with papers. A typewriter balanced precariously at one end of the desk, a telephone sat on the other.

Round the walls were large glossy photographs of men and women. Most of the men were holding microphones and grinning inanely - dressed in dinner-jackets, bow-ties and shiny, patent leather shoes, they smiled their artiste smiles.

The women on the photographs were all half naked. Leaning against curtains or perched on step-ladders they too grinned inanely. Each photograph had an unreadable signature scrawled across it.

The man, whom I guessed was the agent, stepped from behind his desk and walked across the room, hand outstretched, teeth protruding and eyes bulging.

"Hello there, girls." He tried hard to look sexy. "I'm Dave ... Dave McGuire." He shook hands with each of us in turn then pointed to two chairs. "Just sit down for a minute ... pianist should be here anytime now." He held out a gold cigarette case. "Fag anybody?"

We both accepted a cigarette although neither of us could really be called smokers - just the odd one at parties that sort of thing. But we were both in such a bad state of nerves I think we would have gladly accepted a Winston Churchill cigar had he offered one - and smoked it down to the butt.

I guessed that Dave was somewhere in his late forties. He was very slim and had hips like a young man's. A tall man, he held himself well, and had a slight sway when he walked across the room. He was a very attractive man but much too old for me. His suit was well cut but I noticed that the collar of his shirt was creased and curled up at the ends. This often meant no wife or sometimes, a wife who couldn't care less how her husband looked. It would be interesting to see whether or not there was a Mrs. McGuire in his life and the way Rita was looking him up and down we would soon find out — that's if he decided to book our act of course.

"Are you going to take your coats off then, girls?" He offered to take our coats. "They won't bite me, will they? They look like a couple of wild dogs." He laughed heartily at his own joke. We handed over our precious furs and he draped them across the back of his chair.

Rita looked relaxed and I hoped I did too - we mustn't let him see that we were inexperienced and terrified as well.

A few minutes went by and then a pasty-faced man walked into the studio. He sounded short of breath and muttered, "Sorry I'm late, Dave ... I had to stay for the three o'clock race. I'd put my bleddy shirt on it."

"Did you win?" Dave winked at us.

"No ... bleddy thing pulled up." The pianist inhaled cigarette smoke deep into his lungs. "How long do you think we'll be this time? There's a cert in the four thirty ... I'd like to have a chance at getting my money back."

"Shouldn't be too long, Barry. I just want to see what the girls can do." Dave winked at us again. "I keep telling him, girls ... give up the horses and take up women instead. They might be a bit more trouble, but they'd be cheaper in the long run."

Barry sat down on the piano stool and ran his fingers up and down the keys.

"You should try keeping my missis then ... it's cheaper to keep a racehorse than keep my missis in clothes." Barry played one or two chords.

Dave leaned against the front of his desk and tapped on a telephone pad with his pen. He looked at his wrist-watch and said, "Come on then, girls ... let's hear a couple of numbers from you."

I placed the sheet music in front of Barry.

"Right then, how do you want it?" Barry placed his cigarette in an ashtray and flipped through the music using the forefinger of his right hand. I explained how we were going to sing 'Sisters', "All the way through and back to here ... then we sing this bit again."

Barry played our introduction, we cleared our throats and took deep breaths. We moved closer together and posed the way we had rehearsed it so many times in front of the bedroom mirror. I took deep breaths and concentrated on the net curtains which were blowing gently on a breeze's whisper. My throat felt terribly dry and my legs trembled but somehow I kept on going. Rita sang out very well and on the second rendering of the song her voice got louder. I too sang louder so that the harmony would be well balanced.

At the end of our song Dave walked to the back of his desk and sat down. He fussed with some papers but did not say a word. His expression gave away nothing. I was sure he did not like us. We were too inexperienced - he would never put us on his books not at this stage.

We went into our second number. We pouted, smiled, stuck out our bosoms and thrust out our hips. Barry was an excellent pianist. He put in lots of twiddly bits of his own and banged out the rhythm with his left foot. The harmony seemed to sound all right to me but it had to sound good to Dave, he was the one that mattered.

At the end of this number Dave lit another cigarette and blew a cloud of smoke at the grinning photographs on the wall. He smiled at me and asked, "Can I hear your solo now, Helen? You are Helen aren't you?"

Oh God! ... please don't let me faint. I breathed in deeply and went over to the piano once more. The palms of my hands were wet through with perspiration and my heart beats were terribly erratic. Perhaps I'd drop dead in the middle of the second chorus! I could see the headlines quite clearly. 'Singer dies through shortage of breath'. I leaned on the piano, swallowed again and had a dreadful urge to spend a penny.

"The leaves of brown, came tumbling down remember ... that September ... in the rain." I looked straight ahead at the wall in front of me. The grinning men in dress suits stared back. I thought about the words of the song and concentrated with everything I'd got. I took an extra deep breath in preparation for the last three words which I had to hold on to for as long as I could to give the song a really good finish. The notes were very high but I got up there somehow and I held on with everything I'd got. My voice faded — nerves had literally taken my breath away.

There was silence for a moment and the relief I felt after performing my solo must been comparable with a condemned man being pardoned, I thought, as the blood in my veins started to flow normally once again.

I walked back to my chair and then, damn it, I began to feel nervous for Rita. She walked over to the piano looking very confident but I knew what she must be feeling.

Rita's choice for her solo was the very beautiful 'Blue Moon' but unfortunately the music was written in a key higher than she'd rehearsed. Barry soon sorted a key out for her and she was away, with Barry transposing the music to the key of 'F' as he went along. The pianist may not have known much about racehorses, but he certainly knew his piano.

Rita put everything she'd got into the song and although the pauses weren't quite right here and there, the mood and feeling more than compensated for this.

After Rita had finished her solo there was more silence and then Dave said, "Right then, girls ... I think we can do business." He reached for a red, leather bound desk diary. "I can give you a booking tomorrow night if you want it. There's a cancellation I've got to fill in at the Glass Bowl. You can catch the bus from the Market Square ... drop you off outside the door. Be there at seven thirty ... give you time to sort yourselves out and have a word or two with the pianist and drummer. They're a nice crowd up there. Get a lot of miners in, with it being near a colliery of course. They get a bit rowdy about half past nine, but they're a good bunch of lads. They go mad on girl vocalists. You'll go down a treat there ... it'll be free booze all night. Show them a bit of leg and plenty of breast and you'll bring the house down."

"Oh, thank you." I managed to say.

"Right ... thank you ... we'll be there." Rita's face was bright pink.

Dave wrote something down in his diary and added, "I charge ten-per-cent by the way. I'll probably come along to hear your last spot so you can pay me then. I like to keep my books straight ... you can pay my commission on time, that way we'll all be kept happy."

I couldn't believe it was happening. A booking straight away at our first audition. So all our scheming and hard work had paid off. The agent had actually thought we were good enough to sing at one of his venues. I felt almost ready to sing another song — well almost!

Dave's voice bulldozed through my thoughts.

"I said what do you call yourselves, then?"

"Dumonte Sisters." Rita answered him.

"Oh yes ... very nice ... bit of the old French. By the way ... have you got leotards?"

"Yes." Rita and I chorussed.

"Oh, that's good," Dave looked roguish, "perhaps you could wear them in your act a bit later on. You could do a soft-shoe routine with canes and boaters. Won't matter if you can't dance very well. The men will be too busy looking at your legs and thighs and their wives will be busy looking at them looking, if you see what I mean!"

We told him we knew what he meant all right.

"Now then ... would you like to join me in a drink to celebrate our little transaction?" Dave reached inside his desk and produced a bottle of whisky and some glasses.

"What's a leotard?" I whispered to Rita.

"Don't know," she whispered back, "but whatever it is, I'll bet our Vera can make us both one."

Dave poured the drinks and said, "You'll get six pounds at the Glass Bowl. It's not a lot but they don't get a very big crowd in on a Sunday. There's not a lot of room either, but it'll be a start working on my circuit. Most of my artists save their new numbers and gag-routines for places like that. You can try out all your new numbers at the small venues. And I'll tell you something ... if the miners don't like your songs they'll let you know sharpish. If they don't like a song you won't be able to hear yourselves think never mind sing. And if they like your act you'll have a table full of drinks all night."

Dave handed out drinks and said, "Right then ... here's to a very happy and long partnership. You play right by me and I'll keep the work coming. Fail to turn up and that's the last work you'll get out of me."

We raised our glasses just like they do on the films when they've signed a big contract. I was floating with happiness. I looked at Rita and knew she felt the same. She was also flirting like mad with Dave and he was lapping it up. Keep up the good work, Rita ... let's get our diaries filled, I thought. Men can't resist a bit of flattery from a young girl so why not cash in on their weaknesses.

"Are they performing again, Dave?" Barry downed his drink.

"I don't know about performing," Dave winked at Rita, "but we won't be needing you again today."

"I'll be off then ... try and catch the last race." He hesitated and looked slightly embarrassed.

"Would you like to pay Barry then, girls." Dave took charge again.

"Oh ... I'm sorry." I rummaged in my purse for the two pounds.

"Thanks, love ... be seeing you." Barry hurried away to give our money to his bookmaker.

"Have you got steady boyfriends ... or unsteady husbands?" Dave grinned at us and replenished our drinks.

Rita crossed her legs showing a nice bit of thigh. "We have our moments but nothing serious at this time of asking. Have you got a wife?"

Dave laughed showing nice well cared for teeth which were just a little too large to make him really handsome.

"You won't catch me getting hooked. Why buy a book when there's a lending library full of them!" He offered cigarettes again.

We talked for a while mainly about showbusiness, techniques and musical accompaniment, that sort of thing, and thoroughly enjoyed ourselves.

At last Dave gave a signal that it was time for us to depart. He stood up and looked at his watch. "Business calls I'm afraid, girls. Got some people to see and then I'm off to Doncaster this evening. New comedian I've booked ... want to see if he makes them laugh. No laughs ... no bookings ... that's the way it works in this business."

He handed over our coats and opened the door. He patted Rita on the behind and said, "See you both tomorrow night then. Hope you go down well. You should do with the miners. 'Bye then."

Rita and I walked from the building in a daze. A booking, and the agent had heard us sing!

"We're on our way, Rita."

"Yes, Helen, I think we're going to do all right."

We linked arms and talked about our booking all the way down to the Market Square.

★ ★ ★ ★ ★ ★ ★ ★ ★ ★ ★ ★ ★ ★ ★ ★ ★

Sunday afternoon, Rita and I went to Vera's house for our velvet dresses. A few tucks here and there, in with the zips and the dresses were ready. They looked fantastic and fitted skin-tight just as we had envisaged.

"I've put a couple of bones in the bust part." Vera looked pleased. "Give you a nice uplift."

We stayed for a quick cup of tea and asked Vera if she would make more dresses the following week. We planned to change our dresses each time we went on stage so we would have to have two or three more gowns each.

"We'll get some brocade and lots of net." I told Vera. "And you can use the same pattern each time. We're going to get artificial flowers and diamante brooches for decoration so you can leave that to us."

Vera popped the gowns into a bag and we hurried away, both eager to get back to Rita's flat for some last minute rehearsals.

We rehearsed our songs, both duets and solos, and at five o'clock I insisted we give our voices a rest.

"We'll have no voices left for tonight ... let's have a bite to eat and then we'll have a rest before we start out."

Rita made eggs on toast and we also had three cups of tea each. Every time I thought about singing my throat seemed to be extra dry, I kept wanting to swallow but my throat seemed to be abnormally tight.

At six o'clock we started to put on our make-up. Rita insisted we put make-up on our eyes so that they would show up better on the stage. I outlined my eyes with a black pencil and spat on my mascara brush before dipping it into the black mascara.

"Blimey! ..." Rita exclaimed ... "you look like a startled doormouse."

"That's nothing to what I feel like, Rita." I felt quite ill with stage-fright. I can only describe it as feeling like a particularly bad dose of flu, only for stage-fright, there was no medicine to help out.

We packed our velvet gowns into suitcases, together with the sheet music, gold dance shoes and strapless bras complete with padding.

I wanted to lock myself in the bedroom — forget about the whole thing. I remembered what Dave had said. Fail to turn up and that's the last booking you'll get. I applied more lipstick and rouge, breathed deeply and at last said to Rita, "Come on then ... let's go."

CHAPTER SIX

At twenty past seven Rita and I pushed open the door marked 'lounge'. We were greeted with great enthusiasm by a large happy looking man of around forty, I guessed. He had long ginger sideburns and a bushy moustache. His red smiling face peeped out from the spectacular hairy display of facial decoration.

The man walked from behind the bar and nodded towards a door which had Ladies and Gents chalked on it. He took hold of our suitcases and said, "This way, girls ... follow me and I'll show you where to get dressed."

"Oh ... watch him, me ducks." An old man who was leaning against the bar shouted after us. "He means where to get undressed ... watch him, I'm warning yer!"

The landlord led the way down a tiny passage and up some stairs.

"You can get changed in our bedroom." He put our suitcases down and switched on an electric fire. It'll be a bit cold till the room gets warmed up ... wind blows from the North."

"Thank you ... this'll do very nicely." I was trembling from nerves as well as the cold.

"Don't forget to draw the curtains before you get undressed." He laughed and winked at us. "They can see in the bedroom from the road when the light's on. Now don't forget, 'else there'll be a bleddy traffic jam ... you'll have all me customers out in the road if they can see you getting undressed."

The landlord left the room and walked back down the stairs whistling at the top of his whistle.

I took my velvet dress from the suitcase and laid it flat on the landlord's bed.

"Come on, Rita ... let's go and get a drink. I can't sing without having a couple of drinks first. I don't know about you ... but I can't stop trembling."

"I know," Rita answered, "I just keep thinking to myself I don't know how we dare go on. Oh, Helen ... I'm terrified!"

We went back down stairs and ordered two bottles of Guinness.

"Could we have two ports in them as well?" I remembered my old grandad saying something about port being good for steadying the nerves. The way I was feeling I needed a whole bottle to myself.

I led the way over to a table near a fire which was backed up well with coal and slack. There were only seven people in the room. A young couple, a middle-aged couple, two old ladies and the old man who had warned us of the amorous desires of the hairy landlord.

All seven people stared at us a lot and smiled. The old man took out a snuff box and after inhaling deeply sneezed into an off-grey handkerchief. He blew his nose and sounded like the Queen Mary on a foggy day. He walked over to our table and sat down.

35

"Are yo' two the talent, then? We like gel singers here. There'll be more in soon ... it'll start to fill up soon. Don't forget to sing some owd 'uns, me ducks. We like the owd 'uns here." He lifted his pint mug with trembling hands and sucked loudly at his drink. "Sing summat we can all join in. New 'uns is all right but yer can't beat a good owd sing-song."

We agreed with him and promised to sing some old ones. The door opened and four youths dressed in leather jackets with studs on the back, tight drain-pipe trousers and crepe soled shoes walked over to the bar. Eight eyes lit up like hundred watt bulbs when the youths saw us sitting at our table. They sauntered over to the next table to ours and banged four pints of mild on the iron topped surface. They stared and stared - I began to feel embarrassed as though I was part of a freak show. And then I thought, well yes, Rita and I were on show. We were there to be looked at. We were artists now and different to the rest of the people in the room. We would have to get used to the stares.

"Ey up then, blondie." One of the youths smiled at Rita. "Are yer 'aving one with us then? What's it to be, blondie?"

Everyone in the room stopped talking and waited for Rita's reply.

"Thanks, love," Rita returned his smile, "me and me mate are on Guiness."

I winced inwardly at her reply, and then thought, these youths were part of our audience - if we acted snooty they wouldn't applaud our act. I began to feel miserable, the evening was not turning out as I had expected. I thought about something Bette Davis had once said in one of her films. She had arrived somewhere and had said, "what a dump", and given one of her memorable looks of contempt. I whispered what a dump to Rita and she laughed and whispered back, "Shut up ... if they hear you they won't clap us."

The port began to do its job and I began to feel more relaxed.

"They're the talent," said the old man, "we're goin' to have some owd 'uns later on. They said they'd sing some owd 'uns."

"Ooh ... you've got in there quick, Charlie." One of the youths teased him in a kindly way. "Yer want to watch him, me duck ... he's a rum 'un. Had more women than Errol Flyn he has ... 'ent yer, Charlie?" Charlie's eyes sparkled with happiness at the attention he was getting.

"Ah ... I have 'an all. I've had more than your lot'll ever have all put together. I was in France during the war," he turned to us, "them French gels wouldn't leave me alone, they wouldn't."

Rita and I nodded in all the right places we hoped.

"I'm eighty six yer know and I live on me own." Charlie boasted. I gave the standard reply, "You're not are you?" and looked as impressed as I could.

At five minutes to eight a thin man dressed in a grey pin-striped suit walked into the lounge. He was carrying a briefcase so I reckoned he must be our accompanist for the evening. I was right - he ordered a pint of bitter and then walked across to the organ which was standing in the right hand corner of the room furthest away from the fireplace. He nodded a greeting to us then placed some sheet music on the organ stand. He pressed a switch at the side of the organ and moved the microphone to the front of the organ. That was to be our stage, I thought, and stage-fright took hold of me once again.

The organist tapped the microphone and then blew into it. A thudding noise

36

reverberated around the room. He picked up his pint of bitter and brought it over to our table. He pulled a chair up to the table and said, "Are you the Dumonte Sisters?"

"Yes," I was thrilled at being called by our stage name for the first time, "that's us." We shook hands and he explained the programme for the evening.

"You go on at half past eight. There's no panic to get started here ... they don't fill up till about nine. I'll come up and have a look at your music about twenty past."

He went over to the organ and commenced playing. I could feel the atmosphere of the room warming up as he played. People tapped their feet and the four youths whistled along to the tune and old Charlie beat out a rhythm on the table with his fingers. The organist was good - I felt a lot happier now. Two more bottles of Guiness appeared on our table.

"Better not have too much to drink," I told Rita in between sips, "don't want to forget our words."

"That's why I'm laying off the gin," she replied, "if I drink too much gin my mind'll go blank."

At a quarter past eight we took our drinks upstairs and after drawing the curtains together changed our clothes.

I stuffed my strapless bra with two head scarves and my cleavage looked terrific. Rita did likewise, and seeing as she was already quite well endowed, looked stupendous.

The dresses were so tight we could hardly walk. We slipped our feet into the gold dance shoes and put on our long dangling ear-rings. We looked at ourselves in the dressing-table mirror and Rita started to giggle when she caught sight of my bust.

The organist knocked at the door. Rita called out, "Come on in." She held out our sheet music to him and said, "Now this one has a nice steady beat ... we sing it through once and then repeat it once more but a bit faster that time, like this." She clicked her fingers and hummed the tune.

"Right then ... that's your opening number." The organist placed the music face down on the bed. "What's next? Oh and by the way ... the drummer hasn't turned up again tonight. He's a bit unreliable ... got a spot of woman trouble I think. You'll be all right without drums. I'll play extra loud for you."

Rita handed the next song to him. "Really slow the first time. The harmony comes over better if we keep it nice and slow." She tapped her foot and carried on with her instructions, "About like this, please."

I fled along the corridor to the bathroom. Nerves had seemed to attack my bladder - I had to spend a penny before we went on. Rita and the organist were waiting for me when I got back. The organist led the way downstairs.

"Right then, girls ... let's get cracking. Stand just outside the door and the landlord'll announce you. You'll be able to hear him if you stand near the door. I don't think he'll want you to do any solos tonight. Do your first duets and see how we are for time ... but I don't think you'll have time for more than three spots."

I could have kissed his feet. No solos tonight! That's what I had been dreading the most. Singing with Rita would not be quite as terrifying as standing there singing on my own. Luck was with us after all it seemed.

We waited near the door and I looked at the palms of my hands. They were wet with perspiration and my body felt as though it was under an attack of malaria. If this was stage-fright you could keep it.

Rita looked just as scared and confided, "It's a good job I've got all my own teeth. If they were false I'm sure they'd chatter right out of my head."

"Oh, Rita ... I daren't go on."

"Let's run off." She started to laugh.

"What a dump." I laughed along with her.

"Ladies and gentlemen," the landlord's voice reached us through the door, "as you've already seen for yourselves, we have a nice bit of glamour for you tonight. I hope you give them the usual Glass Bowl welcome. Quiet now, please. A big hand for the beautiful ... Dumonte Sisters."

Rita opened the door, we walked across the room and stood in front of the microphone. We both cleared our throats at the same time. The organist was playing our introduction - there was no escaping now. I took a deep breath, opened my mouth and hoped something like a musical sound would come out of it. I forgot all about my bladder - there was something wrong with my heart now. Come on heart, slow down for goodness sake, please slow down a bit. We both came in on the opening note together - I felt more confident and began to belt out the words, Rita did likewise. I remembered the movements, stuck out my padded bust, wiggled my velvet encased hips and smiled, smiled, smiled at the audience.

The audience kept very quiet. They just sat and stared at us from every angle of the tiny room. I tried not to look at them and kept my eyes straight ahead which meant I was staring at the top of the brightly lit bar. I could see the still figures of the landlord and his wife behind the bar so I concentrated on the tops of their heads.

Our song was coming to an end. We held onto the last few notes as long as we could and made the very last note louder than the rest.

The audience applauded. It didn't exactly raise the roof but they sounded quite enthusiastic. The second song would go down better. We were loosening up a little now. I had ceased to tremble too, and my heart beats seemed to be more regular.

They enjoyed our slow song - I felt certain they would like the last song in our first spot. It had a very catchy tune. I was correct, the audience joined in the chorus and the youths whistled through their teeth. Rita and I sang louder and with much more confidence. Our first spot came to an end. The audience applauded, we bowed and then walked over to the bar. I ordered two more bottles of Guiness.

"Have these on me, gels." The landlord twiddled his moustache. "They enjoyed you. Don't bother with solos tonight. Do two more duets and that'll do. I want to get an extra bingo in tonight." He passed our drinks over with a grin.

We made our way back to our table — the youths had moved in closer.

"Ey up, blondie ... me mate says he fancies you."

"Oh, I like the blackhead. I like to squeeze blackheads." A man seated at the next table joined in the fun. He looked down the front of our dresses and added, "You want to mind you don't get a cold on your chests."

"Oh, I wouldn't mind rubbing 'em with Vick if they did," butted in old Charlie, "I'm very good at rubbing chests."

"You old devil," I said, for want of something better to say.

"Don't forget to sing some owd 'uns." Charlie sipped froth from another pint of mild. "Summat we all know." He poked snuff up his nose and added, "I'm eighty six yer know ... and I live on me own if ever yer want a bed for the night."

I realised that most of my tension had disappeared. Must be the drink!

We performed our second spot at quarter past nine and this time I actually enjoyed singing. Rita had really got into the feel and beat of the songs and this helped me tremendously.

The landlord stepped in front of the organ and announced the Bingo, there was much scurrying about for Bingo tickets and our audience sat with pens and pencils at the ready.

"Two little ducks ... twenty two," called the landlord. "Top of the shop ... ninety."

Rita had bought tickets for the two of us so we joined in the fun. An old lady, twin-set clad and hair cut short above the ears, screamed out, "House!" There were cries of "Oh, not you again, Mabel, it's fixed."

The landlord checked the card against his own and then made a great show of handing out the prize which was three pounds seven and sixpence.

"Do your last spot about ten to ten, girls." The landlord came over to our table. "Give 'em 'Side by Side' and 'My Old Man'. They like to join in on the last spot."

"We haven't got the music to that." Rita was apologetic.

"Oh, don't worry about that ... the organist's a good lad. He can play anything. Sort it out with the organist."

The door opened and Dave walked into the room. He waved a hand in greeting and went up to the bar.

I felt terribly nervous again. What if we went wrong - started off in the wrong key! It was possible Rita and I would make a right mess of things if we were going to sing without having the proper sheet music.

Dave came over to our table, found himself a chair and sat down. The youths and old Charlie gave him a friendly greeting so I gathered that he must have visited the Glass Bowl regularly to see his other artists.

"How's it going then, girls?" Dave sipped at a whisky and then lit a cigarette. "Enjoying yourselves, are you?"

"It's been smashing, Dave." Rita leaned towards him giving him a birds-eye view of her bosom. "We're going to do our last spot in a few minutes. The landlord wants us to sing some old songs but we haven't got the music."

"Oh, just sing them all in the key of 'C'." Dave looked appreciatively at Rita's charms. "As long as you know the words you'll be all right. This lot here'll help you out anyway." He indicated with a sweep of his hand the audience which had now grown to over fifty people giving a nice friendly atmosphere to the place.

We went through the same procedure with the organist. He looked through the three songs which we had rehearsed so thoroughly and then we discussed which of the old songs we would finish the evening with.

We decided on 'Side by Side', 'Let the Rest of the World go By' and 'Underneath the Arches'. The audience applauded like mad when we had finished.

"Like a drink, girls?" Dave took out his wallet. I refused his offer because I was beginning to feel rather tipsy but Rita asked for a gin.

"I shouldn't mix it," she giggled, "but I've been so keyed up all evening I feel as though I need something to simmer me down."

Dave fetched more drinks for himself and Rita and then offered us both a lift home. "It's on my way," he explained, "I don't usually run a free taxi service but seeing as it's on my way."

Old Charlie was listening to our conversation and butted in with, "I've just been telling 'em, Dave ... I've got half a bed to let if they're interested."

"When are yer coming here again?" One of the youths hutched his chair up nearer. "How about coming down the Palais next Wednesday? It's a good night on a Wednesday. Me and me mates allus go down on a Wednesday."

"We can't, love," Rita answered him, "we'll be working."

"Where are yer on at then? ... we'll come and see yer."

"Yes ... tell us where you're on at and we'll all come."

"We'll be your fan-club."

"So long as yer don't get 'em in the Pudding-club." Old Charlie again.

"It's a good job I'm here to protect you." Dave was enjoying the friendly banter. "Wait till you wear your leotards ... you'll need an armed guard."

"Time, ladies and gentlemen if you please." The landlord whipped empty glasses from tables and tipped cigarette butts into a waste-paper basket. "See the wife for your money, girls." He nodded towards the bar. "Book 'em again, Dave ... and don't let it be too long before we see them." He moved to the next table. " Come on, your lot ... 'ent you got no homes to go to?"

Rita and I went over to the bar and the landlady pressed the no-sale key on the till. She counted six pound notes into Rita's hand and I felt rather foolish being paid in front of our audience. We went back upstairs and changed our clothes once more.

After we had packed our suitcases we went downstairs again. Dave ushered us into his car and we were on our way home. It was a very comfortable car - a Humber Super Snipe which had soft, real leather seats and bags of room. Rita and I sorted out the fee we had received and I handed Dave his ten per cent.

"That's the idea," he said, "keep the books straight and we all know where we stand."

I snuggled down in the soft leather and felt like a real celebrity. So this was how it felt to be on top of the world! I had the most unusual feeling of floating outside my own body. I seemed to be able to view my surroundings from outside the car somewhere - it was most strange and something I had never experienced before. I looked across at Rita, she had a smile of contentment on her face which, I guessed, was there because of the exciting evening and the amount of alcohol she had managed to consume.

We reached the street where I lived and I told Dave where to stop the car. He turned to face us and took a diary from his inside coat pocket.

"Now let's see what else I've got. You did say you couldn't do any Saturdays, didn't you."

"Yes, that's right, Dave." Rita explained. "We have to work six nights at the Cresta club ... we can only do Sundays at the moment."

"Fair enough." Dave thumbed through the diary. "I'll just concentrate on Sundays for now then. I've got a date at the Blaythorpe Miners' Welfare for next Sunday. The Welfare's got a nice big stage with curtains," he laughed, "bit posher than the Glass Bowl. They've got a good drummer and pianist. You'll probably only have to do two spots. Sing five numbers each time ... that should be enough. If they want any more one of you can do a solo spot. I've booked a comedian as well for that evening and they have two Bingos so you should have an easy night of it. Er ... it's seven quid for that one."

Rita and I wrote the booking in the diaries we had bought and made a note of the directions Dave gave us on how to get to the club.

I thanked Dave for the lift home and said goodnight. Rita moved into the front of the car and winked at me as the car drove away. I hoped she'd be all right with Dave because neither of us knew what kind of man he was. But there it was, I thought, they were both single and free to do as they liked. There was Neville of course. I put my key in the lock and murmured out loud, "That's showbusiness!"

CHAPTER SEVEN

The following day Rita and I used our 'singing money' as we called it to buy some pale blue velvet. Rita also suggested we buy some dark blue lace to wear at the front of the bodice which would make the gowns look slightly different to the black ones.

After we had bought the materials from the market we went to Carlin and Priestley's restaurant and had beans on toast and a pot of tea.

"Oh yes, our Glass Bowl engagement went down ever so well," I told our enthralled audience of waitresses who had gathered round the table. "And we're on at the Blaythorpe Miners' this Sunday."

"Ooh, I say you're not are yer!" Old Edna looked very impressed. "They have some good turns on there. Fancy you being on there."

"I'd love to come and see yer." Nora, the youngest of the girls edged nearer. "I've always wanted to be on the stage."

"Come and see us then, Nora." Rita egged them all on. "You know how to get there."

"Don't you have to be a member?" Old Edna pursed her lips. "I'm sure you have to be a member."

"You'll be able to get in all right." Rita kept her face straight and sipped at her tea. "Just mention our names ... say you're with the Dumonte Sisters. Say you're with the artists."

"Ooooh," came the chorus, "you pair of lairy boggers you."

★ ★ ★ ★ ★ ★ ★ ★ ★ ★ ★ ★ ★ ★ ★ ★

Rita and I entered the Blaythorpe Miners' Welfare like true professionals. The fur coats made us feel really posh.

Once inside the door we were greeted by a man dressed in a dark dress suit, a starched white shirt and a black bow-tie. He walked over to us and introduced himself, "Good evening, girls. I'm your entertainment secretary. Dumonty Sisters, are you?"

"Dumonte," I corrected him with a smile.

"This way then, young ladies ... I'll just show you the dressing-room."

A proper dressing-room — how marvellous. It was just like being on at the Empire, I thought.

The entertainment secretary led the way through a large concert room. Although it was only twenty minutes to eight there were already about a hundred people seated at the tables. Music from a gramophone record was being relayed through loudspeakers which were placed in all four corners of the room.

"That sounds as though they've got good equipment," Rita nodded towards one of the speakers, "they'll be able to hear us tonight."

The stage was very large and, as Dave had mentioned, there were bright orange velvet curtains which must have cost a packet. No wonder the price of coal keeps going up, I thought, it's to help pay for all this lot.

After hanging up our dresses in the dressing-room we walked down the length of the concert room once more and headed for the bar. I ordered our Guiness and ports and we stood at the bar for a while.

Eventually, the entertainment secretary came bustling over to us.

"There's a table 'specially reserved for the artists down at the front if you'd like to sit down, girls. Alfie Seltzer's already at the table if you'd care to join him." He pointed to a table at the front of the room.

Rita and I didn't really want to sit at the table but we decided we had better humour the man, after all he was in a position to give us a return booking.

Rita ordered two more bottles of Guiness then led the way to our reserved table near the front of the stage.

"How'do, girls." The comedian introduced himself. "I'm Alfie ... Alfie Seltzer. Full of fizz I am, so watch out!"

"Hello, Alfie," we echoed.

"Have you been here before?" Alfie had a good guzzle from his pint of bitter.

"No, have you?" Rita sat next to him. "First time for us."

"Oh ... the audience's Bingo mad. They're a noisy lot of sods."

"Bingo seems to be the thing now, doesn't it." I answered.

"You go on first, girls." Alfie toyed with the button on his shirt cuff. "Give them a bit a glamour ... warm them up for me." He looked at his watch. "You'll be on about ten past eight. The pianist and drummer'll play for a while and then you'll be on about ten past."

Alfie was right — just gone eight o'clock Rita and I went through the ritual of explaining how we wanted our music played, to the pianist and drummer. The pianist made notes in pencil where we wanted lines faster or notes held on longer and the drummer tapped on the side of the table and listened how fast we wanted the beat.

I dabbed more powder on my face and applied extra lipstick.

I felt sick with my malaria feeling again and I wanted to spend a penny.

"I've changed my mind, Rita. You'll have to do two solo spots. I can't walk out onto that great big stage. Just look at that massive stage," I said, full of misery, "I'm terrified."

Rita laughed and replied, "You can't escape now ... and anyway ... whose idea was it in the first place? Let's get an act together," she mimicked me, "we can do a lot better than some of the tripe they get at the Cresta."

"We can," I replied, "but I never knew stage-fright would bring such agony of mind. I'm wet through with perspiration."

"Well, you're on in a couple of minutes, there's no escape."

"I can get out of that window." I pointed to an escape route.

"Let's give you a leg up then." Rita looked at herself in the mirror and licked her lips to make them more shiny.

The pianist and drummer had stopped playing — it was too late.

"Good evening, ladies and gentlemen." Starched shirt was doing his stuff from behind the closed velvet curtains. "For your entertainment this evening we have a delightful duo ... straight from their successful tour of West Germany." He beckoned for us to join him on stage and we went over to the middle of the stage. He winked at us and continued, "These lovely girls had got a very busy schedule but luckily for you, the committee at the Blaythorpe Miners' managed to book them for this one night. Order please at the bar ... I said could we have a bit of hush round the bar. Thank you, gentlemen ... we pay out good money for our artists so the least you can do is listen." He handed Rita a microphone which was on his right and gave me the one he had been using. He walked to the side of the stage, took hold of a handle and started turning it — the curtains swayed apart and Rita and I were exposed to the glare of footlights. We grinned at one another for comfort and the grins were frozen on our lips. The pianist and drummer played our introduction and my legs began to shake. Thank goodness for long dresses, I thought, it was like being on the cake-walk at the Fair.

I looked out over the footlights and the bar, brightly lit, stood out like a lighthouse in the midst of a sea of human faces. I decided to focus my attention on the bar. We started our first number which was 'Sisters'. I was thankful for the mike, it gave me something to do with my hands. Oh what joy! The accompaniment was first class. The pianist sounded like Charlie Kunz and the drummer was terrific. The microphones were good and our voices came out of the loudspeakers clear and crisp. I wiggled my hips and rolled my eyes and Rita did the same. And I noticed that it was quiet at the bar — a very good sign, I thought.

Rita introduced our second number — we had decided to take turns at announcing the songs. She did very well, waited till the applause had died completely down then said, "Thank you very much ... we would now like to sing a song made famous by Ronnie Hilton and it's called ... 'No Other Love'." The song had a lovely beguine tempo and the drummer did wonders with his drum-kit. His feet went like mad on the pedals, he tapped with his drum-sticks on the sides of the drums and did a lot of clashing about on the cymbals when we came to the last line of the song.

It was now my turn to introduce a song. My tongue felt numb, rather like the aftermath of a visit to the dentists. I had to say something, the audience were waiting. "Thank you very much everybody." Not very original but my brain had seized up. "We would now like to sing a particular favourite of ours which went down very well in West Germany." I glanced at Rita, her eyes were opened wide as she waited for the rest of my patter. I continued, "But this evening we are going to sing the song in English."

A few men sitting at the tables at the front of the room shouted something about not wanting Jerry songs at their club. I decided that my fortè was obviously not in the comediènne department.

"Ladies and gentlemen ... Sentimental Journey!"

I could sense by the way Rita went at the song straight away with her lovely clear loud voice that she was feeling more relaxed. It brushed off on me and I began to enjoy myself. The harmony sounded beautiful. I stretched out my right arm and Rita did likewise with her left. We looked towards heaven, swayed our hips and tapped our feet in time to the rhythm. The audience loved the song and applauded loudly. We were warming them up nicely for the comedian — he would have a good night.

We finished our spot and the curtains swished gently together again. I suggested we go down to the bar and have a drink whilst the Bingo was being played. We kept on our 'singing dresses' and our cleavages were a huge success with the miners. In no time at all we were surrounded. The miners all wanting to buy us a drink at once. They all wanted to talk to the artists.

"I'll get them in, surry ... put yer money away."

"No yer not ... I asked them fust, din't I, gels!"

"Watch him, gels ... he's a right 'un with the women."

"Have shorts with me, gels ... have a drop of gin ... makes yer sin."

"How's the wife and ten kids, Bill? Not brought the wife with yer then tonight?"

"Oh, don't be jealous, surry ... I can't help it if I'm good looking."

"Bloody 'ell ... 'ark at him. I've seen better looking faces on my whippets."

Rita and I basked in the attention and soaked up the limelight. I felt very excited as though my body had been charged with a battery. I tingled all over and the flattery made me feel quite out of the ordinary. For once in my life I felt really desirable and attractive. I could feel my self-confidence returning — since the break-up of my marriage I had felt colourless, unattractive and quite unfeminine but now, in the middle of all this attention from the miners, a new Helen Linsey was slowly emerging. I was like a singing phoenix, I thought happily, as I smiled and encouraged the men. I was rising out of the ashes — the trauma of a broken marriage.

After a quarter of an hour had gone by the lights were dimmed once more ready this time for Alfie's act. Rita and I hurried back to our seats. We sipped at our drinks and puffed at cigarettes which we had stuck in the ends of long white cigarette holders. I felt a bit self-conscious holding the holders but Rita had bought them from a stall on the Market so we had to get our moneysworth out of them.

"Ladies and gentlemen ... your attention, please. Thank you down there at the bar. You know what was decided at the last committee meeting. Plenty of quiet round the bar while the artists are performing." Starched shirt's voice cut through the cacophony of talking and laughter. "It gives me great pleasure ... ha-ha-ha ... it always has ... to introduce you to your comedian for this evening. He's been to the Blaythorpe before ... here he is ... that man of mirth ... the one and only ... Alfie Seltzer. The man who will cure your indigestion." There were a few giggles from the women in the audience. Starched shirt continued, "Order please! ... plenty of order for ... Alfie Seltzer!"

The curtains opened and Alfie stood in the centre of the stage. He was grinning out at the audience and from where I was sitting I noticed he had a nervous facial twitch. I began to feel nervous for him now. I knew what he was experiencing, out there facing the audience. It was worse for Alfie, I thought, if they didn't laugh at his jokes it would be terribly embarrassing for him.

Alfie was wearing a red plaid jacket which hung over the edges of his shoulders. His trousers were black, the bottom half of an old dress-suit, I imagined, because they were shiny at the knees and old-fashioned. His bow-tie was red with white spots on and his shirt too was red and had a large collar which turned up at the ends. His black patent shoes were cracked and when he turned sideways I saw they were down at heel.

"Good evening, everybody," he went into his patter, "I went to see my doctor yesterday. I'm worried about my health, I said. Oh yes, he said, and what seems to be the trouble? Well, doctor, I said, I can't stop digging great big holes in my garden. I just keep digging all these big holes all over everywhere." Alfie's voice was thin and scratchy, the sort of voice that puts your nerves on edge because you keep thinking it will give out at any moment.

"All these great big holes, doctor," Alfie continued. There were a few guffaws from the men. "Oh, I know what's wrong with you, my man, said the doctor ... you've got

Beri-Beri." A few more guffaws. Alfie battled on. "Now then, lads ... I want to ask you something." He went to the edge of the stage and stared down at the audience. "Listen here, lads ... do you talk to your wife when you're making love?" He paused and pretended to listen to their answers. "What? ... what's that you say, lads? Oh, I see ... only when you're near a 'phone."

Now there was raucous laughter from the men but the women kept silent and gave their husbands nasty looks.

Alfie waited for the laughter to die and then continued, "All you need in this world, lads, is a friend. Ah yes ... a friend. My wife's my best friend. No ... you mustn't laugh ... she's a lovely woman. Got everything a man could ask for, my wife has." He paused for effect. "She's got everything ... big strong muscles ... a moustache." The audience started to laugh. "And a hairy chest ... and a voice like Paul Robeson's. Oh yes, lads ... she's a lovely singer you know. She's sung to full houses all over the world, she has, I'm not kidding you. She's sung in opera-houses ... alms-houses ... glass-houses ... greenhouses." More laughter from the audience. "Still, I'm not complaining, lads. No ... I've got a beautiful girlfriend. She's a lovely redhead ... no hair, just a red head. Lovely girl she is. She's got her bust at the back instead of the front. Bit of a funny shape, lads ... but she's heaven to dance with." More laughter from the audience.

"I don't know what you lot 'ave got to laugh about. The world's full of trouble. Have you heard about them there crooks who were escaping from the police in a cement-mixer full of stolen money?" He paused for a few seconds and then said, "The police had to let them go free. The crooks had a concrete alibi."

He turned to the pianist and drummer. "Now gentlemen ... if you'll just play some nice fast music I'll do my tap-dance. Like to see me dance would you, girls? I taught Fred Astaire all he knows, girls." He leaned over the front of the stage and addressed the women seated at the front tables.

The music started and Alfie did some weird movements with his feet. Suddenly, from the inside of his jacket, he produced an old metal tap which was dangling on the end of a piece of string. He bobbed the tap up-and-down in time to the music of 'Stepping out with my baby.'

Rita and I laughed at his tap-dance and so did the audience — they seemed to prefer silliness instead of the usual filthy jokes and double entendres which so many comedians churned out in the Clubs. He was a real nutcase but his zany humour was just the kind which appealed to my sense of humour.

The music stopped, Alfie put away his tap and addressed the audience once again, "I kept hearing music playing inside my head ... I went to the doctor's and he said let me look at your hat, my man. I took my hat off and he examined it and said, I thought so ... it's the band round your hat."

Alfie battled on for about fifteen minutes and then, at last, the curtain folded him away to the sound of applause. It was time for another game of Bingo. Roughly ten minutes or so and it would be time for another performance from the Dumonte Sisters.

"Time to go and get changed, Rita. Let's take our drinks to the dressing-room." We went backstage and I started to get stage-fright once again.

We squeezed into our black velvet dresses, they would look gorgeous under the full glare of the spotlights. We padded our bras and zipped one another into the gowns, the pianist and drummer were knocking at the door again.

"Got your music ready, girls?" The pianist smiled at us. We sorted through the sheet music and were ready once more for our audience.

When the curtains opened we were greeted with loud whistling from the miners. I loved it. I'd never before realised what an exhibitionist I was. All the attention was certainly helping to build my confidence. I sang my heart out to them. I sang for each man individually — wanted every man to think it was to him alone I longed to cuddle up close to. I wiggled my hips — I could be as suggestive as I pleased, I was safe up there on the stage; ensconced in the warmth and aura I could escape into the unreality.

We concluded out act with 'Side by Side'. The applause that followed was tremendous. Rita and I stood hand in hand, smiling and bowing low. Our cleavages coaxed more whistling and cheering from the men.

★ ★ ★ ★ ★ ★ ★ ★ ★ ★ ★ ★ ★ ★ ★ ★ ★

Later, as we were relaxing in the dressing-room and finishing our drinks, clad only in our pants and bras, the door opened without warning and the entertainment secretary walked in. He looked with delight at the scene before him.

"Would you please mind waiting outside!" I grabbed for my cardigan.

"Yes, clear off a minute," Rita also grabbed at something to cover herself with, "we're in the nude in here!"

"Oh, don't mind me, girls," he continued staring, "I've seen a lot more than this. We 'ave strippers 'ere you know ... every Sunday dinner and every Wednesday night. I've seen the lot I can tell yer."

"Please get out!" I was furious and more so than usual I think because he had seen me without the padding inside my bras.

"All right ... all right ..." he waved a diary at us, "I only wanted to sort out another booking with you. I'll be back in ten minutes then, if you're that shy." He let the door slam behind him.

"Cheeky pig!" Rita finished her drink and stood up. "Now we know why there's no lock on the door ... it's so he can get a cheap thrill." She admired herself in the mirror. "Oh, Helen ... did you hear him? He's going to give us another booking. We'll have to get some cards printed. We'll put, 'The fabulous Dumonte Sisters. Songs from the shows, modern and pops'."

"We can't put that we're fabulous." I laughed at her.

"We can and we are." She whirled round and round. "Fabulous."

"Yes, we are," I agreed with her and got dressed before gawper came back again.

Starched shirt gave us a return booking for the following August. Plenty of time to learn more songs and have different outfits made, I thought. We must have lots of lovely gowns for the women in our audiences to look at and discuss with each other. The women would remember our gowns and, I hoped, the men would just remember us.

The entertainment secretary winked at us and looked slimy.

"Now don't let Dave know about this booking. Keep quiet and you won't have to pay his commission. They liked yer tonight so," he fumbled inside his wallet, "I've decided to give you an extra quid. And I'll give yer an extra quid next time 'an all. A bit of glamour goes down well here."

"Thank you." Rita and I chorussed. "Thanks very much."

47

"Put the date in yer diaries then. And don't forget to confirm a week before. Either in writing or by phone. Freddie Bolton's my name ... you can give me a ring. Just ask for fiery Fred .... I'm hot stuff I am, girls."

I scribbled the date in my diary and Rita did likewise.

"I'll just get you another drink before you go then." Fiery Fred beamed at us. "Shan't be long." He let the door slam again.

"He's trying to see if there's anything doing with either of us." Rita's voice was sarcastic. "They never give up trying, do they!"

"No," I replied, "it's just like a game of chess. You have to think two moves ahead of them all the time. I tell you one thing though."

"What?"

"He's not going to get his hands on any of my pieces."

"Mine neither ... did you see his teeth? I think he must have borrowed them from his grandad."

Fiery Fred returned to the dressing-room with our drinks. He handed us the drinks and then leaned against the sink. He addressed Rita, "If yer want to earn a bit extra I can get yer fifteen quid a time for stripping."

We looked at him in amazement — I was the first to recover.

"Don't be so cheeky ... we wouldn't dream of doing anything like that!"

His face looked sour.

"Oh, I didn't mean you, love. You're much too skinny. And you've got nowt' up top. I wouldn't pay you in washers for stripping. You 'ent got much to show off 'ave yer now." He smirked and looked at my bust.

"Snap!" I answered, but I think my sparkling wit was wasted on him.

We had a word with Alfie before we left the club and discovered that he too had been given a return booking.

"Same night as you again, girls." He looked pleased. "I like working with a bit of glamour, makes it easier for me. I'm working on some new gags. I'll have got a new act together by August."

I doubted it somehow and thought, what did it matter if he was a bit corny. As long as he could make the audience forget their troubles for a while, take their minds off crawling about in the black earth for a living, he was all right. That's what showbusiness is about, I thought, and then smiled to myself as I thought about Alfie's tap on the end of that piece of string. You couldn't get much dafter than that, I thought, as Rita and I waited in the bus shelter for our bus.

CHAPTER EIGHT

My work at the Cresta which had once seemed so interesting quickly changed from exciting to boring. I could think of nothing else but clubs and bookings. Even Christmas passed almost unnoticed.

Rita's boyfriend, Neville, asked if he could come and see our act when next we had a booking. Neither of us were very keen, for different reasons, but we agreed to let him hear us at the Branton British Legion where we had a booking in two weeks time.

Springtime had made us feel frivolous and daring — Rita and I expressed this in the shape of Charleston dresses. We could both dance the Charleston a little and had great fun practising it for our act. The British Legion were in for a treat because we had decided to try the dance out on them. The songs we had chosen for this musical extravaganza were, 'Aint we got Fun' and of course 'Charleston'.

Vera had really excelled herself with our new creations. Bright orange grosgrain material cut two inches above the knee, which was very daring, I thought, even for us. The dresses had orange lampshade fringing sewn all over them which jiggled about when we moved as though we were on a perpetual cake-walk. Thin strips of diamante had been used in place of ordinary shoulder-straps and for a change, loose fitting bodices and so we didn't need any padding in our bras. Vera had also made diamante head bands to wear low down on our foreheads which were held secure by pieces of elastic, hidden at the back of our heads with curls.

Rita wanted to dye some stockings orange but I disagreed and thought black stockings would look much sexier. We completed our outfits with black satin shoes and three rows of long black beads which we whirled round and round in the air when we danced. Vera had screamed with delight when we had given her a preview of the act.

★ ★ ★ ★ ★ ★ ★ ★ ★ ★ ★ ★ ★ ★ ★ ★

The Branton British Legion was a small building hidden at the back of a children's playground and a cricket pavilion.

An elderly man sat in a glass panelled box just inside the door. He looked on his last legs but when he saw Rita, Neville and I walking towards him sprang suddenly to life. He jumped from his seat and thrust one of the glass panels to one side. He poked his head through the hole and asked, "Are yo members? I can't remember seeing yo before. If you're not members you'll have to get a member to sign yer in." A half smoked cigarette waggled up and down in the corner of his mouth.

I envisaged a packed club room ahead of us. They must get very full, I thought, if it was so difficult to get in. I felt another bout of stage-fright coming on again.

"We're the artists." Rita all triumphant. "The singers."

"Oh ... you're the turns, are yer?" The old man closed the panel, stepped out of his box and muttered, "I didn't know yer were the turns. Cum with me then, me ducks ... I'll take yer through."

He opened a door on the left-hand side of the passageway and beckoned us through.

There was a large billiards table in the centre of the room. A few men stood round the table watching another man who was about to take a shot at a ball. The men glanced briefly in our direction and then focussed their eyeballs back on the billiard-ball.

"The entertainment secretary'll put yer right, me ducks." The old man coughed, his lungs seemed to collapse and then decided to have another go. "He'll be here about a quarter-to." He shuffled back to his position of power in the glass panelled box. An old fox going back to his lair, waiting to pounce on all unsuspecting non-members.

Neville put our suitcases down and beckoned towards the bar.

"I think we need a drink after that, don't you?" He looked embarrassed as he led the way towards the bar.

As well as the men playing billiards, there were just over a dozen more people in the club. Mainly elderly couples, but there were four young people sitting at the front near the stage. The young couples had two very small children with them and they it seemed had invented a lovely new game. Screaming and shouting they chased one another in and out of the tables. This was going to be one of those nights, I thought, feeling miserable, Neville had brought us bad luck.

Rita read my thoughts and said, "I don't think the charleston'll go down well here."

"No," I replied, "a minuet'd be more like it." I tried to sound cheerful and make a joke of it all.

"I think I'll have a bat round." Neville smiled at us sympathetically. "I'll come back in time for your last spot. I'll come back about ten." He drank up and hurried from the room.

"Perhap'll it'll fill up later on!" I was glad to see Neville go. "They'll all be watching that war film on television. It ends at quarter to nine."

I was right — the club did start to fill up. People straggled in, I noticed one man in particular because he was wearing a bow-tie.

"He's our man," I whispered to Rita, "bow-tie and dark suit ... I'll bet he's the secretary." I sipped at my drink and smiled at him.

Bow-tie looked shy, he returned my smile and walked over to the bar.

"Good evening, are you the Dumonte Sisters?"

"Yes."

"First time at the Branton, isn't it?"

"Yes."

"If you'd like to bring your drinks with you, I'll just show you the way to your dressing-room. The place doesn't start to get full till about nine. Do your first spot at nine ... before the Tombola. Do your next spot at half-past nine ... and then you can finish off with your last spot about ten-past ten. If you'd just like to follow me then."

He made no move to carry our suitcases downstairs but I gave him the benefit of the doubt and thought perhaps he had got a hernia through carrying too many suitcases. And after all, I thought, hernias could really mess up your love life.

Rita and I followed bow-tie down some cellar steps. He led the way along a tiny passageway and opened a door which had 'Private' chalked on it.

"If you'd like to get changed in there." He did not venture to step inside the tiny room. "Then if you'd come back upstairs I'd like to get you both a drink if I may."

He's not such a bad sort after all, I thought, and told him our drinks were Guiness. Rita and I didn't like to appear too expensive when anyone asked to buy us a drink. We usually bought our own ports and slipped it into the Guiness afterwards.

The dressing-room was very cold and the smell of damp, and empty beer bottles which were in crates piled high against one side of the room, was overpowering.

An old wooden table stood in the centre of the room and there were three metal chairs stacked one on top of the other. The mirror was full length and had lost most of its silver backing. When I stood in front of the mirror pieces of myself were missing. I could see down as far as my neck, then my shoulders disappeared. My right side was visible as far as my knees and then my leg vanished. It was a scream — just like a comic mirror at the Fair. A faded picture of Winston Churchill hung on the wall next to the mirror. Old Winston smiled down at us, resplendent in regal robes.

On the other side of the mirror were photographs of other artistes, these were stuck on the wall with cellotape or attached with drawing pins. There were also some of the artistes' business cards. I took out one of our cards and wedged it into the top of the mirror frame.

At ten minutes to nine the pianist and drummer came down into the cellar for a look at our music. They lady pianist told us that she and the drummer were married. A marriage in perfect harmony, I thought, how nice to share the same interest and be able to have an evening out together and earn money at the same time.

"The mike's a bit dodgy, girls." The drummer informed us. "Plays up a bit if you don't use it right. Don't get too close to it else it'll whistle like mad."

"Oh, and mind where you stand," his wife added more exciting instructions. "There's a couple of loose floor-boards at the front of the stage. Mind you don't get your heels fast."

They went back upstairs and Rita and I had another fit of the giggles.

"We've got a choice tonight, Rita." I looked in the mirror and tried to find the reflection of my mouth in a part of the mirror you could see yourself in. "Either we get electrocuted with the mike ... or we fall through the stage and land up in the cellar."

There were no curtains on the stage. Just the piano and set of drums in one corner and a large box with knobs on which was apparently the amplification unit. An old Henry Hall days type microphone stood in the middle of the stage. To get to the stage we had to walk the length of the room past the billiards table and the bar. We then had to climb some ricketty wooden steps on the left hand side of the stage.

The entertainment secretary announced us, "Quiet at the bar please, everybody. We have for your entertainment this evening two lovely sisters. Give a big hand for the ... Dumonte Sisters."

The audience applauded and the secretary added, "Thank you ... here they are." Or at least it was supposed to sound like that but the microphone began to whistle and screech. The secretary turned towards the box and twiddled about with the knobs. He then took hold of the microphone once more and blew into it. Then he started to count, "One ... two ... three." The microphone behaved.

We hurried up the ricketty steps and stood in front of the microphone which the secretary had replaced on its stand. I looked down to make sure I wasn't standing near the loose floor boards and waited for our introduction from the pianist.

51

The pianist played a couple of bars and we were away. Or rather, we should have been away. I leaned closer to the microphone and sang out louder. But I couldn't hear anything! I knew immediately what the matter was — yes, I had gone deaf with fright — all the worry about falling into the cellar. But no — the microphone had packed up altogether. We carried on singing like stars in a silent movie. Out of the corner of my eye I could see the entertainment secretary, he climbed onto the stage and started fiddling about with the knobs on the box. Now our voices could be heard intermittently. What on earth was he playing at. Oh, I wish I could die. I turned to look at Rita, I think she was just on the verge of hysterics. Again, a high pitch whistle and then, our voices echoed round the room. Success at last. The microphone behaved itself for the remainder of the song.

At the end of our first spot the audience clapped loudly. Perhaps they felt sorry for us. The ordeal with the microphone had certainly been very off-putting. We took our Guiness and ports with us, down into the bowels of the earth once more and changed into our Charleston dresses. We were going to open our second spot with 'Ma he's Making Eyes at me', then go into our Charleston routine.

I was frozen, couldn't make my mind up whether it was mainly the cold cellar or my usual bout of malaria-type stage fright.

"You look terrific." Rita sipped her drink then lit a cigarette. She handed one to me, I could see her hand shaking as she held out the lighter. We looked at ourselves in the mirror, jiggled the parts we could see about a bit. Rita swung her beads round and round.

I noticed her shoulders. Rita had beautiful shoulders, like a lady in a Gainsborough painting. Flawless skin, lovely shoulders. This skin was now covered in duck bumps.

"I'm bleddy frozen," she carried on jiggling about, "it's like getting changed inside a mummy's tomb."

"I think I want to spend a penny again." I crossed my legs.

"Hurry up then," Rita laughed at me, "and mind you don't pee on your fringing."

At half past nine the entertainment secretary knocked on the door.

"Are you ready, girls?"

We opened the door and could tell by the expression on his face that he was knocked out by our outfits. He admired us openly, especially when his eyes feasted on our black net stockings.

"You look very nice," was all he could manage to croak, "very nice." He stepped to one side so that we could go up the cellar steps in front of him. We knew he was having a good look up our legs.

There was an appreciative murmur when we walked onto the stage, whistling from some younger men who were leaning against the bar and a lot of chattering from the women as they discussed our outfits.

We began the first song. The microphone behaved itself. Now for it. Cold terror gripped me. Just like falling through the ice on a pond, there was no escape. I had now got to make a fool of myself in front of all these people. Which leg did I start off with? Was it the left or the right? Which hand did I use for swinging my beads round? I resolved after tonight never, ever, to get on a stage again. My nerves just would not stand up to it.

I looked at Rita. She was smiling down at a group of gawping men who were sitting at a table near the front of the stage. She didn't look frightened out of her wits. The duo played our introduction and we were off. Miracles! We both started off with the correct foot. I charlestoned and swung my beads for all I was worth. The audience loved it. They clapped in time to the music and da de dah'd along with us. When we started our second dance to, 'Aint we got Fun', five elderly ladies got up from their seats and unable to contain themselves started an act of their own. A great cheer went up from the audience. Knobbly knees, thick ankles, varicose veins flashed this way and that in time to our music.

When we had finished our spot the audience clapped and cheered. Our new idea was a success. I felt elated. Couldn't wait to change my dress again and get back up there onto the stage. Stage struck? Show off? Mental? Whatever. Oh, I couldn't give it up now. Besides we were good. People seemed to react favourably to us. They must like our act or else they wouldn't clap and re-book us. Even the women seemed to like us and that was saying something.

At five to ten Neville walked into the room. He had managed to get past the terror of the glass box. We had changed into our black velvet dresses and were standing just inside the room waiting to be announced.

"I say," Neville looked at us, rather surprised, "you both look very glamorous. Just like real artists."

"Well, what do you think we're supposed to be?" Rita put her hand on her hip. Neville put his arm round her, gave her a squeeze. "Having a drink, girls?"

"Thank you. A drop of port please. Oh, we're on! You can watch us from the bar. See you in a few minutes."

The lights at the back and in the middle of the room were dimmed leaving only a few on near the stage. This would show off our black velvet gowns and diamante ear-rings. As we climbed onto the stage for the third and last time, the slits in the sides of our dresses gaped open and the display of fish-net clad thighs, brought more whistling and shouting from the men at the bar. I wondered what Neville was thinking!

We gave them 'Sentimental Journey' and then went into a medley of old numbers. 'Side by Side', got a lot more people besides the five old ladies onto their feet. They danced in and out of the tables, up and down the aisles and along the front, near the stage.

I could see Neville's shape silhouetted against the brightly lit bar. Thank our lucky stars we were having a good night after all. I knew he'd be surprised and impressed with our act. I'll bet he was feeling very proud of Rita.

The entertainment secretary asked if we could 'please' give a return booking in three month's time. We accepted and were also delighted when he gave us a pound extra. "The committee decided you were worth it," he smiled at us, "especially that Charleston bit. The members have had a really good night."

We carried our suitcases up from the cellar. Two men were standing in the passageway. One stepped forward. He beamed at us. "Hello, girls." He held a half smoked cigar in one hand, a large black book in the other. "My fellow committee member and me would like to book you for our Miners' Welfare at Medford, if you have a free date this year that is?" Neville walked towards us and stood listening.

"I'll just have a look when we're free." Rita thumbed through her diary. "Yes, we can do one for you on either the ninth or the sixteenth of September."

"Ninth, lovely," scribble scribble went the man, "that'll be eight pounds for three spots. There'll probably be a group on with you as well. You should have a good night.

You can confirm the booking by phone if you like. Here's my card with the number on. Have you got a lift home by the way?"

"Yes, thank you." Rita looked over to where Neville was standing.

"Goodnight then. See you in September."

"Goodnight." It was marvellous. The bookings were rolling in.

We packed our suitcases into Neville's car and made our way home. It was ages before I could get to sleep. The evening had been quite exhausting. All the worry about the microphone, and the floor giving way. The anxious moments before we had started our new dance routine. But, I decided, it had been worth every moment. The applause, the whistling and cheering from the audience, the envious looks from the women and the appreciative stares from the men had made the evening very exciting.

I was hooked on showbusiness like I had never been hooked on anything before. I fell asleep at last, in the middle of designing a new gown. It was going to be black satin with lots of black net jutting out from the knees. And we would have large red artificial roses pinned on one side of the net.

CHAPTER NINE

On the following Monday afternoon we went to the hairdressers and then took the commission round to Dave's studio. Dave had a visitor but told us to sit down for a while, he had something to say to us.

He introduced us to the extremely large, but well dressed man. He shook hands with us and his brandy breath would have made a good fire-eating act if someone had lit a match near it.

"These are the Dumonte Sisters. I was telling you about them earlier." Dave lit a cigar, handed one to his visitor. "And this is Jimmy Cook. You've probably heard of him, girls. Books mainly for the big clubs and better class of pub. He would like to see your act. Can you do a shop window next Wednesday night at the Metropole club at Coningswell?"

"Well," Rita looked at me, "I think we could both get the night off, but we shall have to make it right with Ray Bowler. He'll have to get two of the casual staff to stand in for us. I'm sure we'll be able to get though."

"You mustn't turn a chance like this down, my dears", Jimmy Cook smiled at us showing no less than three gold teeth, "There'll be a dozen or so agents and entertainment secretaries in the audience. You could pick up a lot of work if they like your act. Have you auditioned for any of the Butlin's camps by the way? They pay very good fees ... that's where the money is, girls."

"Oh, we're not good enough for that sort of thing yet", I lowered my eyes, looked demure, "we're only just starting out really."

"Never", Jimmy roared, "never let me hear you say you're not good enough ever again! If you're offered a job you don't think you can handle say it is inexpedient at that particular time. Remember." He glowered at us from underneath eyebrows which looked like miniature flue brushes. "Inexpedient. Think big and you'll become big, my dear."

He reached inside his jacket, took out a diary, held it in the air and waggled it at us. "There's a lot of money waiting to be earned if you want it. If I like your act on Wednesday, I can have you out practically every night of the week. Take your coats off."

We stared at him. He had caught us by surprise. We took our coats off and stood holding them. Jimmy walked over to us and took the coats.

"Turn round. Emm! You're a big girl." He oggled Rita with obvious delight. Now it was my turn to be mentally undressed. "Emm! You don't look much like sisters. Not on the weight stakes anyhow." He patted my behind. "You want fattening up a little, my dear."

"I drink plenty of Guiness!" was all I could muster.

"Emm!" Now it was Rita's turn for a pat on the bottom. "I don't know about sisters. You look more like Laurel and Hardy." What an ignorant, insensitive man he was. Perhaps he could join our act? We could be a comedy trio. Laurel and Hardy and Fatty Arbuckle. I looked at Rita and knew she had something far more insulting in mind. Still, bite the old tongue. This man was going to be of some use to us. Poor pathetic old lecher. I looked at him with distaste. I wouldn't use him for practice if I'd been born in a nunnery on a desert island. His stomach had reached monstrous proportions. I'll bet he hadn't seen his feet for years! If he wanted a look he would have to stand in front of a mirror.

He sidled up again and put his arm around Rita's waist.

"I know what you could do to make yourselves look more like sisters. Dye your hair. Yes, that's it. Agree on a colour and dye your hair. How about a lovely rich auburn colour? I love red hair. Very fiery and hot blooded red haired women are. Got any more brandy tucked away Dave?" His mind grass-hopped again, he winked at us. "Bloody tight he is you know, girls. He'll be the richest bloke in the cemetery when he goes. Ha-ha-ha. You can't take it with you, Dave."

Dave took a bottle of brandy and a bottle of whisky from out of his desk drawer. He handed the glasses round. We sipped our drinks and all looked towards Jimmy. He may have not been a very charming man, but he had magnetism. Overpowering magnetism. He looked at Dave.

"I've started booking a few strippers. Packs them in at the Miners' Welfares. You can't get in the places, especially Sunday lunch-times when the little woman's at home having fun over a hot oven. Gorgeous, beautiful girls some of them. Are you booking any of them, Dave?"

"No. I couldn't send strippers to any of my places. Some of the committees are very funny about filthy jokes even. Won't have filth."

"Arr", Jimmy knocked his brandy back, "that's what I call a really good night out." His chest heaved and wheezed. "Filthy jokes and strippers."

Oh blimey, I thought, sending signals across to Rita with my eyes. Here we go again. Same old subject!

★ ★ ★ ★ ★ ★ ★ ★ ★ ★ ★ ★ ★ ★ ★ ★ ★

Ray agreed to let us both have Wednesday evening off, but did not look very pleased.

"You can't keep having time off together. You'll have to make your minds up. You either want to work here or do your singing lark." He changed the subject. "Let me know what fresh stock you need for the bar. I'll be down the cellar, Rita. Bring your list down to me."

Rita made a note of the spirits we needed and went to tell Ray. A few minutes later she came back to the bar looking rather flustered.

"It's Ray's birthday today. I think he's a bit drunk. He's just grabbed hold of my breasts and tried to get his whatsit out." I told her about my adventure down the cellar — because I hadn't embroidered on my experience with Ray when it had happened to me all those months ago.

"And he told you it was his birthday too?" Rita doubled up with laughter.

"Yes. That's two birthdays he's had since we've worked here. At this rate he'll be old before his time. I know we asked him for a rise last week, but this is ridiculous. Oh, he's coming. Don't make me laugh."

Ray walked over to the bar, arms laden with bottles. He looked completely in control, as suave and elegant as ever.

"Here you are then, girls. Now I'll have a nice large brandy please. Have a drink yourselves. It's my birthday today."

I don't know how we did it, but we managed to keep our faces straight until he'd gone back into his office.

"It really must be his birthday." I laughed and poured a large gin and orange for each of us.

★ ★ ★ ★ ★ ★ ★ ★ ★ ★ ★ ★ ★ ★ ★ ★ ★

At a quarter to eleven Neville came into the Cresta. He looked as though he'd had enough to drink. Rita told him about our conversation with Dave and Jimmy.

"And so if he likes our act he's going to get loads of bookings for us. There'll be a lot more agents there as well. Helen and I are seriously thinking of packing it in here and turning really professional. We could earn a packet going singing regularly, especially with good agents." Her face was flushed. Enthusiasm shone out of her eyes. She looked extremely attractive. Neville seemed displeased with the idea.

"But I thought you liked working here! And we get to see each other most afternoons. If you get bookings all over the show I'll not see anything of you at all."

He was jealous. Poor old Neville. I hadn't realised. He was in love with Rita, afraid of losing her. Rita was flippant.

"Oh don't look so miserable, Neville. Learn to play the guitar or something, then you can come with us."

Neville sat, shoulders hunched, on a stool at the bar. He sipped his drink and stared past us at the shelves at the back of the bar.

"You won't like going singing every night. It's a rat race. I think you ought to keep it as a sort of hobby. Like my golf."

"Oh don't talk ridiculous, Neville?" Rita washed some glasses, I dried. "I want to do it so that's the end of the matter."

"Well I don't want you to," Neville raised his voice.

"We'll talk about it later." Rita turned away to serve a customer. "Good evening, Mr. Donlan. The usual is it?" Neville was dismissed.

★ ★ ★ ★ ★ ★ ★ ★ ★ ★ ★ ★ ★ ★ ★ ★ ★

The Metropole club was packed to capacity. We arrived later than arranged. Neville, who was supposed to be giving us a lift, had gone sulky and refused at the last moment. The bus we caught had gone the long way round, in and out of two villages and stopping at nearly every bus stop.

The scenery was beautiful although it did not have our full appreciation; our nerves were stretched like strings on a violin.

The entertainment secretary led the way through the crowded concert room.

"You'll have to share the dressing-room," he apologised. "We've got twelve acts on tonight in the shop window. Seven ladies and five men. It'll be a bit of a squeeze I'm afraid but it could be worse. Luckily we've no groups on, they take a hell of a lot of room up. All that equipment they bring. I nearly broke my neck last week, tripped over one of their microphone wires. Six microphones they had ... I ask you. You could hear them in the next village."

We changed into our black velvet dresses and daubed nervously at our cheeks and noses with face powder. The other girls were doing likewise. They smiled politely but seemed suspicious of us, unfriendly. I decided I didn't like them either. If they were better than us they would pinch all our bookings.

A tall, buxom woman with sparse dark brown hair reached into her suitcase. She took out a magnificent curly blonde wig and placed it on her head. The transformation was remarkable.

"I'm on first," she addressed us all, "I sing light opera."

"What, soap?" said Rita. Everyone laughed except curly wig. She put on a pair of long green satin gloves which covered her elbows and looked disdainfully round the dressing-room. "I don't usually do shop windows. No need to really. I have plenty of bookings all the year round, but Jimmy Cook's coming this evening and I would like to get in on the Leicester circuit. I've heard he loves my type of voice."

"He loves her type of breasts as well," Rita whispered.

"What do you call yourselves?" She looked at our velvet gowns, "I like your dresses. Did you make them yourselves?"

"The Dumonte Sisters," I answered her.

"Umm. Never heard of you. Still you're very young aren't you. Are you just starting out?"

"No. We've been at it for years," Rita lied. "What's your name?"

"Carla Danby." She combed the curls on the blonde wig.

"I've never heard of you," said Rita, "and you must have been going some years." The other girls sniggered. Carla tugged at the green satin gloves. "I don't suppose I sing at your type of club." She swept from the room in triumph, like an Amazon in a Tarzan film.

The entertainment secretary knocked on the door, came in flourishing a sheet of paper. "Right then, girls. You'll go in this order. Carla Danby first. Then Billy Rhapsody. Next the Dumonte Sisters. Then, Ricky Carson the tenor," he ranted on, "then the comedian Sammy Sunshine."

Third! We were on third. I wish we could have been nearer the end though — the audience are nicely warmed up by then. Still, there was no changing now.

The pianist, drummer, bass player and accordionist somehow crammed themselves inside the dressing-room and looked our music over. Carla Danby was still outside the dressing-room so I assumed they must have already seen her music.

We had chosen what we considered to be our best harmony songs. We just had to be good tonight. Dear God, please, please let us be good! Carla sang three numbers, the applause was quite loud. I downed my Guiness and port, it seemed to fly straight to my bladder. Billy Rhapsody crooned pleasantly through three numbers. We were next. I froze again. No time to go to the toilet. I fiddled nervously with the padding in my bra. I had forgotten to pack my strips of nylon or scarves, so in desperation, had had to make do with my knickers and a pair of Rita's nylon gloves. Everything looked all right. My cleavage was still there.

We began our spot with 'Sentimental Journey!'

Oh, the accompaniment was sheer poetry. The bass player gave us a spot-on beat and so did the drummer. The pianist was first class and the accordionist's fingers went berserk. And, miracle upon miracles, the microphone behaved itself, was pitched just right.

We knew we were going down well. You get accustomed to the feel and mood of an audience. No noise from the bars. No fidgeting or talking. A complete rapport between artists, musicians and audience.

After we had finished our spot, we went along to one of the three bars in the huge room. We kept our 'singing dresses' on. Our glamorous gowns made us stagey and different. The men crowded round.

"What's it to be then, girls?"

"Hey, Harry, I'll get them."

"How's your wife and six kids then, Alf?" Old jokes poured out.

"Take no notice of him, girls. What yer having?" We soaked it up.

Jimmy Cook was making his way slowly through the throng. He looked like a huge walrus coming up for air. His lips puffed in and out as he struggled for breath. His eyes bulged as he stared at our cleavages. I'll bet he couldn't make out where mine had suddenly come from. I leaned against him on purpose. Gave him a good view. Poor old Jimmy. I noticed that his face was going purple.

"We can't talk here, girls. I liked your act. Come to my office tomorrow at eleven o'clock." He gave us both a business card.

"I'm sorry, but we can't make it tomorrow." Rita's eyes twinkled with devilment. "It is inexpedient."

"Ha-ha-ha. You catch on quick, don't you." He patted her behind and flashed his gold teeth. "Would you like a drink, girls?"

Carla Danby was making her way towards us. The curls on the blonde wig bobbed merrily. "Hello, Mr. Cook. We have met before."

"Er ... um ... yes. Hello, my dear. Can I get you a drink?" She looked smug. "Oh, thank you. I'll have a sherry please. Medium dry please." She carried on the pretence of having met him before. "It's lovely meeting you again, Mr. Cook."

Jimmy handed our drinks over.

"Er ... have you got anything for me?" Carla gushed.

"Oh, give me your card my dear and I will give you a ring." A green satin covered hand dipped quickly into a black plastic handbag.

"I must go", Jimmy put the card into his pocket, "I've still got a lot of people to see. Cheerio." He winked at us and made a way through the crowd, using his stomach as a battering ram.

Carla turned her back on us and sipped daintily at her medium dry sherry.

"Don't ring me, I'll ring you," whispered Rita. We were helpless with laughter, hysterical rather. I think that was because of the awful tension we had experienced beforehand. It had swept from us now, like waves over the sand.

"What are yer laughing at then, girls?" Smiling faces beamed in on us again.

"Oh, I bet that was a filthy one." A red-haired cheeky faced man.

"I like your dress-less straps. You look like Marilyn Monroe and Jane Russell." The men moved in once more. All flashing money and smiles.

Hardly Jane Russell, I thought happily — but with an extra pair of gloves shoved down my bra, I could perhaps pass for the poor man's Lana Turner.

I noticed one man in particular paying a lot of attention to us. He was tall, well made and in his late forties. Hair, going grey at the sides, gave him a distinguished look, a dark moustache added mischief and sexiness. He was with another man, slightly younger, who had kept his hat on. I can't stand men who keep their hats on in a room. Still, ignorance is bliss so they say. They edged their way nearer.

"I enjoyed your songs," said pork-pie hat, "what do you do for an encore?" He looked cheeky. "This is my friend, Jack Sargent, by the way. He would like to give you a booking, amongst other things. Have you got a date a bit nearer Christmas?"

We had the second Sunday in December free. I smiled at them and wrote the date down in my diary. Pork pie hat continued, "Jack's got one or two betting shops, but he's also got an interest in a couple of clubs. They aren't very big, but the accompaniment's good and they're a friendly crowd out at Felford. I think you'll enjoy yourselves. I'm George by the way. I run one of Jack's betting shops." You also do all his talking as well by the sounds of it, I thought.

"What's your poison?" He nodded to our near empty glasses. He bought us a Guiness, insisted on ports to go with them and hemmed us in near the corner of the bar. The other men couldn't get near us now.

I could see that Jack had taken a liking to Rita, so I resigned myself to having to listen to a monologue of witticisms, inuendoes and boring anecdotes from George the hat. I imagined he must have been bald underneath the hat, so decided not to be too hard on the poor soul.

One by one the other acts did their stuff. The comedian was rather near the bone, if you'll pardon the expression, but he made us all laugh. The tenor had quite a nice voice, but I found him terribly boring. He stood in front of the microphone with his hands folded together, resting on his chest. He looked as though he was laid out standing up and had a pained expression on his face all the time. Took himself very seriously by the look of him and seemed completely emotionless. I'll bet his wife has to give him a week's notice in writing when she wants it, I thought.

He finished his spot with 'The Lost Chord' and looked as though he had lost everything. The elderly people in the audience loved it. I even saw one old dear wiping her eyes with a handkerchief.

The girl singers were all quite good, especially one, who was very effervescent. She had dressed herself up in a man's dress-suit jacket with tails, black top hat cocked cheekily to one side, black fish-net stockings and high heeled black satin shoes. She sang old time music hall songs. 'Burlington Bertie' and 'Who were you with last night'.

She would have made an excellent principal boy in pantomime. Jack Sargent and George couldn't take their eyes off her.

"She'll be all right for a booking at Jack's club," I whispered to Rita.

At ten o'clock we were so happy and excited. Like flying at 70,000 feet without a parachute. No less than ten entertainment secretaries and five agents had given us bookings. We still kept to Sundays only up until Christmas, but had decided that in the New Year we would give up our jobs at the Cresta and go singing full-time. It would have been madness not to. The work was there, waiting, and we would have plenty of time to learn lots of new songs and think up different acts.

"Have another drink, girls?" Jack took out his wallet which was absolutely bulging with fivers. Rita's eyes bulged to match.

"Just one then", she giggled. "We've had too much already." Another giggle. "And we've got to catch the ten twenty bus back, as well. It's a hell of a way round the villages on the bus we came out here on."

"Oh, don't worry about getting home", George pulled at the brim of his hat, "we'll see as you get home safely. What do you fancy? A Rover or an Austin Princess?"

I looked at Rita. It was her decision. I was all for a lift home, but Neville wouldn't be too pleased about us taking lifts from strangers. Serve him right. I resented him trying to hold Rita back and felt as though I had more claim on her than he had.

We went back-stage, packed our dresses and music away. The other girls were discussing their various bookings. We had all done well out of the shop window. It had certainly been worth our while going. Even Carla Danby looked pleased with herself as she laid her green satin gloves away in her suitcase on the top of her blonde curly wig.

Rita settled for Jack Sargent's Rover, so I travelled behind in the Austin. Jack had asked us back to his place for sandwiches and coffee and that's all we were going back for as far as I was concerned.

"Jack's got a smashing place," George gushed, "real bachelor pad. Wife cleared off and left him years ago. Ran off with another bookie. Mind you, Jack didn't care. She was a right old cow. She could spend Jack's money faster than he could take it off the mugs in his betting shops. And she was a cold devil. Only let him have it once a week. Every Saturday night when they'd been out for a drink, and it had to be in bed. No fun and games, no nothing. And if poor old Jack didn't feel like it on a Saturday, he had to go without it for a fortnight. Mind you, he's made up for lost time since she left ... one long line of lovely women after him."

"Are you married?" I changed the subject quickly. There was an obvious pause before he answered me.

"No ... I haven't got the time. I'm too busy seeing to all the single girls. I like to leave a bit for all of them."

Oh, blimey, why do I lumber myself like this! "I think I've got a cold coming," I tried to put him off, "and my head aches like mad."

"You know what you want for that, don't you, darling," came the standard reply.

We drove up a gravelled driveway guarded on either side by sentries of beautiful elm trees. The 'olde worlde' type bungalow nestled at the top. It had leaded windows and a charming little porch which had a coloured lantern hanging inside.

Rita and I kicked our shoes off and snuggled down into the luxury of the soft, real leather chairs. There were fitted carpets, beautifully made thick, red velvet curtains draped from shiny brass rods, and an elegant cocktail bar at the far end of the room. Not the usual type with the cheap plastic padding, but real dark oak panelling and carved oak shelves complimenting elegant cut glass decanters and glasses.

"I'll pour the drinks while you help yourselves to food ... tuck in, girls." Jack walked towards the bar. "There's everything you need through there in the kitchen. I'll have a beef sandwich. Cut the meat nice and thick."

The fridge was crammed full with food. I took the joint out of the fridge and began carving. Rita buttered the bread. It was like a dream. I couldn't believe it was happening to me. I had never been in a house as posh as this before. Singing had certainly opened up a new world for me.

I looked at Rita. The devil was in her. She looked in cupboards, opened drawers and prodded about. "Look at this! And what about this! He's not short of a bob or two is he. Just the sort of man I've been looking for. I wouldn't mind living in a set up like this. Would you?"

"No." I answered happily, then crammed a slice of best prime beef into my mouth.

We carried the sandwiches into the lounge. Now for the game of chess. Jack made a move towards the settee where Rita had sat down. George patted his knee intimating I sit on it. I said I was much too comfortable to move from where I was.

We played records and talked and drank. After an hour had gone by I signalled across to Rita with my eyes. She was more than slightly drunk. I stood up and yawned. "Well, it's time somebody made a move."

"What sort of move did you have in mind, darling?" said George, who was still wearing his hat by the way.

"Time to go home." I acted daft. "We've got to be up early. Have to be at Jimmy Cook's office in the morning. He's got a lot of work for us." Still no response from Rita. Just a silly grin.

"I'll nip you home then." George also stood up. "I'm dead tired."

"Rita's not going just yet," Jack walked over to the bar, "she's staying for a nightcap. I'll give her a lift later on."

"I'll bet you will as well." George winked at me. God what a bore. How on earth was I going to get rid of him without a lot of embarrassment? I began to feel nervous.

Rita lit a cigarette and grinned across at me. "See you at Jimmy Cook's office at eleven. Mind how you go you two."

Jack saw us to the door and gave me a little kiss on the cheek. "Nice to have met you, Helen. See you again soon." Why couldn't I have got him? Still, Rita was much better looking. I suppose it was inevitable. I smiled at Jack and stepped with trepidation into George's car.

I arrived home, my honour still intact with no thanks to George, at 2.30. I'd had quite a struggle but managed to escape all right. Why should a man expect to grope and fondle you just because he's bought a couple of drinks? Besides, I still had the gloves and knickers inside my bra. That would have been something to tell the boys in the betting shops about.

Throughout all this carry on his hat had remained where it was. I decided, as I snuggled under the bedclothes, that it must have been glued on.

★ ★ ★ ★ ★ ★ ★ ★ ★ ★ ★ ★ ★ ★ ★ ★

I met Rita at eleven o'clock outside Jimmy Cook's office. We were both very impressed with his set up. Nice, expensive furniture spaced out well in a large sunshine filled office. The adjacent room to the left had been made into a small studio, complete with grand piano and microphone. He even had a secretary who sat in an outer office in charge of a small switchboard and who typed with all her fingers, so she was obviously not there just for show.

He gave us lots of work and also a lecture on reliability.

"You must always confirm your bookings in writing or, if the entertainment secretary agrees beforehand, by telephone. Never, ever let a club down unless you're bloody dying. If one of you can't get, let me know as soon as possible so that I can get somebody to stand in. You both do singles, don't you?" He wrote something down in a book. "So ... I will probably send a male singer or a comedian to double up with either of you. But," he stressed emphatically, "if you let me down more than three times, I shall cross you off my books. There's nothing worse than an audience sitting waiting for an act that doesn't show up. All right? Have you both got that?"

We nodded agreement. This man meant business.

"If I can't get out to see you on the nights of some of your bookings, you can bring the commission here to the office. If I'm not in leave it with my secretary." He finished the interview abruptly. "Right you are then, my dears. Off you go and practice hard. See you at the Rowan Bush on the eighth. You should have a good night there ... a nice crowd."

He pressed the button on his intercom. "Get me Shelley Randle on the phone please, Miss James ... goodbye, girls." We left him huddling over his intercom.

Rita and I walked down to Carlin and Priestley's. We were shown to a table by the window in the restaurant and ordered coffee and toast. The waitresses gathered round once more.

"We're going singing full-time after Christmas." Rita lit a cigarette and handed one to me. We put the cigarettes in our white and gold cigarette holders. The waitresses looked at the cigarette holders and then looked at one another.

"I came to see you at the Welfare," little Nora dusted crumbs from our tablecloth, "I brought my boyfriend with me and he thought you were smashing. We thought you were really brilliant."

"Why didn't you come up to us?" I popped a sugar-lump into my coffee.

"Oh, we didn't like to. You were sitting at the front anyway ... at the artists' table."

I could feel the distance between us and felt rather sorry for Nora.

"Well next time come and sit with us. Come and have a drink with us you daft thing. Fancy not saying hello. You could come back-stage if you wanted to and have a look inside the dressing-rooms."

The other girls smiled but with their lips only. I could tell by the looks in their eyes that they were jealous. Not the vindictive sort of jealousy, but the sort that said, I wish it were happening to me and not Helen and Rita.

I felt rather stupid waving my cigarette holder in front of them and lowered it a bit. I decided not to go to Carlins again for quite some time because it felt like showing off in front of the girls who had once been my friends.

"I'm seeing Jack at one o'clock." Rita's voice sliced into my thoughts. "We're going to have some lunch at a posh pub just outside town and then he's going to take me for a ride round in his car. He's going to show me some of his betting shops."

"What about Neville?" I sensed trouble bubbling up. "Neville wouldn't be very pleased if he knew."

"Oh him ... he's playing silly boggers because of our singing. Did I tell you ... he's been talking about our getting engaged?" She laughed and poured more coffee into our cups. "Can you imagine it, Helen. Me tied down to Neville? Not on your Nelly. I'm really enjoying going round the pubs and clubs. It's all so exciting, isn't it! I'm very fond of Neville but I don't want to get engaged to him."

"But I thought you were ever so keen on Neville?" I persisted. "You said he was a good catch, with all his newsagents' shops and everything. I thought you were keen on hooking him?"

"Well I was! ..." She paused and looked thoughful. "But Jack's rather dishy isn't he? And I love his house. I'd love to live in a house like that. I've never been in a house before where they've got their own cocktail-bar."

"Oh well," I laughed at the way her mind worked, "if poor old Neville's got to compete with cocktail-bars he doesn't stand much chance."

"You know what I mean, Helen. And anyway, Neville won't find out where I've been today because I'm going to say I was with you all afternoon."

"All right then." I finished the last of my toast.

"Oh and by the way," Rita looked slightly embarrassed, "Jack's booked me to do two singles. Two Saturday nights after Christmas."

The toast felt suddenly dry and I had a hard time swallowing. My survival-radar switched to full power. So that was it! Rita was contemplating going solo. And Jack, blast him, was helping her. I began to feel very annoyed. After all I had done for Rita. If it hadn't been for me she would have gone on working at the Cresta club till she drew her pension.

Then my confidence began to sag. Perhaps Jack didn't think I was worth a booking at his clubs? I felt my stomach begin to churn. If Rita left the act that would probably be the end of me. I didn't like doing the solo spots in our sister act because it made me terribly nervous. Singing with Rita was different, the nerves were still there but we supported each other.

Rita was now chatting to two of the waitresses — my mind raced on and on sifting through what she had just said. She's getting carried away with herself, I thought, and it was all that damn Jack Sargent's fault. And poor old Neville was getting pushed out too. I began to feel angry with Rita. I would be left without the other half of the act and after all the hard work and planning I'd put into it. Rita's voice was very good, I thought miserably, I'd noticed the applause she got when singing solo. Sometimes, but not always, the applause she got was louder than mine.

For the first time since I had started up the act, I felt that the magic sparkle had gone out of my life.

CHAPTER TEN

Two weeks before Christmas, Rita and I gave in our notices to Ray Bowler. He didn't seem surprised at the news and took it quite well.

"I'll be able to give you both a booking at the Cresta now then. I'll be sorry to see you go, girls. You're both very popular with the customers. But there you are," he shrugged his shoulders, "and I'll not have to order so much gin now you're leaving me." His eyes seemed to look straight through us.

I blushed with guilt but Rita pretended not to understand.

"Oh I know, I'm one for me gin. I can't resist a drop of 'Mother's Ruin'. It costs me a fortune." She changed the subject quickly, "Will you really give us a booking, Ray?"

"'Course I will ... give me a chance to see what you can do. How much are you going to charge me for a Saturday night? I'd like to see you both perform." He laughed and added, "On stage of course."

He gave us a booking for the third Saturday in March. I was thrilled because I knew the accompaniment would be first class. I was also secretly pleased that we would have a chance to surprise all our regular customers. It would certainly seem strange singing to them instead of serving their drinks.

Ray also invited us to his Christmas party and said it could be our going away celebration too. He arranged to hold the party at his home on the Sunday before Christmas.

Our act had been booked at one of the local pubs that same evening but we promised to go to the party straight afterwards.

In the middle of all these preparations Neville walked into the club. He was included in the invitation and also said that he would be coming to the pub to hear our last spot. He seemed to be in a very amiable mood — not a sulk in sight on his face.

Christmas always makes me feel wild — feelings left over from being a child I expect. I get terribly sentimental about Christmas carols and pretty window displays and long for excitement, something different to happen. I was in this mood when I suggested to Rita that we take Jimmy Cook's advice and dye our hair the same colour. Rita agreed without thinking about the consequences and we booked our appointments with a hairdresser.

"I think the blonde hair will take all right, duck," said Madamoiselle Arlene alias Marlene Crowe, who had her front-room converted into a salon. "The black'll take a bit of doing though." She ran her fingers through my hair and frowned. "We don't want the bleddy lot to drop out, do we?"

I agreed to chance losing my hair and she commenced mixing some sort of mixture which looked like red mud.

Madamoiselle Arlene did a terrific job on our hair. We were now both redheads.

Dark, rich auburn hair with a lovely sheen. The hairdresser set our hair in natural waves and curls. Rita and I were delighted with the colour and both agreed that now we really did look like sisters.

New make-up was bought to match our new hair. Beige face powder, pale orange lipstick and dark green eye shadow.

On the day of the party I stayed in bed until lunchtime then I had a meal and caught the bus to Rita's flat. We rehearsed the harmony to a few Christmas carols and as we did so I felt the hairs in the nape of my neck stand on end. I enjoyed singing the carols with Rita so much; derived a tremendous amount of satisfaction from the lovely sound we were both making. How fortunate we were, I thought, that next year we were going to earn our living doing something we thoroughly enjoyed. That is, if Rita stayed with the act of course and didn't decide to go solo.

That evening the booking went very well. The audience were in a frivolous, free spending mood because of Christmas. They were rowdy but it was a happy, festive kind of rowdiness. They joined in all the carols and clapped our other songs until their hands must have ached. Bottles of Guiness were sent over to our table faster than shells on the front line. By the time Neville arrived at the pub we were well and truly tipsy.

The young unattached men bore down on us brandishing mistletoe. And married men got carried away with the spirit of Christmas when their wives left the room to go to the toilet — they too wanted a kiss from us. I proffered my cheek for the barrage of kisses and so did Rita. She kissed away like mad despite the presence of a now outraged and very jealous Neville.

And to make matters much worse for Rita, half an hour before closing time, Jack Sargent and George The Hat walked into the room.

Rita caught sight of them and waved and beckoned them to our table. She introduced them to Neville who forced a smile and said hello.

George had a sprig of mistletoe pinned to his hat. I knew he was fond of his hat, I thought with some amusement, but decorating it up for Christmas was a bit much.

Neville asked the two men to have a drink then made his way through the crowd towards the bar.

"I didn't think you'd turn up." Rita leaned closer to Jack.

"I had to come and bring you a little bit of something for Christmas, Rita." Jack felt in his inside jacket pocket. He handed her a small box which was decorated with a red satin bow. Rita slipped the box into her handbag and squeezed Jack's hand.

"Thank you, Jack. Neville's coming back from the bar ... I'll look at it later." She released his hand and sat up straight again.

George did not have much to say to me. After his unsuccessful journey back to my flat I could see that he was decidedly off me.

"We're going to a party afterwards," I addressed Jack. "It's a sort of farewell party as well as a Christmas one. We're going to our boss's house. Ray Bowler from the Cresta club. Do you know him, Jack?"

"Everybody's heard of Ray." Jack sipped at his whisky. "Got a finger in a lot of pies in this town. Good bloke Ray is ... I'll bet he gives fabulous parties."

"Pity you can't come with us." Neville butted in. "But he's got a full house ... we can't take anybody else."

"Oh that's all right, Neville," Jack smiled at him, "we've arranged to go to a party anyway. Can't get round to them all can we, George?"

"No, I'm about blotto now." George blotted up more whisky.

"Oh, by the way," Jack moved nearer to my chair, "would you like to do a couple of single spots at my clubs?"

I felt my heart jumping about.

"Yes, I'd love to, Jack."

"Right then ... get your diary out, me duck, and we'll see what we can do." He thumbed through the pages of a large red diary. "Rita's on here and here ... so can you do this one? ... and this one?"

I felt elated. This was like a Christmas present. All my doubts about Rita leaving the act were dispelled. I wanted to hug and kiss Jack he had made me feel so happy. So there wasn't anything sinister about him after all. I wrote down the dates with trembling fingers. I didn't like going solo but it would be good practice, I had to get used to singing on my own. Every pub and club couldn't afford a sister act.

I felt the magic sparkle return to my life and sat with a smile on my face that wouldn't go away.

At the end of the evening we all stepped outside the pub. Rita, Neville and I talked to George and Jack for a while then said our goodbyes and Merry Christmasses.

The sky was navy blue and the glimmering stars reminded me of cut out cardboard covered in gently vibrating tinsel.

It was extremely cold but my body felt warm, nice and snug in my lovely warm rabbit fur.

The car spluttered then purred to life and we were on our way to Ray's house.

I felt elated and yet, parodoxically, very sad somehow. I was sitting in the back of the car and watched as Rita snuggled up close to Neville. They whispered things to each other, but I was not interested in their conversation.

I knew what was wrong with me. It came to me suddenly, as though a bolt of lightning had stabbed clean through the car window and struck me straight between the eyes. I needed to be loved. I wanted someone to care for me once again. The awful feeling of desperation and anger since my divorce was beginning to fade. I was still very suspicious of men but my normal feelings were beginning to return. I longed to hold someone in my arms again, had an overwhelming desire to be made love to by a warm, caring man. Now I knew what the trouble was I felt happier and decided that I would do something about it in the very near future.

I was terrified of being hurt again and the thought of being married sent me into a kind of panic. And anyway, I thought, as I snuggled down in the warmth of Neville's car, I had my career to think of now. I wanted to be a success. I would be like Rita and play the field. Our act had to come first.

By the time we reached Ray's house I had my life all neatly planned and organised. Or so I thought.

We arrived at Ray's house and were greeted warmly by him. I decided not to have anything else to drink for a while. I felt quite tipsy from the amount of Guiness and port I had already consumed at the pub. My feet felt heavy when I walked as though they were encased in a pair of Al Capone's gangster-made cement shoes. When I spoke to anyone it sounded to me as though I had got my head stuck in a vase — my voice had a tremulous echo.

I helped myself to a glass of lemonade from Ray's well stocked bar and then found a seat. I knew quite a few of the guests but there were also one or two men I had never seen before.

Rita came across to where I was sitting and perched herself on the arm of my chair. She had a glass of whisky in one hand and a sausage roll in the other.

"Hang on to this, Helen," she thrust the glass into my hand, "let me show you what Jack bought me. Quick, while Neville's out of the room!" She opened the lid of the box and a beautiful gold brooch, in the shape of a rose, nestled in black velvet. It had tiny pearls encrusted in the petals which represented dewdrops. It was exquisite.

"Where on earth will you say you got it?" I rubbed my fingers along the pearls. "It looks terribly expensive."

"I'll tell Neville that you bought it me for Christmas. I'll say it's off the market. He won't look too closely at a piece of jewellery. I'll say you bought it for me to wear on stage ... on one of my evening dresses. Hey, watch out, Helen, he's coming over." She snapped the lid shut and popped the box back into her handbag. "I might not wear it at all. I might save it for a rainy day and then flog it."

Neville held out his arms to Rita.

"Come on, gorgeous ... let's have a nice smoochy dance." He held her close to him and pressed his face against her cheek.

As they danced by my chair Neville had his back to me. Rita mouthed the words, 'I can flog it', and pulled a comical face. She was incorrigible but I had to laugh despite myself. Poor old Neville, I thought, you don't have a parson in hell's chance of reforming her.

I began to sober up a little bit and decided to eat something. I selected a couple of sandwiches and a sausage roll and poured myself a glass of port.

I returned to my seat and had just bitten into a sausage roll when a good looking man pulled a chair up next to mine and introduced himself, "Hello ... aren't you one of Ray's barmaids?"

"Yes ... I haven't seen you at the Cresta. How do you know me?"

"I've been down there a couple of times ... didn't stay long though. But I stayed long enough to notice you."

"Oh, thank you, that's nice of you to say so."

"I don't work in this neck of the woods. I travel about quite a lot with my job. I work mainly in the north west."

He pulled his chair up closer and added, "I'm a rep. for a brewery company. I like the travelling about though ... don't like to be stuck inside all the time."

"Same as me then." I sipped at my port. "I've just given my notice in to Ray. I liked working at the Cresta but I work on the stage as well and I've decided to do that full-time." He looked very interested which I thought he would when he knew I was an artiste.

"What do you do then? You're not a stripper by any chance, are you? I'll have to come and watch your act if you are."

"Don't be so cheeky," I was indignant, "do I look like one then?"

"I'm pulling your leg," he added hastily, "anybody can tell you're a dancer. You've got beautiful legs." He eyed my legs up-and-down. "I knew the minute I saw you that you were a dancer."

"Well they'd be wrong then." I kept him in suspense. "Because I'm a singer. Me and my friend over there." I pointed to Rita. "We're the Dumonte Sisters. Have you ever heard of us?"

He looked very impressed indeed at the news and answered, "No, I don't think so. Have you been going very long?"

"Not all that long," I admitted, "we're just getting started, but the work's rolling in now. As I just told you we're going to sing full-time. They've got loads of pubs and clubs round here ... keep us going for years."

"Would you like to work in the north west?" He seemed genuinely interested. "The people up there are very friendly and they go for entertainment in a big way. You'd go down a bomb ... a bit of glamour in the working men's clubs. I tell you what ... give me a few of your business cards." He paused and added, "You have got business cards I take it, have you?"

"Of course we have." I rooted about inside my handbag and found a couple of cards.

"Right then," he looked at the cards, "I'll hand these out at a couple of the big clubs and spread the word around."

The thought crossed my mind that he was shooting me a line, I still didn't trust any man, but it couldn't do any harm giving him the cards — something may come of it.

"Oh, I'm Ralph by the way. I've been rattling on and haven't introduced myself properly."

"I'm Helen. Helen of Malperry with the face that launched a thousand chips." I was beginning to enjoy myself and still felt very high from the booking at the pub. It usually took quite a while for me to come back down to earth after a performance.

"Shall we have a dance, Helen?" He put his glass on a coffee table. "There's not much room but we can have a go."

Ralph held me tightly in his arms and I liked being there. I pressed up against him and he reacted by stroking the back of my neck with his fingers. I closed my eyes and surrendered to the mood of my mind and the longing of my body. I was safe, here in the midst of all these people. I didn't want to tease Ralph, give him the wrong impression, but I couldn't stop myself from pressing up to him as closely as I could. Tonight I needed affection, attention and flattery from a man. Tonight I wanted to feel like a real woman once more. Not the caricature I had become since the traumatic ending to my marriage. I swayed to the music and let my thoughts wing off out into space. The glass in my self control barometer began to crack and I closed my eyes and let it.

"Who's your dishy friend?" Rita asked, as we powdered our noses in front of one of Ray's bedroom mirrors. "I don't know where you found him but you want to hang onto him."

"I'll introduce you when we go back downstairs. But you can keep your maulers off. You've got quite enough to keep you going with Jack and Neville."

We went back downstairs and I introduced Rita and Neville to Ralph. "Ralph's a rep. for a brewery," I told them, "plenty of free samples."

"Nice to meet you, Ralph. If you get any free samples of gin I'll take them off your hands."

"We're going home now, Helen," Neville said, after shaking hands with Ralph. "Rita's had more than enough to drink, I'm going to tuck her up in bed."

"Yes, and guess who's going to be tucked up with me?" Rita swayed about a bit and giggled. "Neville's staying at my place tonight." She looked Ralph up-and-down and then winked at me and added, "We can all have a lie in tomorrow, can't we?"

"Goodnight, Rita. I'll be at your place about half-past four. Don't forget I'm coming up to rehearse on Christmas Eve afternoon."

Rita and Neville thanked Ray for a lovely evening and departed. I snuggled up to Ralph once more and we danced for another half an hour before finally deciding to go home. I sought out Ray and found him chatting to a scatty looking little blonde. Ray was giving her the full treatment. Flashing teeth, sexy half closed eyes and full attention that most women find hard to resist. As I approached I could smell his after-shave which easily overpowered the blonde's perfume if she was wearing any.

"Oh yes, Ray ... thank you. I'd love to see upstairs." The blonde pressed her leg against Ray. "And fancy it being your birthday as well! If I'd have known it was your birthday today I could have given you a present."

You'll be giving him a present, I thought, and you won't need to tie a bow of ribbon round it.

"Goodnight, Ray. Thank you for a smashing evening." I held out my hand. Ray held both of my hands in his own and gave me a kiss on the mouth.

"Goodnight, Helen. And the very best of luck to you and Rita with the singing. I really mean what I say, gel. I'm looking forward to hearing you at the Cresta in March." He released my hands. As I turned to go I whispered, "Oh and by the way, Ray ... have a very happy birthday." He raised one eyebrow and roared with laughter, the blonde smiled happily and joined in the laughter.

Ralph drove me home and out of the intimate atmosphere of the soft lights and seductive music, we seemed shy of one another.

We arrived at my flat and Ralph got out of the car and took a hold of my suitcase. He carried it to the door and then looked embarrassed as though unable to say what he was thinking.

"I'd ... er ... I'd like to come and hear you sing on Christmas Eve, Helen. I know the place very well. If you wouldn't mind I'd love to come along because I'm not doing anything that night, and I hate being on my own on Christmas Eve."

"Yes, come along then, Ralph." I decided not to say that I would be nervous and didn't want him to arrive until the last spot. "I'll see you there then. Neville's giving us a lift."

He handed over my suitcase and said, "Are you going to a party afterwards? Because if you're not, perhaps we could have a Christmas drink together? Either at your place or mine."

"Yes, all right then." I thought it was a good idea because I had enjoyed being in his company very much. "I've got some drink in, if you want to come back here."

He leaned forward, kissed me quickly on the cheek and got back into his car and drove away.

★ ★ ★ ★ ★ ★ ★ ★ ★ ★ ★ ★ ★ ★ ★ ★

I washed off my make-up and rubbed mercalised wax into my face. One of the customers from Carlin's had told me that if you used the wax on your face every night your skin would stay wrinkle-free and lovely. Mind you, it was best not to use it if you had company because the wax made you look like Marley's ghost which was rather off-putting to would-be lovers.

I brushed my new auburn coloured hair and then tied my hair back away from my waxy face with a ribbon. No need to set my hair in grips tonight. I had three whole days holiday, apart from the bookings of course, but I didn't call that work. I was going to live just like those actresses who stay in bed all morning and float around in a flimsy negligèe all afternoon before going to work in the theatre. I decided to get Vera to make me a flimsy negligèe. Ah yes ... Vera. I made a mental note to buy her some really exotic perfume for Christmas then I settled down and drifted gently off to sleep and hoped I would dream about Ralph.

★ ★ ★ ★ ★ ★ ★ ★ ★ ★ ★ ★ ★ ★ ★ ★

When Rita and I arrived at the Jolly Ploughman on Christmas Eve, the place was already packed to capacity. The landlord had written in white chalk on a board at the front of the tiny stage ... 'The Dumonte Sisters. First appearance of the most fantastic act in town.

They're Dynamic ... They're Dynamite ... They're Delectable. Come early to get a good view ...'.

All around the edges of the board he had drawn springs of holly and faces of fat faced laughing Father Christmasses. Someone had stuck a sprig of mistletoe on the microphone and there were bunches of multi-coloured balloons all around the back of the stage. The pianist had three pints of bitter lined up on the top of the piano, the drummer had likewise on the floor beside his drum set. The latter also puffed on a huge cigar but did not look as though he was enjoying it very much.

The audience went wild when we appeared in our orange charleston dresses. Four men near the front of the stage threw their hats into the air and shouted 'Yoohoo'. It was like a scene from a western movie. I hoped that we would be able to make it back to our changing-room, which was the landlady's kitchen by the way, through all those hot blooded, eager-to-touch-us men.

Ralph came into the pub at nine thirty and joined Neville who was squeezed up near the bar at the far end of the room.

The place was really jumping; atmosphere electric. The people were happy and excited. They had made up their minds to enjoy themselves. Conversation and beer flowed like a river at high tide. If Rita and I had drunk all the Guiness and ports that had been bought for us, we would have been unconscious for a month.

After our last spot, we made our way slowly through the forest of smiling, happy people and joined Ralph and Neville at the bar. I enjoyed my Guiness and port. The room was terribly hot and stuffy and my throat was rather hoarse from singing. We had really had to belt it out because of all the noise. We must have nearly deafened the poor devils sitting directly underneath the loudspeakers.

I mentioned to Rita that Ralph could perhaps get some bookings for us.

"Oh good", she smiled at him, "perhaps you could come with us to some of the clubs if you've got contacts. Show us around. Of course we would give you some money for petrol."

I tried to tell by his expression if Ralph was interested in Rita, but he didn't seem to be. He only had eyes for me. I relaxed, flirted with him a little.

Rita told me that Neville was sleeping at her place again that night and also staying with her for the Christmas holidays.

"He'll have you washing his socks next," I teased her. "Have you heard anything of Jack by the way?"

"Seeing him when I do the solo at his club next Friday."

71

The landlord of the Jolly Ploughman came into the kitchen at the end of the evening and counted out our money.

"Can you come back about June or July? I'll let Dave McGuire know about the booking." He paused and then continued, "You don't want to let on about some of your return bookings. Then you wouldn't have to cop up any commission to Dave."

"Oh, that's all right," I answered, "Dave's been very good to us. He's helped us to get a lot of work ... it's worth ten per cent of anybody's money."

"Just thought I'd mention it, that's all. Lot of the artists don't let on about some of their bookings. But of course it's up to you."

We fixed the date for a return booking and packed our gowns away.

I thought about what a marvellous Christmas I was having. Earning good money doing something I enjoyed tremendously and also, I had met a man I liked and whose company I would have over Christmas.

We left the Jolly Ploughman at eleven thirty, there had been a late night extension and so the bars had done a roaring trade.

"Merry Christmas, Rita."

"Merry Christmas, Helen ... and just behave yourself."

"Merry Christmas, Ralph ... mind how you go."

"Merry Christmas, Neville ... see you next weekend, mate."

Ralph headed the car in the direction of Malperry and soon we were relaxing in the front-room of my flat. We played records, drank coffee, sipped at whisky and talked and talked about ourselves.

Ralph kissed me and when I responded moved his hand slowly up my thigh. I took hold of his hand and moved it away from my thigh — he did not persist and I was glad. I did not want to be rushed into anything.

I wanted to talk, get to know him more, before we went any further in the relationship. What was it someone had once written? Women are like delicate flowers — all right if left to blossom in their own good time. But a forced bloom or love affair quickly fades and dies.

I decided I was like a precious orchid, Ralph would have to wait.

But not too long of course or else I would end up a wallflower.

Ralph helped himself to more whisky and said, "I've never been out with a singer before. The audience really liked your act tonight. And I must say your harmony is beautiful. You must have rehearsed for hours and hours."

"Yes, we have. The audience did give us a lot of applause, didn't they! What did you think to our evening gowns?"

"I don't know how you get into them. They look as though they've been sewn on. And pardon my saying ... your bust seems to be bigger when you're on stage."

I blushed and replied, "That's one of the tricks of the trade. I'll let you into our secret when you're a bit older."

"You've got a beautiful figure, Helen." His voice sounded husky. "I love slim girls. I always feel as though I want to protect a slim girl." He leaned towards me and kissed me on the lips again.

He pulled me down onto the carpet and gently eased himself on top of me. His body felt exciting, I felt faint and could feel my resistance fading fast. I pushed him away, not roughly but firmly and meaning it.

"All right, Helen ... all right. I can wait." Ralph's smile was tender, full of understanding. "It's all right, Helen."

It was at that moment I thought I had fallen for him. Here we go again, I thought, hang on to your hat.

★ ★ ★ ★ ★ ★ ★ ★ ★ ★ ★ ★ ★ ★ ★ ★

Ralph gave me a lift to Jack Sargent's club and agreed to go somewhere else for a drink because he could see I was terribly nervous.

"I'll see you about half-past nine, Helen." Ralph handed over my suitcase and left the club.

The Bodega was a large club and had quite a big stage. There was a proper dressing-room furnished with table, four chairs and a sink with hot and cold water. There was also a full length mirror which had all of its silver backing intact. I looked at myself in the mirror and patted at my hair.

I put my gowns on coat hangers and hung them on the hooks on the back of the door, then I grabbed hold of my handbag and hurried to the bar for my Guiness and port.

The pianist and drummer were at the bar having a drink and they introduced themselves.

"I'm Harold." The pianist was a sad faced, no-sort-of-shape man. "And this is Paddy, your drummer ... best drummer in the business, he is."

Paddy had a broad flat nose, like a boxer, with black hairs creeping out of his nostrils. His face was very pale and black bushy eyebrows accentuated the paleness of his face.

After we had replenished our drinks I led the way back to the dressing-room. The fellas had a look at my sheet music and I told them how I wanted the different tempos.

"A word of advice." Harold tucked my music underneath his arm. "Don't stand too near Paddy when you're singing. He's not choosey what he does with his drum-sticks."

"Oh ... right." I was baffled.

"He's got a thing about womens' arses. He'll have yer if you stand too close to his drums."

"Yes, and don't worry if the dressing-room door's locked when you want to get changed." Paddy took a large gulp of his pint of mild. "The mens' toilet's right down the far end of the room ... I 'aint got time to go all that way everytime I want to pee. I'm a ten pints a night man, me duck."

I didn't know what on earth he was on about and it obviously showed on my face.

"He pees in the sink." Harold put me right. "Here in the dressing-room."

"He's right there ... I do that," Paddy had opened the door of the dressing-room. "And I wipe me dribbles on the curtains over there." He pointed to the curtains in the dressing-room which were regency striped and rather creased at the ends. This is going to be quite a night, I thought, and made a mental note not to use the sink for anything.

Harold and Paddy were extremely good musicians and the microphone was terrific. I sang a selection from Oklahoma and ended with my dad's favourite, 'Out of my Dreams'. The audience liked, 'Oh What a Beautiful Morning', the best and joined in with the singing and some of the men whistled the tune.

I joined in the games of Bingo and was asked to select the winning numbers for the Tombola. Then it was time for my second spot. I selected my green brocade gown for

73

this spot and decorated the bodice with a large artificial gold rose.

After I had finished my second spot I walked down the steps at the side of the stage and took hold of the handle of the dressing-room door. Paddy had beaten me to it. He had nipped off the stage in front of me whilst I was taking a bow and popped into the dressing-room for a pee. I chatted to some people who were sitting at a table near the front of the stage and waited for Paddy to 'do what a man's got to do.'

My third and last spot went down very well and I think this was because I had become more relaxed. I opened up with, 'I can't give you anything but love', and all the men in the audience loved this song. I wiggled my hips, shook my bust, complete with padding, for all I was worth. I finished up with some old favourites and the audience sang along with me. When I had finished my spot they shouted for 'more' and so I had a quick word with Harold and sorted out two extra songs. The audience applauded enthusiastically at the end of my performance and I asked them to give a big hand for the pianist and drummer. They deserved it too because they had given me first class accompaniment.

Ralph arrived too late to hear me sing but he looked very pleased when he heard the entertainment secretary ask if I could do a return booking.

"Jack Sargent's over at his other club tonight, me duck. But he leaves all the bookings to me. Can you do one on the sixth? I've got a comedian booked that night ... so we need a nice contrast. Put the sixth down, me duck, and confirm it by telephone if you don't mind."

Ralph took hold of my suitcase and ushered me through the crowded club room. I sank down gratefully into the comfort of his car.

"I was late on purpose tonight, Helen." Ralph inserted the car key into the ignition. "I know you're very nervous doing solos. You'll soon get used to it though. When you've done a few more bookings you'll wonder what all the fuss was about."

"I don't think so, Ralph. It's just like I'm going through a nightmare in slow motion when I first have to walk out onto the stage by myself. I get nervous when Rita's with me ... but it's nothing like it was tonight. I wanted to turn round and run away from the club. I felt sick with stage-fright."

"It's just like any other job." Ralph tried to console me. "Everything seems strange and frightening at first. In the end you'll love singing on stage that much they won't be able to keep you away, you'll see."

"Yes, I suppose you're right." I didn't mean a word of my reply. "But with Rita it's a lot of fun. When I'm on my own, like this evening, it's like going to work. Oh, I know you're right, Ralph," I changed the subject, "so where did you get to this evening then? Did you try one at the Pigalle?"

"Yes, it was packed. The new owners are making it pay by the look of things. They've employed some hostesses, real glamour-pusses. But if they fetch your drink from the bar it costs you. They expect a short for themselves."

"Bit of competition for the Cresta." My mind cascaded back into yesterday and it seemed like a lifetime ago since I had first put my handbag behind the bar at the Cresta and served my first drink.

Ralph and I talked for a while over coffee and this time he didn't attempt to make love to me. I looked at his face, it was an honest face, nothing classic about the features but a good-looking, pleasing countenance. I leaned towards him and kissed his cheek.

"I enjoy your company very much, Ralph. And thank you for the lift to the club."

"You are very special to me, Helen." Ralph stroked my hair and the feeling of desire began its slow tingling journey right through my body. He kissed my lips and I responded passionately. "Let's go to bed." I stood up. We walked through to the bedroom hand-in-hand and I switched on the bedside lamp. Our bodies locked together in an embrace of impetuosity and for a few moments I forgot about what I should have been doing, what my mind should have been thinking — all I could think about were my needs as a woman — the desirability of the man who lay beside me. I surrendered to him and all the imprisoned emotions which had been locked away inside, since the break-up of my marriage, were released in great tidal waves of passion.

We were still locked in each other's arms when the first light of dawn spilled through the blue black morning skies.

CHAPTER ELEVEN

The ferocity of chill winter winds gave in to the gentleness of spring's soft breezes. Rita and I discarded our rabbit furs and warm woollies for two piece outfits and light-weight dresses. A good part of the money we earned from singing was spent on clothes. Having Vera for our dressmaker helped enormously of course because she saved us pounds and our outfits were always of the latest styles and materials.

Vera's 'piece de resistance' of the moment was her Grecian creation. She had made gowns of black chiffon, a most difficult material to handle but Vera had triumphed. Draped at the left shoulder in the Grecian manner, the dresses then flowed down in elegant swathed pleats. A diamantè clip was pinned on the shoulder where the material was gathered. Rita and I saved these gowns for our last spot and wore our hair up high on the top of our heads and had little kiss curls hanging down at the sides of our ears - just like the Grecian goddesses you see on Wedgwood pottery.

When we sang anywhere near to Rutledge, Vera and her husband Bill would come along to hear us sing.

"I made those dresses." Vera chatted to people in the audience. "I get the material off the Market you know. I made that pattern up out of me own head."

The women sometimes placed orders and Vera started a nice little sideline in glamour-wear for miners' wives and factory workers' girlfriends.

The idea I had first had, all that time ago at the Cresta, had opened up a whole new world for quite a few people.

Bookings were now coming in from all directions. Jimmy Cook kept us busy mid-week whilst Dave McGuire concentrated on Sundays and sometimes, Sunday lunch double-up as it was called.

Rita and I didn't like Sunday noon and night bookings because, if the venue was a long distance away, we had all the afternoon with nothing to do and this was quite miserable if it happened to be raining.

Ralph had given our cards out to pub landlords and committee men and soon quite a few of these tentative venues came to fruition. Ralph had become one of our best agents and he didn't cost a penny. I do it for love, he told me one evening, and so far that was the nearest he had come to saying that his feelings for me were more than shallow ones. Otherwise, the word love had never been mentioned between us, it was still early days.

I had grown very fond of Ralph, but didn't think I was really in love with him. He had come along at the right moment, when my scars were beginning to heal and he had fulfilled the need in me for romance and companionship.

Neville, I was almost certain, had fallen for Rita in a big way and had also quietened down considerably. I think he had realised that tantrums and moody sulking would not keep Rita by his side. He was attentive and very pleasant to her and, I noticed, he was always there when we went on a booking. No chance of anyone else giving her a lift home.

Rita had taken to the stage as though she had spent years entertaining instead of the short time since we had first started singing along to records in her flat. She did not seem to be affected by nerves either and had many a laugh at the state of me before I went on stage.

I still could not get out onto the stage without first having a drink. This perhaps would seem ridiculous to other people but to me it became a psychological thing. The moment I had sorted out my gowns in the dressing-room I was flying to the bar for my 'Dutch-courage'.

One evening, owing to difficulty in finding the place, Rita and I arrived late at a Miners' Welfare. The entertainment secretary was, unfortunately, one of those nasty little jumped-up fellows - all bustle and greased down hair - I'm in charge and you'll do as I say type of man.

"You're late! ... should have been on by now."

"Sorry, love ... won't be a minute." I bumped my shins on my suitcase as I hurried. He followed us through to the dressing-room.

"I keep a tight ship here. Everything runs like clockwork here. It'll be time for Bingo soon and you 'ent even been on."

"I'm just going to fetch some drinks, Rita." I turned to leave.

"Drinks ... no time for bloody drinks, Miss. I'll send the pianist and drummer in."

I conceded defeat and could feel my throat tightening up. I wanted to swallow and when I tried I couldn't swallow. I coughed and then panicked because I was sure I had hurt my throat. We had to go on stage cold sober and it was awful for me. I decided that I would never be caught like that again - with my throat closed up with nervous tension - a stuck on a raft in the middle of the ocean kind of throat. I bought a flask and took it everywhere with me, filled up with gin and dry martini, like a baby needs a dummy for comfort, I had to know my flask was there if the need arose again. If any other bossy entertainment secretary tried to rush me on stage I would be able to have a big swig from my flask first.

Having a drink before I went on stage became an obsession with me - I knew I could not sing without first having a drop of false courage. And we needed courage all right! Microphones packed up in the middle of our act. Pianists played the wrong tempo or did not seem to be able to read our music very well. Drummers played beguine tempos instead of waltz-time, and quick-steps instead of slow dramatic beats.

Curtains became stuck half-way across the stage and once, horror upon horrors, the pianist did not turn up at all. Rita and I went ahead, probably like many other poor souls before us, and sang to the accompaniment of drums only. The audience applauded loudly admiring our bravery and the committee members would not let us buy our own drinks. All our Guiness and ports were bought out of the 'Pensioners outing to Skegness' fund we were told in confidence by an old age pensioner who cleared empty glasses from the tables. And we were given an extra pound each on top of our fee for being such good sports.

This sort of thing was very nerve-racking but it certainly stopped us from ever getting bored with the entertainment business. It all added spice and a great deal of laughter to our work.

One evening, in the middle of a particularly hot week we did a spot right out in the wilds of the countryside. We were booked to sing at a farmers' social evening. Just before we were due to go on stage for our first spot a terrific thunderstorm brewed up. The building where the venue was being held was a large wooden hut with no curtains to the windows. The thunder roared and the lightning flashed like a scene from a Frankenstein picture.

The organist came back-stage to have a glance at our music and as he did so I laughingly remarked to Rita that perhaps if we held the switched on microphones there was a chance we could get struck by lightning as electricity attracted lightning like moths to a flame.

My comments were soaked up by the daft organist who promptly refused to play his organ during the storm.

"But we'll have to make a start soon." I flinched as another streak of lightning lit up the sky outside.

"I've never heard of anybody being electrocuted while playing about with his organ," Rita's face crinkled into a cheeky smile, "I think your organ'll be quite safe."

"I'm not touching it till the storm dies down." The organist had no sense of humour.

The audience began to get very noisy and soon, a few of the farmers who had supped more than their share, started up with a slow hand-clap.

All at once I had an idea. I had noticed that some of the farmers were wearing Wellington boots. I left the dressing-room and went out into the concert-room. I selected a merry looking red-faced farmer and told him of my plan. He thought my idea was hilarious and handed over his wellies with a flourish.

I hurried back to the dressing-room and asked the organist if he would be willing to wear the boots. "You'll be well earthed ... good thick rubber."

The entertainment secretary came back-stage to find out what the delay was and when he saw the organist struggling into the wellies offered him a packet of Durex and said, "Here you are, Norman ... blow these up and tie them to your organ."

"Which one?" Rita looked the organist up-and-down and started to giggle.

"You can laugh," the organist adjusted his black bow-tie, "but I once read in the newspaper that a woman who wore steel bones in her corsets was struck by lightning. The lightning struck her corsets, it did."

"You'd better take your corsets off then, Norman." The entertainment secretary was enjoying himself. "Come on then, girls ... come and give 'em a song before they smash the bleddy place up."

At the end of the evening I suggested to the organist that he play the "Thunder and Lightning Polka' for an encore but, as I remarked earlier, he had no sense of humour and replied, "I've a good mind to pack this lot in ... it isn't as though I need the money you know."

"Have a drink," I said, and for the first time that evening I thought I could detect a smile on his face.

★ ★ ★ ★ ★ ★ ★ ★ ★ ★ ★ ★ ★ ★ ★ ★

On and on we went, gaining experience with every booking, it was the hard way but the only way. Small stages, huge impressive looking stages and quite often, in the pubs, no stages at all.

We learned microphone techniques, stage presence and lots of other little tricks many of which we picked up through watching other artistes.

The old stagers, such as ageing comedians, magicians, has-been tenors and never-was sopranos taught us the most. We learned from their years of experience and from their mistakes.

We both knew instinctively now that it was no good going onto a stage and just standing there and singing a song. You had to project your image and get the act over to the audience so that they remembered you, and more importantly, wanted to see and hear you again.

By the time Christmas arrived once more I think I can honestly say without appearing boastful that Rita and I had a very pleasing and polished act.

The bookings rolled in and of course this snowballed because once we had appeared at a club or pub we were invariably asked to do a return. Our diaries began to look very good and so did our futures.

I had a new idea for the act. We would sing two numbers dressed in long gowns then nip to the side of the stage where two straw boaters and walking canes would be ready on a chair. Whilst the pianist played an introduction we would slip out of our gowns and reveal two stunning, emerald green leotards.

We would then don the boaters, flourish our canes and sing, 'Toot toot tootsie', and then go in to a soft-shoe-shuffle routine.

"Vera can make the leotards out of green jersey wool." I told Rita of my new idea. "They'll cling like mad to our bodies ... show our figures up a treat."

"Oh, I don't want to do that." Rita look petulant. "I'd feel daft doing that. I can't do a soft-shoe-shuffle."

"Of course you can. You do the Charleston beautifully," I tried coaxing her, "anybody can learn the shuffle. We could wear black fish-net stockings and have some green garters made. The men'll lose their eyeballs when they get a load of that lot."

"No, I don't want to wear a leotard."

"But you'll look terrific! ... you've got a beautiful figure."

To my astonishment Rita suddenly burst into a flood of tears. She held her hands over her face and rocked backwards and forwards as though in some sort of agony. I hurried over to her and knelt down — then I attempted to take her hands away from her face.

"What's wrong? Oh, Rita, tell me, love, come on. Please tell me what's the matter. You can confide in me. I'm your friend."

There were real sobs now and in between them she managed to tell me what was wrong, "I'm going to have a baby. That's what's wrong."

I sucked in some air and became transfixed in my kneeling position like a stone Pompeii figure. I did not know what to say to her.

The sobs subsided and Rita uncovered her blotchy, tear stained face.

"Oh, Helen ... isn't it terrible. I've missed two periods and I've been sick in the mornings. I won't be able to continue with the act. That's why I can't wear a leotard ... everybody'll be able to tell I'm pregnant."

Misery made her shrink, her head hung down almost level with her chest. I put my arms around her, stroked her hair back from her face and went through half a dozen meaningless platitudes. My thoughts were in a tangled mess, like barbed wire all mixed up with sheep's wool. It would mean the end of our act. We would have to split up. I felt ashamed but these thoughts were paramount in my mind. Our marvellous little act — and after we had both worked so hard. And all for nothing! I felt sorry for Rita but still could not help feeling angry. I decided we both needed a strong cup of tea and went over to put the kettle on the stove.

"Have you told Neville? What's Neville got to say about it?"

"I told him last week," she blew her nose, "but I daren't tell you because of the act. I've been dreading telling you. I'm so sorry about the act, Helen ... I really am so very sorry."

"Ah, well ... don't worry about it too much, Rita." I handed her a cup of tea. "You've got the baby to think about now. The baby'll turn your life upside down."

"My life is upside down now. Neville keeps putting pressure on me for the wedding date."

"Well of course he is. You can't leave it much longer else you'll be able to tell when you walk down the aisle."

"I didn't want to have a church wedding. I've always said I wanted to go to the registry office. But he says he wants us to have a big do."

"Oh, you must have a church wedding. Ey ... your Vera will make you a lovely wedding dress."

"Would you like to be my bridesmaid?" Rita brightened up and smiled at last. "I know you're a bit old but ..."

"... Ey, less of the old. I'd love to be your bridesmaid."

We sat in silence for a few moments thinking about the wedding. Rita was the first to speak, "I can get a maternity corset from Johnsons and pull the stays really tight."

"You won't have to do that for ages," I answered her, "some of our evening gowns are quite loose. You'll be able to carry on with the act for a few months yet."

We both thought about this and suddenly the future did not look so black. I would have time to get another partner. If I wanted to of course. I could always go solo till after the baby was born. There would be plenty of work for me doubling up with comedians, and magicians.

"Yes, that's what I'll do." Rita helped herself to a chocolate biscuit and handed the plate to me. "Get a corset and pull the stays tight."

"Poor little mite!" I pulled a face. "It's got to have room to breathe you know."

"We'll go down the market tomorrow then," Rita poured more tea and added, "I fancy myself in cream and lace and I think you'd look smashing in pale blue. I'll tell Neville tonight ... put him out of his misery. He suggested we had the reception at the Regency Rooms in town. What do you think, Helen? Do you fancy the Regency Rooms?"

"I think that would be ideal, Rita. Bit expensive but Neville's got plenty. Wait a minute," I had another one of my ideas, "we could get some publicity out of this. Nice piece in the Evening Chronicle, about the other half of a singing act getting married. Leave it to me, I'll give them a ring and see what I can fix up."

Rita seemed almost like her old self again and munched away at the rest of the chocolate biscuits.

"You'll be sick if you eat any more." I warned her.

"Don't forget I'm feeding two now." She carried on munching. I'm not likely to forget that, I thought, Neville had won after all.

★ ★ ★ ★ ★ ★ ★ ★ ★ ★ ★ ★ ★ ★ ★ ★ ★

Rita and Neville were married in a lovely little church just on the outskirts of the city. Vera had transformed the wedding into a fairy-tale one. Our dresses were exquisite creations.

Rita's dress was pale cream lace worn over coffee satin. High at the neck it had dainty Victorian style pleats on the bodice. The sleeves had deep cuffs fastened at the wrists with tiny mother-of-pearl buttons. Rita had insisted that my dress should be of the same design seeing as we always dressed the same in our sister act. My dress was therefore identical to Rita's except for the colour which was pale blue lace over dark blue satin.

Rita had cream satin shoes and I had blue ones. Rita carried a bouquet of deep pink roses nestling in trailing green fern and decorated with bows of red satin ribbons. I had a bouquet of yellow roses also nestling in fern and adorned with yellow ribbon.

Mademoiselle Arlene had whirled and twirled our hair into Grecian styles and roses from our bouquets had been entwined into the curls at the back of our heads.

The newspaper did a nice piece in their Monday edition.

'ONE OF THE DUMONTE SISTERS MARRIES. MISS RITA DUMONTE ONE OF THE FAMOUS SINGING DUO WHICH IS WELL KNOWN ROUND THESE PARTS IN THE CLUBS AND OTHER ESTABLISHMENTS ON THE ENTERTAINMENT CIRCUIT MARRIED MR. NEVILLE BLAKNEY COMPANY DIRECTOR OF A CHAIN OF NEWSAGENT SHOPS. THE WEDDING TOOK PLACE ON SATURDAY AT SAINT ANNES CHURCH A DELIGHTFUL 17th. CENTURY CHURCH AT CUMLEY-ON-THE-HILL. THE BRIDE WAS ATTENDED BY THE OTHER HALF OF THE SINGING DUO MISS HELEN LINSEY AND RONALD BIRCHALL WAS THE BEST MAN.'

The piece then described our gowns and wedding bouquets and then ended with a fantastic lie concocted by Dave McGuire who insisted it would be good for our image.

'THE RECEPTION WAS HELD AT THE REGENCY ROOMS AND THE HONEYMOON IS SOMEWHERE IN THE SOUTH OF FRANCE.'

There was to be no honeymoon. And anyway, I thought, they'd had their honeymoon weeks ago. That evening after the wedding reception was over Rita and I had to rush off to do a booking at an undertakers' reunion dinner. And by the reception we got when we did our first spot, I began to wonder whether the audience had been embalmed — they were that quiet. But, after a few more drinks, the undertakers showed that they were just as capable as anyone of enjoying a night out. But it gave me a funny feeling when we started to sing 'There was I waiting at the church'. You needn't wait at the church for me yet, boys, I thought, as I looked down at their smiling faces and had a funny feeling they were weighing me up to see what size coffin I would need when I popped off.

I will never forget Rita's wedding day, partly because of the undertakers' reunion dinner and also because of the peculiar feeling I got in my stomach as I walked up the aisle behind Rita. I knew instinctively that the exciting, close friendship that had been built up over the last couple of years between us was soon to come to an end. I felt desolation.

★ ★ ★ ★ ★ ★ ★ ★ ★ ★ ★ ★ ★ ★ ★ ★

Rita grew larger and larger and we eventually looked like an advertisement for a

81

before and after body building course. Rita's bust grew mountainous and made mine look even smaller. I did not dare stuff any more scarves into my bra because I already looked top heavy. I could not put on an ounce of weight and every time he saw me Jimmy Cook called me 'Lark's Legs'. I kidded myself that what he really meant was I had a beautiful singing voice like a lark.

After the morning sickness had ceased Rita began to look quite radiant in her new role as mother-to-be. She seemed to thoroughly enjoy playing wife and slave to Neville, and if it was all acting, should have been awarded an Oscar. She even got involved with coffee mornings and flitted from house to house with all the rest of the young housewives.

She bragged about the lovely detached house she and Neville had settled into with its landscaped garden and statue of a nude in the middle of the lawn. And Neville's Jaguar car sent her into raptures.

"Neville says I can take driving lessons after I've had the baby. He says he'll buy me a car of my own if I can pass my test."

"That'll come in handy for our bookings if you learn to drive." I tested her reaction as to whether she would be carrying on with the act after the baby was born.

"Yes, and I'll be free to nip about all over the place without having to ask Neville to give me a lift every time." She paused and did not look me straight in the eyes. "Neville's not ever so keen on my coming back with you after I've had the baby. But I said I wanted to and that was that."

"Maybe you won't feel like it, not once you've got used to resting and being at home all the time." I sipped at my Guiness and port and acted nonchalant. "But I'd like you to let me know for sure, Rita. I'd like to find somebody else to take your place if you decide not to come back."

"I'm coming back ... I couldn't give up all those smashing nights out. Talking of nights out ... Jack Sargent wants to take us both for a drink next Friday." She plucked a stray hair from her eyebrows and added, "I haven't told him the news yet. Do you think you can tell I'm expecting?" She turned sideways and held her stomach in as far as it would go.

"Well, your bust looks bigger, but you wouldn't know if you didn't know," I reassured her. "Is 'George the Hat' coming next Friday?"

"You bet your life he is," Rita teased me, "he's got a thing about you Jack says."

"What about Neville?" I had misgivings about the night out.

"Oh, he's not invited." She laughed and added, "It'll be my last fling, Helen ... my very last."

"Don't say that, Rita ... you're only a spring chicken yet." But I felt she was right. You don't have to be a prophet to know — know when something was coming to an end.

As Rita's stomach grew we had to be more discriminating in our choice of venue. We had to make sure that there was a stage, preferably with curtains, so that we could be standing ready on the stage facing the audience and not have to walk on. Rita did not like to walk on or off the stage sideways because then everyone could see her condition.

Rita was magnificent. If there were no curtains she would shuffle off and on the stage keeping her stomach facing front and this was no mean feat after she had consumed a couple of Guiness and ports. She said that it felt like walking a straight line down at the police station. The months scurried away, Rita tightened her stays, struggled into her by now rather tight fitting gowns, and did not seem to worry about a thing.

At the end of the seventh month Neville put his foot down and Rita put hers up as they say.

December gave birth to screeching winds and cold swirling fog — Rita gave birth to a screeching pink and warm baby girl.

Little Katherine was obviously going to be a singer like her mother. She practised her lung control for hours on end. In no time at all she seemed able to hit top 'C' with very little effort.

I adored her — she was such a pretty, dainty baby. She reminded me of a Dresden china doll. She had Neville's looks and a tiny thatch of dark brown hair that was scraggy and stuck out like a baby chick's.

Neville adored her and would obviously spoil her like mad.

One afternoon as Rita and I cooed and sighed over the baby Rita told me that she was beginning to have slight misgivings about all this domesticity.

"You see, Helen ... I love her," she nuzzled her face into the baby's neck, "but I feel so tied down. I'm getting a bit browned-off with coffee mornings and local chit-chat. I'm really missing going on the bookings with you."

"Well, you'll soon be on your feet again." I didn't like to admit it but I felt rather smug. She had put me to a lot of upset and bother.

"But Neville says he doesn't want me to come back till Katherine's a lot older. He says my place is in the home ... looking after him ... and Katherine. And he's right, I know he's right, but I'm beginning to feel like a prisoner."

"How much older is he thinking of then?" I stroked Katherine's dainty feet. "About a year old ... something like that?"

Rita hesitated and said, "He's thinking more like when she's ready to go to school. He says he'd like us to have another baby while I'm still young. I've had it, Helen, if I do. That's the end of me."

"But surely, Rita ... it's up to you? If you don't want another baby he can't make you have one! You love going singing. It's changed your life completely ... and mine. Goodness knows where it was leading. Jimmy Cook was only saying the other day that he was concentrating on getting radio and television work for some of his best artists. And he's always said that he regards us as one of his top acts. We could get on television, Rita ... I know we could. Oh, you can't pack it all in now, surely?"

"The time spent with you, Helen, round the clubs has been the most exciting and interesting time of my life. But I'm caught in a trap, can't you see. Neville is such a good husband, I can have anything I want ... anything. And for some reason he is really against my going back to singing."

"It must be jealousy then." I sighed and felt miserable. I knew instinctively that Rita was somehow hiding behind what Neville wanted. I realised that she was not being completely honest because she was embarrassed, afraid to hurt my feelings. I decided to let go of the idea that Rita would return to the act.

By the time April came along and Vera and I were choosing new and daring patterns for my new creations, Rita was choosing new and boring knitting patterns for Neville's latest creation.

Neville had won easily. He was quite a little schemer on the quiet, I thought, Rita would have a high old time getting her own way now.

83

I conceded defeat and concentrated on my solo act. But the act had lost more than the lovely bubbly personality of Rita. It had lost that newness. The exciting, thrilling newness that tears away at your guts when you are first trying to achieve something out of the ordinary.

I felt ordinary now when I stepped out onto a stage — and missed the laughter and fun backstage which I had shared with Rita. And I was also beginning to drink more. The awful stage-fright I experienced before a performance seemed much worse now there was no Rita to laugh it off with. Sometimes I had consumed two Guiness and ports before starting my act, especially if the club was a large one and the audience particularly noisy. But nevertheless, it always seemed worth the dreadful nerves when I heard the applause from the audience at the end of my act. Always seemed worth the awful throbbing in my brain and the sick dizzy feeling the next morning when I awoke.

CHAPTER TWELVE

It took me a long time to adjust to the fact that the Dumonte Sisters had finished as an act. But, adjust I had to and quickly. I decided that I would much rather work on my own or with different partners than go back to being a waitress at Carlin's or a barmaid at the Cresta. The sheer boredom of it all would have finished me after having once tasted the thrill and excitement of showbusiness. I was determined to make a go of things no matter what happened.

I very rarely went to visit Rita and Neville but I did telephone occasionally. I almost knew what Rita would have to say before I telephoned. She told me about Katherine, complained about Neville and said that when she had sorted herself out she would like to come back to the act once again.

I could not afford to wait that long and soon fate dealt me another winning card.

I was booked to do a stint at a club just outside Newark where the audience consisted mainly of air-force personnel. They were rowdy but a good natured crowd, a bunch of airmen let loose for a few hours.

After my second spot I was approached by a very pretty girl of around twenty two, I guessed. She was similar to me in height and weight, and had a lovely dark mane of shoulder length brown hair.

"Don't you sing with your sister now then?" She came over to where I was leaning against the bar.

"Er ... no, not at the moment. She's decided to get married and have a family. She wasn't my real sister ... just a friend."

"I've seen your act a couple of times. You'd got a very good act there. And your evening gowns are fabulous. I think it makes all the difference when you look good as well as sound good."

"Rita's cousin Vera makes all our gowns." She seems very friendly, I thought, as I weighed up the reason for her friendliness. I soon found out.

"I was wondering whether you were looking out for another partner? I've been in the business nearly six years now. Usually go round with my dad. He does a comical magic act. I do the vocals and help him with his tricks. I'd love to be in a sister act though ... much rather do that."

I had to think quickly. If I said yes and she couldn't sing very well it would be embarrassing.

I was non-committal in my reply. "Well I've got a lot on at the moment with my single bookings ... but I could be interested in a new act."

"Would you like to join us for a drink?" She nodded and pointed across the room. "I'm with my boyfriend, over there look. Come and join us."

I followed her to a table near the door. She had a nice, neat little figure. I noticed she got more than a few appreciative glances from the airmen. She could dye her hair auburn, I thought, planning ahead, and with a few alterations could easily fit into Rita's gowns.

"What are you drinking?" the boyfriend asked after being introduced to me. He looked a bit shy and was very good looking. A bit like Charlton Heston.

"I'm drinking Guiness and port but I'll just have a small port in here if I may. Daren't drink too much because my boyfriend can't give me a lift home tonight and it's nearly an hour's ride back on the bus."

"Oh, I'd like to try a Guiness and port please, Tony." She smiled at him and nuzzled her lips to his neck. When he had gone out of ear-shot she turned to me and said, "I'm game to try anything new, aren't you?"

"Yes, join the club," I answered her and then thought, but can you sing?

"If you like," she continued, "I'll sing a couple of songs for you, they know me here. That's if you don't mind of course."

She was a mind reader. There must be something in magical acts after all, I thought.

"Have you got any music with you?"

"No ... the fellas have accompanied me a couple of times, they can follow me."

She seemed very confident and showed no signs of stage-fright. She walked over to the stage and had a few words with the pianist and drummer. There was a roll on the drums and the pianist introduced her.

"Ladies and gentlemen ... quiet please! With our lovely artist's permission we have another delightful singer to entertain you this evening. Order please, you lot round the bar there. Give a bit of order for ... Sylvia Clifford."

The airmen did not let her down, they whistled and cheered. Tony looked very pleased and, I thought, what a difference to the way Neville had reacted when men had whistled after Rita.

Sylvia was good. A nice melodious voice, clear diction and she had her breathing under control too. I hummed along with her, very softly, to see if she was in a similar key to the ones I felt comfortable singing in. It was there all right. I felt certain we could get a good act together. Lots of hard work of course, but it would mean plenty of good bookings.

Sylvia got louder applause than I had received but I was used to this — if a local person or someone out of the audience who looked like an amateur got up to sing they were always supported like mad by the audience.

The pianist and drummer played for a while and then it was my turn to sing once more. I changed my gown ready for the last spot and hoped I'd go down well because I wanted to impress Sylvia. I was not disappointed. The airmen were well oiled by now and would not let me off the stage. They shouted for more every time I finished a song — they were in a singing mood so I kept on going with some of the old songs. The audience sang along at the tops of their voices.

Now it was time for my dramatic ending. I had chosen 'Who Are We' a song not many people would know the words to, this always kept them quiet. I had learned that you had to finish the evening with something rather dramatic so that it was the artist who closed the show without too much audience participation.

The song went over well and the airmen quietened down to listen. I needed plenty of breath for the last line of the number because it went extremely high. I knew my face had a look of agony on it when my voice soared to the top notes but this added to the performance and kidded the people on a little. It certainly did the trick with the airmen. They applauded and whistled at the end of the song. One or two people started to applaud before I had rounded off the last note, this was always a sign that they were really enjoying your singing.

I changed my gown and rejoined Sylvia and Tony.

"I must rush now," I told them, "get the last bus back."

"Tony'll give you a lift into town. Whereabouts do you live?"

"Malperry. I've got a flat there."

"Oh, that's not far from me," Sylvia organised everybody, "we'll drop you off first ... it's hardly out of our way at all."

"Got time for another drink then, girls." Tony stood up. "Two Guiness and ports for two of the best looking girls in the room."

"Have you thought over what we were talking about?" Sylvia fidgetted about on her chair. "Do you think we could make a go of it?"

"I'm game to give it a try. Of course it all depends on whether or not I can harmonise with your voice. Rita's voice was lovely and deep, I can only harmonise with deep voices, because I have to sing a lot higher of course to make the harmony sound good." I handed her one of my business cards. "Give me a ring and I'll arrange for you to come over to my place for a rehearsal."

"I can fix a time now if you like," Sylvia looked excited, "I can get anytime in the day. You say when."

"Next Saturday then ... and I'll give Rita a ring, see if she'll let us have her gowns. It'll save a lot of money if we have them altered to fit you."

"I'm sure we'll be able to team up." Sylvia's face was flushed with excitement. "I've been looking for a chance like this for ages."

We finished our drinks and at last made our way through the crowd of jostling, flirting airmen.

It had been a good night, I thought, one of the best.

★ ★ ★ ★ ★ ★ ★ ★ ★ ★ ★ ★ ★ ★ ★ ★

The following Saturday afternoon Sylvia turned up at my flat as arranged.

"I'm glad you said Saturday," she confided, "I work as a telephonist receptionist during the week but I didn't want to let on in case you had said you wanted to practice during the week. I was going to take time off work if you had said a day during the week."

"You really are keen, aren't you?" I sorted through some records.

"I told you, I've been looking for an opportunity like this for ages. I'm a bit fed-up with my dad's magic act. He's a bit old-fashioned, poor old sod. Who wants to see somebody pulling doves out of his trouser-pockets? And swallowing razor-blades? People want more than that nowadays. They want glamour and something a bit different. Look how strippers pack them in at the 'Old Captain'. You can't get through the door there on a Saturday night."

"Oh, I know ... I did a booking there the other Thursday night and the men kept shouting, 'Gerrum off' while I was singing." I put a record on the turn-table. "I felt ever so embarrassed. The men were behaving like raving lunatics. Somebody's told me that the strippers move about amongst the audience and the men feel hold of them."

"They get ever such good money though." Sylvia smiled cheekily.

"Yes," I replied, "they get ten pounds a night some of them. That works out at about five-bob a feel. You can keep it thank you very much. I wouldn't want men feeling hold of me."

"No," Sylvia looked cheeky again, "I'd want at least ten-bob a feel."

The music began and we got ready for the first run through.

"We get too hungry for dinner at eight."

I showed Sylvia how to stand, how to hold out her arms and wiggle her hips. She was a very adept pupil and soon the harmony blended into shape.

It gave me a very strange sort of feeling, standing there in front of the bedroom mirror, just like Rita and I had done almost two years ago.

As our confidence grew we sang out more loudly. Sylvia was good, not quite the beautiful sound Rita had made, but nevertheless she would do.

"I think we'd be all right, don't you?" I felt very happy.

"I thought our harmony sounded smashing." Sylvia looked radiant.

"That's it then, Sylvia. Sylvia Dumonte I mean."

"Will it be O.K. with Rita if we keep the same name?"

I hadn't thought about that but was sure Rita would not have any objections. She would feel pushed out, I knew that much, but it was her decision. Rita had only to have said yes — and I would have welcomed her back with a glad heart. But now it was too late — I had teamed up with Sylvia and that was the end of Rita. I couldn't keep changing my mind, I had to know where I was going. My goal was radio and then perhaps television and Sylvia seemed just the right person to help me get there. She had the looks, confidence and voice. I felt the old feelings of elation returning and again my life seemed to tingle with excitement.

"Your bust's even smaller than mine, Sylvia. Here, let me show you one of my tricks. Your dad's got nothing on me." I pushed a couple of scarves down my bra and paraded in front of Sylvia.

"Blimey! ..." Sylvia stared at my bust. "And last week I was feeling jealous of your cleavage, when you were singing at that club in Newark."

"It's all done by mirrors," I laughed, "now you know where your dad stuffs his doves."

★ ★ ★ ★ ★ ★ ★ ★ ★ ★ ★ ★ ★ ★ ★ ★

I now had to reorganise things, let everyone know that the Dumonte Sisters were back. I telephoned Jimmy Cook and went round to see Dave McGuire. They, of course, both wanted to hear Sylvia, so arrangements were made for them to hear the new act at a little club in Ilkeston where the audience was well-behaved and friendly. I knew despite her outward appearance that Sylvia would be nervous for the first few times at least so I wanted her to have an easy-going audience. Also, I knew that the accompaniment was first class and that was important if Jimmy Cook and Dave McGuire were going to listen to our songs.

I rehearsed Sylvia until we were both exhausted but she tried very hard and soon everything was fine. Sylvia decided that she would like to sing songs with a fast beat for her solos and so I settled for slow sentimental ones. The harmony came without any problems at all, Sylvia's voice was pitched just right for me and I knew it would come over well when we had practised some more and lifted our act to a high standard.

At the Ilkeston club we were greeted with enthusiasm by the committee members and they all drooled over Sylvia. The first two spots went down well and Jimmy Cook and Dave McGuire both liked the new act.

"Another pair of lark's legs," moaned Jimmy, "you want to get a bit of meat on you."

"I'll have a bit off your stomach then." Sylvia gave him some back-chat.

"How about a nice meat injection, my dear?"

Here we go, I thought, another man thinks he's the world's greatest lover — in his mind that is.

But Sylvia had the right idea — her saucy remarks and effervescent personality soon had both agents reaching for their diaries. And the entertainment secretary booked us to sing at a bird-fancier's dance and buffet.

"Plenty of sandwiches and meat-pies, me ducks. As much as you can get down yer. And it won't cost yer 'owt for yer drinks. You'll have a good night, me ducks ... and your fee'll be paid by the bird-fanciers, you should get a bit extra."

"Will there be plenty of cocks on show that night?" Jimmy Cook blew cigar smoke all over us and laughed making his stomach bob up-and-down.

"You want to enter yours, Jimmy," Sylvia latched on to the fun, "it'd look lovely with a bow of ribbon tied round it!"

"Time for your last spot, me ducks." The entertainment secretary grinned at us. "Have yet got any owd 'uns? Give 'em some owd 'uns."

"Put your leotards on, my dears." Jimmy Cook guzzled at his brandy and looked us up-and-down. "Let's see a bit of bum."

"We can't sing 'My Old Man' and 'Waiting at the Church' in leotards," I told him, "we only wear them when we're doing our dancing."

"Put one of your gownless straps on then." Jimmy's eyes were getting that glazed-over look.

"Put one of your Bingo frocks on." Dave sat smiling at us.

"What's a Bingo frock?" I asked.

"Eyes down ... look in." Dave roared with laughter at his own silly joke. "There's gold in them there hills."

"No there's not," I whispered to Sylvia, "there's scarves."

★ ★ ★ ★ ★ ★ ★ ★ ★ ★ ★ ★ ★ ★ ★ ★

As the months disintegrated, leaving behind them fragments of cheering, applauding, smiling audiences, the act grew more polished. Inevitably, Sylvia had to give up her daytime job as the late nights and travelling began to wear her down. I was very satisfied at the way the act had taken shape and Sylvia never complained at the amount of rehearsing we had to do. She tackled new dance-routines with terrific enthusiasm and seemed to enjoy every minute. And she had her hair dyed without a murmur of protest and looked really stunning, with her glorious halo of flaming red hair.

One evening Sylvia's father came along to see our act.

"Ooh ... you are good, girls ... you've got a lovely act together." He did not seem bothered that I had more or less pinched his partner.

"Our Sylvia would never have got anywhere with me. I only need somebody to hand me things and help me to get me rabbits and doves off stage. I've got me sister's gel to help out. She's only sixteen but she's got a nice pair of legs ... she wears them there black tights ... gives the blokes a treat while I'm boggering about with me tricks."

"I've got a nice surprise for you, dad." Sylvia smiled and looked pleased. "You're booked at the Ransmoor Social Club next Saturday ... same night as us."

Her father's face lit up with happiness as he replied, "I'll bring some booze then, Sylvie. Not paying their fancy prices. They stick the prices on at the Ransmoor you know," he addressed me, "it's just been done-up, so they've put the prices up."

"I'll look forward to working with you, Mr. Clifford."

"Call me Harry, me darlin' ... call me Harry."

"I'll bring my flask along as well, Harry."

"Oh, we don't want no coffee. Don't bother with coffee."

"Who mentioned coffee?" I winked at him, "it keeps you awake."

★ ★ ★ ★ ★ ★ ★ ★ ★ ★ ★ ★ ★ ★ ★ ★

The rain poured down as we set out for the Ransmoor Social Club. When we arrived the place was almost empty. The club members must be finding it hard to leave their nice cosy fireplaces, I thought, and who could blame them.

"Don't worry, girls," the entertainment secretary clapped his hands together and smiled a non-convincing smile, "they'll be rolling in later on. They'll turn up for the Tombola if they have to swim for it ... we usually draw the numbers about half past nine."

"We're not getting dressed up for these few," I whispered to Sylvia, "we won't bother with out leotards and you can forget the soft-shoe-shuffle."

"Poor old dad." Sylvia looked anxious. "We'll go on first ... it's no use doing your act till it's filled up a bit."

Ralph, who had given me a lift to the club, suggested to Tony who had given Harry, Sylvia and Muriel, Harry's niece, a lift, that they nip off into the main part of the town and see what the night-life was like. Ralph and Tony had become quite friendly since the forming of the new act and enjoyed a tour of the pubs together.

We crowded into the dressing-room and opened our suitcases. Harry put his cases in a corner out of the way and said, "I'm not using the rabbits tonight ... bogger em! ... there's only a dozen out there. I'll just do me playing-cards trick ... and me fire-eating. Ha-ha-ha ... that'll warm the audience up a bit. And I'll do me razor-blades and me sword-swallowing."

"Aren't you doing yer budgies, uncle?" asked Muriel. "I like yer budgie act. I think they're ever so pretty."

"Yes, all right then ... I'll do the budgies. And I'm going to do me everlasting clay pipe as well." He placed a clay pipe on the window-sill and warned, "Don't go near this ... if yer touch it you'll melt yer hands off yer wrists."

No chance of me going near the pipe, I thought, it sounded too dangerous.

Harry poured vodka and lime into glasses smuggled in with his budgies and rabbits no doubt, I thought, and we talked and laughed about showbusiness and its pitfalls and disadvantages like this evening, with its lack of audience.

"We ought to go and show ourselves," I stood up, "we don't want them to twig on we've brought our own booze."

"Ooh ... bogger 'em," said a very relaxed and bleary eyed Harry, "you don't have to worry."

Sylvia and Muriel agreed with me that we ought to show ourselves so we trooped down the concert room and made our way over to the bar. After the first Guiness and port had played a duet in my stomach with the vodka and lime I felt ready for anything. I was still experiencing stage-fright but only in a mild form.

At half-past eight Sylvia and I did our first spot. The audience warmed up, the pianist and drummer cheered up.

Now it was time for Harry and Muriel to have a go. Muriel cavorted about on the stage whilst Harry shoved a large sword down his throat until it disappeared right down to the hilt. Then he drank something which must have been petrol, put a lighted match to his mouth and breathed flames high into the air. The audience warmed up a bit more and so did the ceiling I should think.

The entertainment secretary had been correct. People began to trickle in with the rain.

Sylvia and I did not do any solos but concentrated on the harmony. Our second spot went down well, we wore our black velvet gowns with the slits up the side and gave the men a good look at our black fishnet clad thighs.

"Ladies and gentlemen ... order please once again for Goldello." The entertainment secretary introduced Harry again. Harry walked on stage, bowed to the audience and produced ten twittering budgies from out of thin air. The audience were intrigued by his pipe that went on smoking even after he had broken it in half and then half again. In the end he was smoking a piece of pipe the size of my thumb nail.

There was a loud roll on the drums and Muriel tottered in her high-heeled red satin shoes over to a table which Harry had placed in the middle of the stage.

"I will now have a nice snack," he leaned over and addressed the audience, "a delicious meal of razor-blades, straight from Sheffield."

Muriel held out a small plate to him and on the plate was a heap of razor-blades. Harry held out the blades one-by-one before he shoved them into his mouth. He made a big show of gulping each blade down and then walked down the steps at the side of the stage and taking hold of a giggling woman's hair cut through a strand of her hair with one of the razor-blades before placing the blade onto his tongue and swallowing it down to join all the other blades in his stomach.

It was horrible to watch but I couldn't avert my eyes because it was so fascinating to see him swallowing all those razor-blades.

When he had swallowed about ten blades he beckoned the same woman from the audience to approach the stage. He opened his mouth wide and let her examine the inside.

"Oooh," she squealed, "he's swallered them, he has! All of 'em!"

Suddenly, Harry put his forefinger and thumb into his mouth. A razor-blade popped out of his mouth, then another and then another. They were all attached to a long thread of black cotton. Out they came one after the other looking like a miniature line of washing. The applause was loud and long but Harry did not stay on stage until the applause had died away. Instead, he rushed from the stage with the razor-blades waving about on the cotton.

After a few minutes Muriel beckoned us to go to the dressing-room. As we walked into the room we could see that something was wrong with Harry. He was bent over the sink and was making funny gurgling noises.

"He's swallowed one of his razor-blades," explained a worried Muriel, "one of the blades came off the cotton ... he's cut his Adam's-Apple by the looks of it."

Water gushed from the tap and swirling round in the water was poor Harry's blood.

"Dad! ... what can we do? ... Oh, dad!" Sylvia leaned over him. Harry stood up and turned to face us, blood running out of his mouth and down his chin. He made more choking noises and swallowed some water. I was horrified and just stood in a trance looking at him. But it was all right. He managed to speak at last, "I nearly did it that time, girls," he spat the water into the sink, "nearly lost me bleddy Adam's-Apple. One of me blades came off the cotton and cut me bleddy tonsils. I've managed to get it back up though." We sat him on a chair and Sylvia dabbed at his face with a handkerchief.

"You frightened us to death, dad." She put her arm around his shoulders.

"I frightened meself to death," he whispered, "I'd have been the first man to die from cutting his throat from the inside." He tried to laugh and made a spluttering noise instead.

"You're sure you've got the blade back up, dad?"

"Yes, that's what caused all this mess. It ripped into me tonsils when I pulled it out. Oh, bogger this lot, pour us a drink, Sylvie."

Luckily, after a while, the blood stopped flowing and a much calmer Harry sat sipping at his vodka and lime whilst Muriel fussed around packing budgies away.

Sylvia and I rounded off the evening with a medley of old songs and then it was time to go home.

"Bit of a dull night was it, Helen?" Ralph put my suitcase into the boot of his car. "I expect it gets a bit boring when you don't get many in."

"Sylvia's dad cut his throat," I replied, "he nearly died."

"Oh yes," he was only half listening, "I should have liked to have seen him do that. It was a bit dull at the pub we went to. If you get another booking with Goldello I'll stay to watch his act. How did you say he cut his throat? They're clever aren't they ... some of these magicians."

"Yes," I answered him, "but you can get too clever you know. If you try and be too clever you can cut your own throat."

"You're in a frivolous mood," Ralph gave me a cuddle, "did they book you again, love?"

"Yes, we're going back a week before Christmas ... and Sylvia's dad ... they booked him as well."

I settled back in the car and thought how much I liked Harry. He was a character, not many of them about. He really would have to do something about the cotton in his razor-blade act, I thought, and then squeezed Ralph's hand as we journeyed home.

CHAPTER THIRTEEN

A fitting had been arranged at Vera's house for three o'clock one Saturday afternoon. I was going to meet Sylvia for a snack in a Lyon's coffee-house down on Long Row. I kept away from Carlin and Priestley's now because it still felt as though I was showing off in front of the waitresses I had once worked with. Sylvia arrived at the cafe looking rather flustered, she waved when she saw me and came hurrying over to the table.

"Oh," she sat down, "what a time I've just had."

"Why ... what's happened, Sylvia?"

"I've just been to take Dave McGuire his commission. There was only him in his office."

"What happened then? Tell me quick and then I'll go and fetch some coffee. Do you want beans on toast?"

"I need a stiff brandy if you ask me." She kept me in suspense.

"Tell me then, you torment ... what did he say?"

"It's not what he said, it's what he did." She started to giggle. "He got hold of me and pinned me down on top of his desk."

"Dirty devil ... what did you do?"

"I put up a bit of a struggle," she was still giggling, "but I thought I'd better not upset him else he might cut our bookings down."

"Oh, that's right, Sylvia ... the show must go on." I was impatient to know what happened next.

"He'd just put my coat on top of the piano ... had given me a glass of whisky. I was standing near his desk when he grabbed me and tried to pin me down on his desk."

"Did you spill the whisky?" I pulled her leg a bit.

"The whisky went all over the place ... all over the papers on his desk. He got my skirt up over my thighs and tried to get my knickers off."

"He didn't?"

"No, he didn't ... but he had a bloody good try. I was bent over his desk, all among his papers and whatnot."

"Over his desk ... that must have been very uncomfortable?"

"You can laugh, Helen, but it's a wonder I didn't slip a disc in me back. When I started to fight him off he got even more passionate and threw himself on top of me with all his weight. I skidded and fell right on top of his typewriter."

"Oh dear, that must have come keen!"

"You're not kidding. The keys were going up and down like mad." She started giggling again and added, "I'll bet I'm the only girl in this city who's had 'The quick brown fox jumped over the lazy dog' typed on her bum."

We laughed some more and I fetched the food and coffee. When I returned to the

93

table Sylvia told me that despite the unfruitful attack on her virginity, Dave McGuire had still given us lots more bookings.

"He knows when he's on to a good thing," I told her, "he earns a lot of commission from our engagements."

"Yes, and he tried to get a bonus today," she added, "but he's not getting any encores from my body."

Men are all fools, I thought, but if we girls knew how to handle them they came in handy now and then.

★ ★ ★ ★ ★ ★ ★ ★ ★ ★ ★ ★ ★ ★ ★ ★ ★

The Klondyke club was on the outskirts of town. It stood in an acre of land and as well as being a nightclub, did accommodation for reps. and businessmen. It also hired out rooms for business conferences and functions.

Sylvia was like a little girl lost in fairyland when we arrived at the club. She peered closely at antique vases and touched velvet curtains and chairs.

She stared open mouthed when we went inside to the ladies' toilet. It had a cloakroom at the back and all round the room were ceiling to floor mirrors. The sinks had individual linen hand towels and luxury perfumed soap. Hanging from the ceiling was a huge four tier, twinkling cut glass chandelier. In the centre of the marbled floor was a large goatskin rug. Sylvia sat on the rug and then stretched out and kicked her legs in the air.

She started to sing, 'If my friends could see me now.'

If only they could, I thought, especially the waitresses at Carlin's. How they would have loved to be in my shoes instead of plodding up and down all day long serving food. I concentrated on thinking how lucky I was to be here, at this fabulous nightclub and then a feeling of nausea hit me — my stage-fright was here again. I rushed to spend a penny whilst Sylvia carried on kicking her legs in the air from her position on top of the goatskin.

We had been given an unoccupied bedroom to get changed in and this had an adjoining bathroom. The bedroom was very luxurious and had central heating and a telephone. I began to feel sick with fright — I had never done a booking at anywhere as opulent as this before. Perhaps the audience would not like our act. They would all be very sophisticated. I hurriedly took out the flask, poured a good stiff drink into the plastic cup, then poured the liquid even faster into my throat.

"Come on," said Sylvia, after also having a good drink of the vodka, "let's go down to the bar and see what's doing. I'm glad your Ralph couldn't give us a lift tonight, it ties us down too much, don't you think? We'll soon get somebody to give us a lift back home. These reps. have all got company cars. And they work a good fiddle on the petrol ... lots of dough."

I patted at my hair, checked to see I hadn't any lipstick on my teeth and followed Sylvia down the long, thickly carpeted corridor and into the cocktail bar. We were an immediate success with the men who were standing in front of and leaning onto the bar.

"Hello there, Ginger. Would you like to have a drink with me?"

"Hello, gorgeous. Haven't we met somewhere before ... like in a bed?"

"May I have this dance?"

After the Guiness and port had caught up with the vodka and lime I began to feel less uneasy. The men here were no different to the miners and the good old factory workers. Just a little more variety in their patter and they could afford to spend more.

A very good looking young man in dress suit, lavender-lace-down-the-front shirt and deep lavender velvet bow tie approached us, smiling an absolute dazzler. He introduced himself as the assistant manager and said that he hoped we would both have a very enjoyable evening as, he was sure, everyone in the audience would.

We were to perform four spots, so I decided on two doubles and a solo spot each. We did not have to go on until nine o'clock and our last spot was just before eleven which would give us just enough time to catch the last bus home if we did not get a lift back.

Our first spot was quite well received and my bladder settled down a little. Sylvia seemed very carried away by the lush surroundings and flirted with every man in sight. The assistant manager whose name was Adrian, stuck by her side like a motor bike on the wall of death.

I did my single spot at a quarter to ten and my nerves were now quite steady. The microphone had a long flex which allowed me to step down from the stage and mingle in and out of the tables whilst I sang my numbers. Proper nightclub stuff this.

When I went down into the bar once more after changing my gown, Sylvia and Adrian left the room together. I chatted to some of the men at the bar and had a couple of dances.

I enjoyed the dancing and lapped up the flattery from the men. Sylvia concentrated her attentions on Adrian and when they danced together it was like watching a scene from a Rudolph Valentino film. He kept thrusting out with his leg and he held her so closely to him I began to wonder how she was managing to breathe. The chemistry between them was really hot stuff and I wondered how Tony would fit into the picture after this evening.

"Adrian's going to give me a lift home, Helen. He'll give you one as well of course if you don't get fixed up. Have you got fixed up, that tall blonde fella seems to have taken to you?"

"He's offered me a lift," I replied, "but I'm being a bit wary. I'll let you know later on."

Sylvia rushed away to get changed and came back into the concert room wearing a beautiful low-cut pale green chiffon gown. A collective murmur of appreciation circulated round the room and when Sylvia stepped onto the stage and the footlights held her in their beams it wasn't hard to see what the men had experienced. A young, beautiful, full-of-life-and-energy dream woman. Not the kind of woman who waits at home with a meal and slippers. But a woman every man yearns for in his innermost thoughts. A sex-goddess full of passion and excitement. Sylvia began to sing, 'Blue moon.' The music drifted through the room. It sounded beautiful.

A hush fell over the room, even the men standing round the bar turned to face the stage and listened attentively.

The musical accompaniment was also beautiful, the pianist improvised notes of his own and the bass player, trumpet player and drummer blended in with the music perfectly.

I sat at a table near the front of the stage and thought, what a strange feeling I was experiencing, sitting there listening to Sylvia singing. I had made the right choice, she had turned out perfect for the act. But now there had to be something more — a new mountain to climb — or rather a new stage to find.

I made up my mind to telephone Jimmy Cook and see if there was any chance of working for radio or perhaps, television. We had gone down very well at the Klondyke — a high class place with a very critical audience. We had a nice polished act, lovely clothes and, according to all our return bookings, two good voices.

My mind raced with future plans and by the time Sylvia had finished her spot I was beginning to feel reckless.

The tall blonde's name was Bill.

"I'm having a lift home with Bill," I told Sylvia, "so just mind how you go."

"Don't worry, I will." She looked at herself in the bedroom mirror and smeared more lipstick on her lips. "I'm still bruised from the other day." Her eyes twinkled with mirth. "The quick brown fox has gone, but the lazy dog is still there." We laughed just as much as Rita and I had done — I was so glad that we got on well together.

★ ★ ★ ★ ★ ★ ★ ★ ★ ★ ★ ★ ★ ★ ★ ★

Ralph and I got engaged. We did it quietly without any party or announcements in the newspaper. He did not pressure me into naming the day of our wedding and I was glad. I liked the idea of being engaged when he had proposed but the thoughts of marriage once again sent me into a panic.

Ralph said he understood how I felt and would be quite content to wait until I was ready for a full commitment to married life. I never discussed with him how I felt about showbusiness and our sister act. Never disclosed how I wanted more from the life, craved to be famous and recognised up there with the established artistes. But, I was very fond of Ralph and could see no harm in becoming his fiancèe. Sylvia told me I was very lucky to 'hook' such a dishy fish and thought I ought to get married as soon as possible before someone else snapped him up.

I thought about the lift home I had accepted from Bill and told myself that I could not have let Bill kiss me goodnight if I had truly been in love with Ralph. It had got to be real love the next time I looked a parson in the eyes and said, I do, and I wasn't sure that this was it.

But, being engaged to Ralph felt good and I flashed my glittering diamond proudly whenever anyone asked to inspect the ring. Marriage plans were pushed to the back of the queue and Ralph seemed content to wait.

Ralph managed to obtain lots of work for our act in the north west but he did not seem to want to become too involved with showbusiness. He very wisely appreciated that a man tagging along harmed the image of our act. The men in the audience liked to flirt and have fun with us and this could not be done with boyfriends hanging around. If Ralph was not working away he always chauffeured me to and from the venues especially if I was booked to appear on my own at some club which was hard to get to by bus — but he rarely stayed all evening and that was the way I liked things. My Ralph had turned out to be the perfect man in every way it seemed. I tucked him away into a nice little compartment in my life and told myself that one day, when the time was right, I would let him out of the compartment and marry him. But not yet — the timing was all wrong at the moment.

CHAPTER FOURTEEN

The installation of a telephone at my flat was a major event. Neither my parents nor any of my friends had ever possessed such a luxury but of course now, since my transition from waitress to artiste, a telephone was a necessity.

I was looking forward to an evening of sheer laziness. Ralph was away working for the whole of the week-end and I had a Saturday free. Sylvia had gone on a booking with her dad so I curled up by the fireside with a bar of nut chocolate and a good book.

The telephone rang and Jimmy Cook's voice said, "Hello, my dear ... can you help me out this evening? My girl singer's let me down at the last moment. It's the last bleddy booking she'll get from this agency." His breath crackled down the telephone wires like a heavy breathing, rude 'phone call. "I'll pick you up, my dear. You'll have a terrific night. It's at the air-force base at Allinton-le-Marsh. I'll only need two spots from you ... I've got two more artists besides you."

"Oh, Jimmy ... I haven't done my hair or anything," I protested a little, "can't you get somebody else? I'll have an awful rush to get ready on time."

"I want you, Helen. You're just what those poor airmen need to cheer them up on this cold miserable evening. Put your curlers in and plonk a hat over them. You can titivate yourself up when you get there. I'll pick you up in an hour's time. Be ready for half-past seven, there's a good girl. It'll take us about half-an-hour to get there, but you won't be doing your first spot till about nine."

"All right, Jimmy ... I'll be ready." Already I was planning which gowns to take with me.

"It's ten pounds, less my commission of course," rasped Jimmy, "they lash out at these air-base bookings. The government's got plenty to throw around. See you later then, my dear."

"All right, Jimmy ... I can't resist a man in uniform."

"I'll put mine on then."

"Oh, what uniform have you got, Jimmy?"

"I was an air-raid warden. I won't tell you what I used to get up to ... among the sandbags."

"You can tell me later, Jimmy ... I must start to get ready now." I hoped he would have forgotten about the sandbags by the time he came to pick me up.

I set my hair and selected three evening gowns. I decided to take an extra gown in case of accidents — zip failure or spilled drinks.

I began to look forward to the evening — all those gorgeous airmen. And there were two more artists on with me Jimmy had said. I liked meeting new artists, I hoped one of them would be a comedian, I love a good laugh.

★ ★ ★ ★ ★ ★ ★ ★ ★ ★ ★ ★ ★ ★ ★

Jimmy arrived at my place and we set off straight away. It was a bitterly cold evening so I was grateful for the lift in his car. All I had to do was keep Jimmy at a distance. He had not forgotten the sandbags. I had to listen to all the details of how he had seduced practically every woman who ever set foot in an air-raid shelter. I could smell the inevitable brandy breath and hoped he would not drink too much at the R.A.F. camp or he would never be able to drive the car back home.

"There's two strippers on with you tonight, my dear." He patted my knee and I steeled myself for worse to follow. "Coming up from London. One of the girls teaches stripping, she's a real first class artiste so you're in for a treat tonight. It's an art you know, this taking your clothes off. I mean to say ... any girl can take her clothes off, can't she?" Pat-pat went his left hand on my leg. I moved my leg away and thought, I know my knees are a bit bony but I'm sure they can't be mistaken for gear sticks.

"I've never worked with strippers before." I began to have mixed feelings about the evening now.

"They charge the earth. Still, that's all right with me. The more they get, the more commission I get."

Jimmy lit a cigar and the car filled up with smoke. My eyes smarted and my throat dried up but at least it kept his left hand from wandering in the direction of my knees.

"When you do your two spots, look at the first two rows." Jimmy gave instructions. "Make up to the men sitting at the front. That's where all the big nobs'll be sitting. Officers, flight whatsits and the like. You'll be invited into the officers' mess afterwards I should think. And mind the rye whisky if they offer you any. It's strong enough to rot a vicar's collar. They're a great bunch of lads, my dear, you'll enjoy yourself."

We were greeted at the door of the air-base by a young, smiling airman who took hold of my suitcase and led the way through a large concert room. He knocked on the dressing-room door which was on the left hand side of a large stage and ushered me inside.

The two girl strippers were already inside the dressing-room. Their make-up jars and tubes were strewn all over the shelf in front of a huge mirror.

"Hello, luv."

"Wotcher, luv."

"Hello." I smiled at the two girls and tried to avert my eyes from their bare breasts.

The young airman had a quick look, gave an embarrassed cough and shut the door behind him.

The taller and older looking stripper had an enormous bosom. It looked quite abnormal to me and I thought how uncomfortable it must have been for her carrying all that surplus flesh around.

"I'm Marlene, luv." Big bosom smiled at me. "My stage name's Marietta, bit more exotic sounding." She picked up two tassles from the shelf and fixed them onto the ends of each nipple. The tassles must have had some sort of suction on them like a sink plunger, I thought, because they certainly seemed to cling tightly to her nipples. She noticed the expression on my face and explained, "I whirl them round and round. I can do them in different directions both at the same time. Takes a lot of practice mind you."

"Oh yes, I'll bet it does." I replied enthusiastically.

"What's your name, mate?" The other girl applied bright green eye-shadow to her eyelids. "I'm Sheila, but my stage name's Shareeta."

"I'm Helen ... I usually work with another girl. We're called the Dumonte Sisters. But they only wanted a solo spot tonight."

"You're like the Beverley Sisters then?" Sheila nodded her head. "I like the Beverley Sisters ... they've got a lovely act together. I wouldn't mind joining a sister act."

"You could call yourselves the Stripping Sisters." Marlene took some sticking plaster from her suitcase and said, "Let's get your plaster on, mate." She looked at me and added, "She sags a bit since she had her last kid. We have to give her lils a bit of an uplift."

I watched fascinated as Marlene took the thin strip of sticking plaster and pressed it firmly underneath Sheila's left breast. She pressed and pressed and then pulled it tightly across, underneath the right breast. The sagging breasts, once the sticking plaster had been stretched across them, shot upwards and immediately looked high and firm like a young girl's. A very skimpy bra, covered in sparkling material, was then fitted over the plaster.

"Does it hurt when you pull it off again?" I winced at the thought.

"Course it does, luv ... it makes your eyes water, don't it Marl?"

"She's usually too sloshed to feel much pain by the end of the show." Marlene stepped out of her skirt. "She still gets nervous ... has to have a drink before she can face them."

"Oh, I would have to as well." I nodded sympathetically.

"I don't bother about the silly sods." Marlene removed her half-slip. "It's the men who need a drink by the time I've done with them. I just treat it as a job. The men are disgusting ... sitting there gaping at nude women. If I was a man I'd find something better to do with my time. They're all filthy minded twerps ... but the money's good and the hours we work are even better. I like to stay in bed till dinnertime."

"Marlene's been stripping for ages now, haven't you, mate?" Sheila applied far too much rouge to her cheeks. "It's my first time at an air-base ... I'm terrified! I haven't been stripping very long but I needed the money for my kids. Their dad's cleared off with a ticket-collector off the Underground." She started to laugh and added, "And a nicer fella he couldn't have hoped to meet."

"I've started to add a bit of comedy to my act," Marlene was now naked. "Sometimes I dress up in a bowler hat and as I take my clothes off I pack them away in a briefcase ... like I'm a city gent."

"I'm going to wear a Donald Duck beak." Sheila was now also naked, except for the bra. "And big Donald Duck feet. And stick a fluffy tail on me bum."

"That should go down well," I tried not to laugh.

"The men get a bit fed up with French-maid outfits and leather outfits and whips," said Marlene, "they roar with laughter when I do my Dracula act. I flop my lils in front of their faces and when they have a feel I bite their necks with great big fangs I have fixed to me own teeth. The men I bite don't laugh ... but all the other men do because I leave a nasty red mark on their necks. They have a bit of explaining to do to their wives ... because you can bet your lives they don't tell their wives where they've been."

I listened to their chatter and half the time couldn't believe what I was hearing. These two lived in a world I knew nothing about. I was fascinated by them, and stared as they put on their tiny 'G' strings.

Both girls now put on three pairs of panties each. They sorted about in suitcases and produced suspender belts which they wriggled in to. Marlene's was black and Sheila's coffee coloured. The suspenders attached to the belts were long and the stockings they put on short, so that a lot of bare flesh was exposed.

"Now don't forget, Sheil," Marlene gave out advice to the less experienced girl, "keep in time to the music. Listen to the drum beats. Nature'll take care of the other beats." Both girls shrieked with laughter.

Marlene continued, "Keep your eyes half shut ... and have your mouth half open and your tongue sticking out, silly sods like that."

"I was doing that the other week," said Sheila, "and I tripped over a bloke's feet and fell and bit me tongue."

"Well just watch where you're going," continued Marlene, "and do plenty of running your hands up and down on the inside of your thighs. Look as though you're dying for a man ... not like you did it at the Sailing-club last Sunday ... you looked as though you were dying for a pee instead of a man." Again the raucous laughter.

"It's ever so hard keeping in time to the music," Sheila addressed me, "dancing about and trying to look sexy at the same time. It's like having a bit in time to a quick-step." She fixed a pair of eyelashes to her lids and they reminded me of a tarantula spider's legs.

"When you get about two thirds the way through your first spot, don't forget to give them plenty of bum. Touch your toes and waggle your bum from left to right like this," Marlene demonstrated, "they love to see me do this," she shouted out from underneath her legs. "I'm thinking of having a pair of eyes tattooed on me bum ... so's I can get me own back on the gawpers."

I was most embarrassed and tried to look nonchalant as though I was quite used to seeing and hearing this sort of thing every day of my life.

Sheila now emulated Marlene. She touched her toes and waggled her bottom from side-to-side and said, "This'll give 'em a thirst, mate." She peered at me from between her legs and added, "Can you think of a gimmick? I want to have a gimmick for when I'm bending like this. I mean when you've seen one you've seen 'em all, haven't you? I want mine to look different. I must think up a gimmick."

The door opened and Jimmy walked into the dressing-room. The strippers did not bat an eyelid — even though their lashes were about six inches long! Jimmy walked over to Marlene and placed his hands on her breasts.

"Umm, I like your new tassles, my dear."

"I'll bet you do, you naughty boy." Marlene slipped out of his grasp. "And if it's true, what we've been hearing about you, it's about time you had a new tassle."

Jimmy had to take the cigar out of his mouth because he was laughing and choking at the same time. His stomach wobbled up and down like an enormous jelly-fish having a dance and his chest crackled and croaked.

"I'm going to put Helen on first," he recovered again, "she can open up with some nice happy numbers ... put the boys in the mood. Wait till you see the lovely spread they've got ready in the Mess. And the prawn cocktails ... well ... I've never seen such big ones."

"He's talking about you again, Marlene." Sheila butted in.

"That's all you think about, Jimmy," Marlene teased him, "your belly."

"I love these functions," Jimmy continued, "they really do us proud. It's worth coming out here just for the food and booze." Jimmy turned to go. "They're sending your drink in any minute now, my dears. Bottoms up."

I began to panic — I had to open the show and I hadn't been able to have a drink. I also had to get changed in front of the strippers, they would see how I had to pad my bra, it would all be so humiliating.

There was a knock at the door and an airman came into the dressing-room carrying a tray absolutely crammed full with drink. Bottles of gin and whisky, one of rum and another of brandy. These clanged together against tonic-waters, dry-gingers and a soda-syphon. Piled on top of one another were three glass bowls full of nuts, crisps and pickled gherkins.

"Shall I pour?" I was eager to get at the drink. "What's it to be, girls?"

I was beginning to wish I had been adamant and refused to take the booking for this evening. The men would only want to watch the strippers. It would all seem very tame, me standing there singing songs when all the men wanted to do was look at tassles being whirled round at great speed on the ends of nipples.

I poured the drinks and passed Marlene and Sheila theirs. I drank a large mouthful of the whisky I had poured for myself, the warmth went cascading down my throat and started swirling about in my stomach. I began to feel better, my face began to glow and my hands felt less shaky, but I still had the feeling that I wanted to spend a penny. I had to get changed, the time was approaching nine o'clock. I turned my back on the strippers and took off my dress. I removed my underskirt and fumbled with the fastener on my bra. After replacing my ordinary bra with a strapless one I then fumbled about in my suitcase for the nylon scarves.

"Haven't you got a cute little figure." Marlene sipped at her half tumbler full of brandy and stared at me. "I used to have a neat little figure like yours ... before I had me kids that is. Kids really bogger up your figure." She sat on a stool and continued staring at my body.

I blushed and held the scarves out in front of me.

"Oh, I'm much too skinny." My face burned with the shame of my secret. "I even have to pad my bra. I haven't got a cleavage if I don't pad my bra with something."

"You'd make a damned good stripper," Marlene continued, "men like a girl with a figure like a boy's. Some of the men go crazy when they see a slim figure like yours naked. They say it's got something to do with the hips ... the trimness of the hips. Takes all sorts you know."

Some sort of compliment, I thought, telling me I look like a boy. My breasts were small but they would still look ridiculous on a boy.

I padded my bra and hurriedly slipped into my red velvet gown. And I hurriedly slipped another large whisky into my glass.

Jimmy, cheeks bulging with food, looked inside the dressing-room and called out to me, "Can the boys come and have a look at your music, Helen?"

I selected three songs, showed the music to the boys in the band and gulped down the remainder of my drink.

The room was crowded out with airmen. News must have got round about the strippers, I thought, they wouldn't have turned out in such numbers to hear me.

I stood on the stage and looked down on rows and rows of blue uniforms. The band started up with my introduction and I was away.

"I get too hungry for dinner at eight." I smiled a bit extra towards the front two rows but could not see the faces of the men because the spotlights were shining in my eyes.

I breathed deeply, reached the last line, and then held on to the last note as long as I could. I bowed to the audience. That was my first number over with. I smiled, acknowledging the applause, and felt my nerves beginning to unjangle themselves a little. Trembling hands, dry throat and fluttering bladder were all forgotten now as I basked in the warmth of the applause and reaction from the airmen.

The musicians were excellent — they had made me sound good — my confidence began to grow.

"Give us 'Blue Moon'" came a voice from the back of the room. I smiled out into the darkness and began my next number and as I did so tried to remember whether I had packed the sheet-music to 'Blue Moon'.

At quarter-past nine it was time for Marlene to do her first spot. I hurried over to the bar and sat on a high-stool making sure I had a good view of the stage.

Marlene's opening number was to 'The lady in red' and this she well and truly was. Red satin gown, red high heeled shoes — even the fur stole which was draped around her shoulders and flowing down to the floor had been dyed red. Long pointed crimson finger-nails and crimson glossy lips.

Very slowly and expertly she removed the trailing fur from her shoulders. Next, she undid the gown which was held together by press-studs all the way down one side for quickness. Underneath the gown she had on her very sparse red lace bra, the black suspender belt, three pairs of panties, black stockings and a frilly red garter. The bra was soon removed and draped over an officer's head. The tassles jiggled about on the ends of her nipples as she danced in time to the music.

Next she sat on a chair and lifted her left leg into the air, stroking the insides of her thighs, and toying with the red garter. Shoes were removed, then stockings and the suspender-belt and garter. Marlene then danced her way over to a different row of airmen. They stared goggle-eyed as she took hold of her breasts and pressed them together making an enormous cleavage.

Now she removed the first of the three panties. Whistling started up at the back of the room. Another pair of panties was now eased slowly down over her big white thighs. She bent down to touch her toes.

The three members of the band played with great enthusiasm as Marlene looked through her legs at her audience. It really was quite impressive, I thought, to see how the musicians could all keep on playing their instruments without once taking their eyes off Marlene. But they did manage it — all of them.

The third pair of panties was removed leaving only the very skimpy red 'G' string. The music slowed down a little and gave Marlene time to get back onto the stage. Now for her final bow, I thought, the lights will go out now and give her time to get off the stage. But I was wrong, there was more. Marlene took off the 'G' string and whirled it round and round in the air. The airmen went wild, the noise men make at a football match when someone has just scored a goal. But Marlene was still not quite naked. Fastened to her pride-and-joy, made out of cardboard, was a replica of an airman's badge. The spotlights were trained at full beam on the badge. There was more whistling, shouting and stamping of feet.

Now the lights were turned off — they came on again — and she was gone.

"Oh, did you like the badge?" Marlene applied more lipstick to her lips. "I like to have a gimmick. You wouldn't believe some of the things I use in my act! ... you want to see some of the things I use."

I'm sure I wouldn't, I thought, and seeing's believing.

102

I did my second spot and included 'Blue Moon' as requested earlier by one of the airmen, the one who had called out of the darkness.

Sheila, who was getting nicely tipsy by now, followed my act ten minutes later. Even I, who had never seen strippers in action before, could tell she lacked experience. She kept in time to the music reasonably well but her movements were too rigid. She gave the impression that she might trip over her own feet at any moment. Marlene's dancing had more of the black people's easy, sensuous, natural movement about it.

Sheila had chosen a cha-cha-cha beat for her opening number. She danced her way over to the first two rows as instructed and shook her breasts in a young officer's face. He made a grab for her bra but she managed to slip out of his grasp. She cha-cha-chaed over to the same chair Marlene had used and did almost identical movements as her friend had done. The men were really warming up to the mood now, the atmosphere was teeming with excitement.

The cheering grew louder as Sheila discarded her garments one by one. The room had a pulsating jungle kind of atmosphere — as though the men were being controlled by some unknown power which they could not resist. They stamped their feet, shouted, whistled, and clutched at thin air whenever Sheila danced within a few feet of them, as though they wanted to tear at her body.

It must be the drink they had consumed, I thought, that had turned well-behaved quiet young airmen and sophisticated, probably well-bred officers, into raving, lustful beasts. Surely, the sight of a woman's naked body could not alone have produced such an effect!

I felt a peculiar tingling at the top of my spine and shivered involuntarily — a feeling of revulsion towards the men engulfed me and I felt the humiliation that Sheila should have been experiencing.

Money — all for money. Every man has his price, as the saying goes. Many times I had heard it said of someone, 'He'd sell his soul for a few quid'.

I looked at the expression on Sheila's face. Eyes half-closed, mouth half-open, silly smirk alcohol induced, but her face looked childlike, exposed and as naked as her body.

It was all a question of mind over matter, I decided, you had to build a brick wall between yourself and the audience, insulate your mind.

Sheila danced over to the stage and tried her hardest to get up the steps without tripping over. She danced to the middle of the stage and threw her last pair of panties into the air. Now she turned her back to the audience and looked over her left shoulder at them in a coquettish manner. She undid her bra and placed it on the drummer's head. The drummer took the bra from his head and whirled it round and round on the end of a drum-stick.

Sheila turned to face the men again, she was clad only in her 'G' string.

"Gerrit off ... gerrit off ... gerrit off ... come on ... come on," the men chanted louder and louder, "off ... off ... off!"

Sheila leaned forward and slipped the 'G' string down over her thighs. She offered her nakedness — but they could only look. The lights should now have been turned down to give her time to leave the stage with a small amount of dignity, but nobody dimmed the lights and Sheila had to run down the steps and into the dressing-room in the full glare of the spotlight.

The two things I will remember most about Sheila are the stretch-marks on her legs, from bearing children, and the vulnerable expression on her face. There was something very poignant about a young woman with the marks of motherhood on her body exposing those marks to jeering, slack-mouthed men. And the expression on her face when performing her strip-dance seemed to belong to the face of an entirely different person.

I wish I was rich, I thought sadly, then I could help Sheila financially, ensure she would never have to endure such an evening again. But then reality seeped through, she would probably spend the money on silly things; the Sheilas and Marlenes on the strip circuit could not be helped. We all did the best we could, people have to work out their own private hells.

I cheered up and became more determined than ever to make it to the top in showbusiness. Men would never have the opportunity to jeer at or look down on me — naked or otherwise.

I returned to the dressing-room and poured myself another drink.

"My boyfriend's out there somewhere." Marlene pulled a dress over her head. "He's a taxi-driver ... a London cabbie, mate."

"He comes in handy 'an all, don' he?" Sheila poured herself another drink. "When we get gigs outside London he gives us a lift. Bloody nuts on Marlene he is ... do anything for yer, mate, won't he?"

"Yeah ... he's all right I suppose". She started to giggle. "He likes having it with the lights on. I hate it with the lights on ... they can tell you're faking enjoying it when they can get a look at your face."

"You're a good actress, Marlene ... that shouldn't bother you."

"No ... it makes me feel uneasy when they want to gawp at yer."

"But what about the airmen tonight?" I was surprised by her admission. "You had about a hundred men gawping at you out there!"

"But that's all they can do ... aint it, mate? They can't touch you," she paused, "or get at your mind."

"Oh, I wanted to ask you about that." I said eagerly. "What sort of things do you think about ... when you're out there stripping your clothes off and everything?"

"Oh ... let me remember what I thought about tonight." Marlene lit a cigarette and watched as the smoke made a halo around her head. "Tonight I thought about what I was going to get for Monday's dinner ... and told myself I must remember to give the kids their dinner-money for their school-dinners. And you know when I pushed my bum in front of that officer's face? ... him with that walrus moustache?"

"Yes, I remember," I prompted her, "the one who fell on the floor."

"Well, when I was doing that I was wondering whether or not to make a trifle for tomorrer's tea or open a tin of peaches. And can you remember that bit where I leaned over that airman and pushed my cleavage together? ... the one who made a grab for my lils?"

"Yes, he was ever so boozed," I replied.

"At the moment I pushed my lils at him I sucked on a piece of nut that had got stuck between me teeth. I then thought that I must remember to make an appointment for the kids to go to the dentist's for a check-up. They're due for another check-up. I've got a thing about teeth ... I love to see a nice set of teeth."

"But don't you think about anything sexy?" I asked hopefully.

"You're kidding, aren't you, lovey?" She wore an amused expression on her face as

104

she added, "I don't feel a bit sexy when I'm performing ..." she laughed and so did Sheila. "Neither on stage or in bloody bed. I've had enough to last me two lifetimes, mate. I'm here to earn money ... make a living nothing more. They're all a load of silly sods out there."

"But you look as though you're feeling sexy when you're doing your act," I persisted.

"Let me tell you something, mate," Marlene continued, "it's bloody hard work, dancing fifteen minutes non-stop and trying to look like every man's dream girl ... every man's fantasy come-to-life. Your lungs are nearly bursting, your leg muscles are hardening up and your face feels as though it'll crack wide open from smiling at the silly boggers."

"I'm sexy." Sheila closed her eyes and ripped the sticking-plaster from underneath her breasts. "Owwwww!" She rubbed at the part where the plaster had been. "I like to imagine all that room full of men desiring me ... wanting to do awful things to me."

"Oh yeah ..." Marlene snorted, "you want to watch yourself else you'll be up the spout again." She turned to face me. "She's had three kids in four years ... silly sod. Give me a plate of steak and chips any day."

Sheila shrugged her shoulders and replied, "My old man was very potent you know."

"Yeah," Marlene rubbed Sheila's shoulders in a most gentle, maternal way and added, "best day's work he ever did when he ran off with that ticket-collector, mate."

Sheila looked sad and changed the subject, "I'm famished, let's go and get some grub, girls."

We walked, or to be honest, tottered into the officers' mess. The spread they had laid on was terrific by anyone's standards. White damask tablecloth almost hidden by plates of sandwiches, pots of patè, pork pies, pickles, nuts, trifles, sausage rolls, five different kinds of cheese and vol-au-vents filled with salmon and chicken. I tucked into the salmon vol-au-vents and selected a prawn-cocktail.

"I enjoyed your singing, Helen." A good looking officer smiled at me from the other side of the table. "It was I who requested 'Blue Moon'. Thank you very much for singing it ... it's my favourite."

"Mine too," I replied as soon as I had swallowed a delicious prawn I had been enjoying.

The music started up again.

"May I have this dance?" The officer took hold of my arm and guided me on to the dance-floor. He held me very close and I was thankful I had taken the padding out of my bra. We danced three dances and then he turned to me and said in a very gentle voice, "Shall we go outside for some fresh-air? It's very stuffy in here, isn't it?"

Although I had consumed quite a lot of whisky the warning bells still clanged loud and clear inside my head. I declined his offer.

"It's pouring with rain out there ... and freezing cold."

He excused himself and went back into the Mess. I did not see him again but soon dismissed him from my thoughts as I tried to cope with lots more airmen clamouring to dance with me.

It was now one o'clock — my body as well as my eyes began to feel droopy. I sought out Jimmy Cook who, miraculously, was still on his feet, he had gone easy on the booze but made up for it with the delicious food.

"Just let me finish my coffee and sample another one of these gorgeous vol-au-vents,

Helen." His fat cheeks swelled out as he crammed more food into them. They reminded me of bicycle tyres being pumped up. "And I must take a few of those prawn-cocktails home with me. Never seen such big prawns in my life. I'll be ready in a few more minutes, Helen. Have another sandwich or something ... you're nothing but skin and bone ... try and fatten yourself up a bit, my dear."

I returned to the dressing-room and packed my evening gowns away. Sheila and Marlene were in there having a last cigarette before starting out on the long journey back to London. Sheila's hair looked a mess as though she had been out in the rain.

"I've done well tonight," her voice was slurred. "That officer ..." she nodded towards me. "that one you were dancing with, Helen ... the Blue Moon bloke."

I stared at her and did not understand.

"He gave me ten quid," Sheila continued, "it only took a couple of minutes. He took me into the hanger across the field. Ten quid for a couple of minutes. It's not such hard work as stripping ... it don't make yer legs ache so much."

"Where did he take you then?" Marlene joined in, "to the cockpit?" Both girls screamed with laughter.

"He said he liked you, Helen," Sheila said generously, "he kept on about how he'd enjoyed your singing. He was ever so good looking, wasn't he?"

"You want to watch yourself, mate," said Marlene, "else you'll be up the spout again. Some use me training you for showbusiness if you carry on like this." Again Marlene stroked Sheila's shoulders in a protective, motherly way. Then she looked at me and held out her hands in a gesture of despair. "What can you do with 'em?"

"My kids need some new clothes," Sheila explained, "you've got to think about yer kids."

All through history, I thought, women had struggled and demeaned themselves for the sake of their children. Sheila was made of much stronger stuff than I was, I thought, an iron-clad woman with generous sprinklings of humour and the ever present vulnerability hiding deep inside.

I wished the strippers good luck as we said our goodnights — maybe I needed it more than they did, I thought, as their laughter reverberated round the quiet airfield and echoed after them as their taxi sped away into the rain-sodden morning.

CHAPTER FIFTEEN

The first Saturday in June, one of my favourite months. Gardens full of beautiful flowers showing off their magnificent displays of colour, delighting the senses with glorious perfumes.

Ralph was coming to lunch but it was now only eleven o'clock. I had two full hours in which to wash and set my hair, manicure my nails and relax to some soothing music. Sylvia was arriving later at about three so that we could rehearse a new number.

The telephone rang and I walked leisurely over to the receiver. It was probably Ralph ringing to ask if I needed anything from the shops. He was very thoughtful and I glowed inside as I said my telephone number and waited to hear his voice.

"Helen ... is that you, Helen?"

It was not Ralph's voice.

"Yes, this is Helen ... who's that speaking please?"

"It's Neville."

"Oh hello, Neville. How are you? How's Rita and Katherine?"

"Something's happened." He made a strange gasping noise and continued, "We've lost the baby! The baby's dead!"

An ice-cold hand seemed to grab at my heart and squeeze it, made it pound and thud. Not my darling little Katherine. The lovely Dresden-china baby!

"Oh my God, Neville! ... oh no! ... oh no!" I stood holding the telephone, I was in a trance and could not think of anything more to say to him.

"Helen, are you still there? Rita's in hospital. They admitted her last night." He mumbled something I did not understand and then added, "Poison in her bloodstream."

"What? ... Neville what do you mean? Why is Rita in hospital?"

"I told you, she's had a miscarriage. She's lost the baby."

The fright he had given me had numbed my reasoning but now I understood. Little Katherine was all right. He was talking about the baby Rita had been carrying.

"Are you listening, Helen?" His voice anxious and childlike. "She said she'd like you to visit her, Helen. Could you possibly manage it this afternoon? I could pick you up at your place, we could go together. A neighbour's looking after Katherine for the time being. Visiting times are half-past two to half-past three at the week-ends."

"Yes, of course I'll go with you, Neville. I'll be ready for about two then."

I replaced the receiver, hands shaking like an alcoholic's after the supply of booze had been cut off. I felt like someone had shoved a bicycle pump down my throat and sucked all the air out of my lungs. I lit a cigarette and made a cup of coffee.

Suppose Rita died? People did that sometimes without the slightest warning. My mind flitted into the past. Rita standing behind the bar at the Cresta, her cheeky grin and beautiful figure. I remembered her zest for living and happy carefree outlook. I reminisced about all the fun we'd had when first starting out with our brand new act. They had been exciting, invigorating times — every new booking different from the rest, challenging and fun.

I sipped the coffee and my bottom teeth chattered against the side of the cup. I was terrified of hospitals. The last time I had been inside a hospital was over fifteen years ago when I visited my grandma. I had a vague recollection of a tiny framed, grey haired old lady propped up in bed with lots of pillows and everywhere smelling like disinfectant and burnt porridge.

My grandma had been smiling and talking about coming home and then they had said she was dead. That's what happened to people in hospitals, I thought, they died.

I told myself to stop being morbid, millions of people live to tell their friends about operations and journeys to death's door and back.

I washed my hair and felt much better.

★ ★ ★ ★ ★ ★ ★ ★ ★ ★ ★ ★ ★ ★ ★ ★

Neville led the way down a long passageway, we followed the signs to the ward where Rita had been admitted.

Poor Neville, standing there in his best suit, clenching his teeth and white faced, holding a bunch of flowers all wrapped up in fancy paper.

We approached the bed and it was all rather frightening. Rita lay with eyes closed, arms resting lightly on the outside of the bedclothes. A plastic tube was attached at one end of her wrist, the other end of the tube was fixed to the bottle. Every now and then some of the fluid would flow down the tube making bubbles spurt up into the bottle.

Neville and I sat down and did not speak and after a few minutes a nurse came up to the bed. She smiled at us then looked at the notes which were attached to a board at the end of Rita's bed.

The nurse then gently eased a thermometer into Rita's mouth.

"That's it, dear ... let's have a look at you then."

Rita's eyes opened and when she saw us sitting there managed a smile in spite of the thermometer.

"That's a good girl." The nurse looked at the thermometer and wrote something down on the chart. She smiled at us again and said, "We've had a lovely long sleep and we've eaten all our lunch. She slept all through the night, Mr. Blakney." She talked as though Rita were a small child.

"Feeling much, much better, aren't we?" The nurse popped the thermometer back into its case above the bed and proceeded to the next patient.

Neville squeezed Rita's hand and kissed her forehead.

"You're looking a lot better, love."

"Where's Katherine? Who's got Katherine?" Rita looked bothered.

"Oh, she's all right ... Diane's looking after her and spoiling her to death."

There was silence for a while then Rita turned to me and asked, "Have you got a booking tonight, Helen?"

"Yes. How about coming with me? Do you think you could cope with the Charleston?" I tried to sound cheerful.

Rita laughed and replied, "Oh yes, I'm full of those sort of tricks. Huh," she sighed, "if my friends could only see me now, eh Helen? Thanks ever so much for coming to see me. You must be pushed for time. Where are you singing at tonight? Is Ralph taking you?"

"We're booked at a Liberal Club in Leeds. Ralph's taking us, yes. He's certainly come in handy, hasn't he." I winked at her.

I kept the conversation flowing and tried not to let Rita talk too much. Neville did not let go of her hand — stroked it gently and patted reassuringly at her wrist.

The smell of the hospital gave me a peculiar frightened feeling and the time seemed to drag on interminably. I glanced at my watch, only ten minutes left. Neville and Rita would want a little time to themselves.

I stood up and said, "I'll come and see you again tomorrow, Rita. See you outside, Neville. I'm just going to let you have a few minutes on you own, to whisper a few sweet nothings."

I kissed Rita's forehead, it was really hot against my lips. As I waited outside the ward it occurred to me that none of us had discussed the miscarriage. Surely, I thought, Rita ought to talk about the baby she had lost. You just couldn't pretend it hadn't happened.

Neville waited until they rang the bell before he left the ward. On the journey back to my place Neville talked a lot but not about the miscarriage.

"Rita's let herself go I'm afraid, Helen. She's lost all pride in herself ... won't eat proper meals ... never wants to go out."

"Yes," I agreed with him, "I noticed what a mess her hair was in."

"I think a lot of it has been my fault, Helen," Neville could not stop talking. "You know how she loved being part of your sister act. She was really keen to come back to your act after she'd had Katherine. But I thought I knew best. I was sure she'd settle down if she had a couple of kids."

"Perhaps the change was too sudden for her." I was beginning to get rather bored with him. "Maybe you should have waited before you got her pregnant again."

"I'm sure you're right, Helen. I wish to God I had. Maybe it's fate she's lost this baby."

"What went wrong do you know? Did she have a fall or anything?"

"Can't find out very much. They said she'd got some sort of poison in her bloodstream. She started to lose a lot of blood ... then she had terrible pains, like labour pains she said. Next thing we knew she was whisked away to the hospital. Then I got a call in the early hours of the morning to say she had lost the baby."

"Well, we'll just wait till she's strong again and then we'll have a talk about her coming back to the stage. I think you were a bit too possessive, Neville. You tried to tie her down too soon. Rita's a very gregarious person, you ought to know that. And she took to the singing like she'd always been performing on stage."

"You don't think she'll die do you, Helen?" He looked tense.

"No chance of that. Rita's as tough as old nails. Look how she was laughing and joking with us. I'll come with you to see her tomorrow. You'll see a big difference tomorrow." I did my best to comfort him.

"Can I pick you up same time then, Helen?" He looked grateful for my support.

"Yes, I'll be ready ... and try not to worry. She'll be home in no time at all. She'll just have to take things a bit easy that's all."

He dropped me off at my flat and drove away looking less tense. I went into the flat and Sylvia rushed to make me a cup of tea. She chatted a lot and questioned me about Rita.

Ralph seemed rather quiet, not his usual self at all, I put it down to the fact that he did not like hearing about illnesses.

Sylvia and I drank our tea and carried on with the rehearsal. I was not in the mood for singing — I could not get my mind off Rita. She had looked so frail and ill.

★ ★ ★ ★ ★ ★ ★ ★ ★ ★ ★ ★ ★ ★ ★ ★ ★

The booking at Leeds went down very well and the entertainment secretary gave us another engagement for nine months later.

Ralph stayed to watch our act because Tony was not with us, he had been invited to a friend's birthday party and Sylvia was joining him there after the show.

Ralph and Sylvia seemed to have a lot to say to each other, I noticed. Sylvia laughed at his corny jokes and leaned against him although managing to make it all look quite harmless. I tried not to be jealous, because I knew Sylvia was only flirting, a thing she could not help doing, she flirted with any man. But I did feel a bit jealous at the way Ralph seemed to be playing up to all the flattery he was getting, especially after he had consumed a couple of whiskies. I couldn't help feeling slightly annoyed — their behaviour was very juvenile, I thought, and then told myself I was being ridiculous, they were just enjoying themselves and after all that's what life's all about.

On the way back home we all sang to the accompaniment of the car radio, Ralph was in particularly fine voice, if not always tuneful.

Ralph drove the car to my place first because he had arranged to give Sylvia a lift to the party. He helped me with my suitcase and kissed me goodnight. I invited him for Sunday lunch. I had already asked Sylvia for tea so that we could have a rehearsal before starting out on the booking. Sylvia and Ralph could keep each other company we had all agreed, whilst I was at the hospital.

★ ★ ★ ★ ★ ★ ★ ★ ★ ★ ★ ★ ★ ★ ★ ★ ★

Rita seemed tons better and the hint of colour in her cheeks appeared to look much healthier than yesterday's high temperature flush.

Neville and I had only been by her bedside for about ten minutes when we were joined by cousin Vera and her husband Bill. Soon after them came two more cousins and then three of Rita's neighbours arrived.

Bad news travels like lightning, I thought, and planned my getaway.

"Look, if you don't mind, Neville," I whispered to him, "I think I'll be getting back now. They only allow two people at the bedside usually, so it'll give somebody else a chance. I've got a booking tonight, and I have got rather a lot to do. Don't worry about giving me a lift back," I read his mind, "I can easily get a taxi."

I kissed Rita goodbye and promised to visit the following evening. I telephoned for a taxi and ten minutes later I arrived back at the flat.

The record-player was turned up rather loud. I pushed open the door to the living-room, ready to say something about the loud music disturbing the neighbours.

Sylvia and Ralph were sitting on the sofa, backs to the living-room door. They had their arms around each other and were in the middle of a very passionate kiss. I stood and watched them in silent horror. Ralph caressed one of her breasts and she gave a little moan. I still could not move — I felt as though I were part of a French-farce. My mind felt trapped in sludge and would not think clearly. I seemed to have fallen into a deep black-hole and could not climb out or cry out.

Sylvia came up for air still unaware of my presence. Ralph smiled at her in a sickly, silly way. I could not remember him ever smiling at me in such a way.

Now my horror turned to rage. How dare they — how bloody dare they! I wanted to fly at them and smash them to pieces with heavy metal. I wanted to mangle them into the earth with a steam-roller, blow them into little pieces with a bomb.

Instead, I walked quietly over to the record-player and switched it off. My mind built a brick wall, Ralph one side and I the other; a barrier that would now be impossible ever to knock down or pierce a hole through.

Ralph jumped to his feet and looked so startled and ashamed I felt almost sorry for him. Sylvia could not look at me but patted at her hair self-consciously.

I tried to act sophisticated and said, "Anybody fancy a nice cup of tea? I'm just going to put the kettle on."

I fumbled with tea cups and poured milk into a cream jug. I felt numb — pins and needles in every part of my body. Peculiar thing though, I thought, I did not feel like crying, there was only the numb feeling.

Ralph followed me into the kitchen, he leaned against the draining-board and said in a soft voice, "I don't know what to say to you, Helen. I can't imagine how it happened. It didn't mean anything ... you know that, don't you?"

"And what were you both up to yesterday?" I remembered how quiet Ralph had been on my return from the hospital. "Been in love long, have you both?" I laid on the sarcasm. "Don't let me come between you."

"I love you, Helen ... I idolise you." He took a step nearer to me. "I've never loved anyone like I love you. You believe me, don't you?"

I poured the tea and did not answer him. His declaration of love after what I had just witnessed made me feel sick. I walked away from him and entered the living-room once more.

"How was Rita?" Sylvia had recovered from the shock.

"Lot better." I answered her.

"Oh, that's good news." Ralph nodded his head. We drank our tea in silence and oh, how I hated them!

★ ★ ★ ★ ★ ★ ★ ★ ★ ★ ★ ★ ★ ★ ★

The drive to the booking was filled with embarrassment and false, forced conversation. Tony was in the car and did not seem to notice anything wrong between the three of us.

Ralph and Tony did not want to stay at the club so they bought our first Guiness and ports and left. I wondered if Ralph would tell Tony what had happened earlier that day but didn't think he would because it was plain that Tony was very much enamoured of Sylvia despite her flirting ways and indifferent treatment of him.

In the dressing-room Sylvia pulled two chairs close together and said, "Right, we've got to talk ... clear the air, Helen." She handed me my drink and took a large gulp of hers. "First of all I'd like to say I'm sorry."

111

"So, you're sorry. All right."

"Look, Helen ... this afternoon ... it didn't mean a damned thing. You know how I am sometimes. I like to flirt with men. I don't think about the consequences, I just do it."

"All right, so you've done it."

"It was all my fault. Ralph loves you, and only you. Blimey! ... he's asked you to marry him. You are engaged. What more proof do you want?"

"None ... it doesn't matter if he makes up to my friends the minute I'm out of the house. That's true love for you. I couldn't ask for anything better than that, now could I?"

"But no matter what happened this afternoon Ralph does love you. There's no harm in a bit of a kiss and cuddle. We didn't go any further than that."

"And how far did you go yesterday?"

"We only kissed ... we ... er." Her face was scarlet, covered in guilt. Too late, she had fallen into my trap. So they had been carrying on whilst I was at the hospital yesterday. I now knew that I could never let Ralph touch or kiss me ever again. He was loathsome, a traitor.

"You know what men are like, Helen," Sylvia had another drink of her Guiness and port, "it doesn't take them long to get a bit carried away."

"But not when they're engaged to someone else?" I fiddled with my finger-nails. "And you're supposed to be my friend." I felt spiteful. "Not some old bag."

"Honestly, Helen," she pleaded her case, "we were just larking about and it sort of happened. I don't want Ralph. I've got Tony. Please let it drop, Helen ... Ralph idolises you, and you're really good for each other. Don't let a few silly kisses with someone else spoil your lives."

"It's not only you, Sylvia," I tried to save face now, "I was getting a bit fed up with him. And he's a rotten lover you know. I expect you do know." I aimed more sarcasm at her. "Couldn't have put up with that for the rest of my life." I began to feel better now that Sylvia and I had talked about things. Sylvia could see I was beginning to come round.

"We're still going on with the act then? You're not giving me the sack? I wouldn't blame you, Helen, but! ..." she grinned at me.

"No, I'm not giving you the sack," I grinned back at her, "but the next time I find you messing around with my man, you'll get more than the sack, so don't say you haven't been warned."

Sylvia hurried to fetch two more drinks, she waited on me all the rest of the evening and behaved like a naughty little girl who had just escaped a spanking. She seemed to have forgotten the incident completely by the end of the evening and made a date with the bass player for the following Tuesday.

★ ★ ★ ★ ★ ★ ★ ★ ★ ★ ★ ★ ★ ★ ★ ★

Rita was ill for quite some time, but gradually the girl I had known at the Cresta came back to life again. I visited her as often as I could and always received a nice welcome from Neville. He stood by his promise that Rita could go singing again once she was strong enough and even hinted that he would like to accompany us sometimes, not too much though, he said, because he realised it would put a damper on things as far as the men in the audience were concerned.

Neville had changed, I observed, and for the better too. But his plans had given me a new dilemma to face. I would have two partners to choose from — how do you get out of that situation?

I decided to worry about it when Spring came round again — that was the time Neville had said Rita would be ready for her come-back.

Ralph tried to make things right between us again but I had lost interest. Also, I could not bear him to touch me. If he came round to the flat and tried to talk to me I felt irritated. Whenever he telephoned I felt bored with his pleading and cajoling. It was goodbye Ralph time and he had only himself to blame. Eventually, he gave up trying but insisted I kept the engagement ring as a keepsake, which I did.

The thing I found hard to understand was why he did not chase after Sylvia once he was free to do so. As far as I knew they never saw each other again, which seemed to me most odd after the episode at my flat.

It saddened me that the unfortunate experience with Ralph had made me even more suspicious of men. I was beginning to look at men with the same coldness as the strippers. Men were weak, stupid and not to be trusted at any price. I decided that I could do without all that heartache and upset, thank you very much.

And as for Sylvia — she never mentioned Ralph again. It was as though he had never existed.

One good thing had come out of the whole affair — I knew that I felt more determined to succeed. Make something out of my life and do it all on my own. I had hardened up and I wasn't sure whether or not I liked the feeling.

CHAPTER SIXTEEN

Summer hurried into autumn and stored away her flowers for a few months. The forests showed off their exquisite mantles of red and gold. Soon I would be able to sing 'Autumn Leaves', one of my favourite songs; each time I sing this song I feel as though it is for the first time. The words and music go so beautifully together that everytime I hear them I want to cry.

On one of those lovely autumn days Sylvia and I set out to keep an appointment at Jimmy Cook's office. He had telephoned the previous evening and said he had the most marvellous opportunity for the act. He would not disclose the details but kept us in suspense. 'Put something sexy on and bring some music, my dear,' was all I could get him to say.

Jimmy's secretary nodded and smiled and pointed to two chairs.

"You're a bit early, take a seat ... they won't be long." The door opened and two men walked into reception. They smiled at us and then one asked, "Are you the Dumonte Sisters?"

"Yes." I wondered who they could be and looked in the direction of the 'ladies' — my bladder was rumbling with fright again.

The men also sat down and we sat silently, smiling pleasantly. Sylvia did not look nervous, she seemed to thrive on suspense and intrigue.

"We're your pianist and drummer," one of the men spoke, "can we just have a quick look at your dots?"

I handed over the music and pulled a face at Sylvia. I hurried to the 'ladies' and thought, why-oh-why hadn't I remembered to bring my flask! I should have known I'd get stage-fright. I began to tremble and the palms of my hands felt moist. I stood in front of the mirror in the ladies-room and told myself not to be so stupid. There was nothing to be nervous about.

I went back into reception. Two other men were there. Extremely well dressed, Saville-Row-type suits that shouted expensive and shoes that were hand-made without a doubt. The men had that look of confidence about them — that look which journeys with success and good living.

The secretary buzzed on the intercom through to Jimmy's inner sanctuary, "The gentlemen from 'Sea Stars' are here, Mr. Cook. And the Dumonte Sisters."

"Show them all in," Jimmy's voice crackled on the intercom, sounding like a creature from outer space.

Jimmy introduced everyone and then said, "Right then, my dears ... if you'd just like to do a couple of numbers. Do a fast one and then a nice slow song."

"We get too hungry for dinner at eight." Sylvia and I belted out the first song. We writhed our hips, thrust out our bosoms and gave the number all we'd got.

We had chosen 'Sentimental Journey' for the slow song. The drummer picked up the nice, easy beat straight away and made lovely swishing sounds on the cymbals. When we got to the last four words of the song he thrashed out a terrific crescendo and the pianist seemed to be using every note on the piano — sounded as though he had twenty fingers instead of ten. First class accompaniment, good microphone system and we had got through the numbers without any bad notes or forgotten words.

The entrepreneur types looked pleased. The pianist and drummer slipped discreetly away and as there had not been any mention of a fee for their services I imagined Jimmy must have paid them.

I was so curious I felt as if I would burst out at any moment and shout, 'What's happening? ... I must know! ... I must!' But instead I just sat and smiled at everyone and tried to look sophisticated. Huh, that reminds me of the Cresta, all that while ago, when I had first gone for the interview with Ray Bowler. It seems like half a lifetime away, so much has happened to me since then.

One of the men — a fair-haired, suntanned, good looker smiled at us and said, "Yes, very nice. Very nice indeed, Jimmy. They'll go down well." He talked about us as though we were invisible and Jimmy started to do likewise, "I told you didn't I? They're sex personified. Just what tired old businessmen need to perk them up."

"And there are plenty of those on our holidays," the other man joined in, "all with pots of money to chuck about as well."

So that was it, I thought, they were going to book us for some type of holiday-camp. I was confident I knew what they were talking about. I'd always fancied a booking at somewhere like that. Lazing around during the day and singing to the holiday-makers in the evening.

"Now then, Jimmy," the fair-haired man continued, "are you sure you can get replacements for the full six weeks? As you mentioned, they have got rather a lot of commitments ... it'll give you quite a headache finding replacements, won't it?"

Jimmy sniffed and pulled at the lobe of his right ear.

"That will all be taken care of. I've got plenty of good acts on my books." He paused and looked crafty. "But of course, it is out of the question without the figure I mentioned."

The two men exchanged glances, stared at each other for a few seconds as though taking part in a thought transference act.

"That's fine then," said the other man, who had beautiful high cheek-bones and sensuous full lips, "we'll just exchange contracts then and that's it."

I looked at Sylvia and pulled a face. I opened my eyes wide and shrugged my shoulders. What on earth was the old walrus planning?

Sexy lips stood up and walked over to where I was sitting. He flashed a smile and said, "Jimmy tells me you've never worked the boats before. You don't know what you've been missing. Free holidays in the sun and plenty of good food."

So that was the surprise! I had to make myself believe it. They had booked the act for a cruise. Oh, if only I could put down on paper the thrill I was experiencing. I sat silently taking everything in and had a hard job keeping my mouth closed, it kept sagging open with every new wonder I was hearing. Me, Helen Linsey — the little girl who used to be a waitress at Carlin and Priestley's restaurant — booked to sing on a cruise ship.

And all because of a crazy idea I had spawned one night at the Cresta club.

115

"And which one are you?" Sexy lips leaned over me. "Did they say you were Helen? I can never remember names but I never forget a face." He looked me up and down and his eyes flitted back down to my legs again. "You'll love the life aboard our ships. Meet all the right people, if you know what I mean." He winked at me.

"Isn't it a lovely surprise, my dears?" Jimmy opened his drinks cabinet and poured drinks for everyone. "You'll be gone for six whole weeks. The ship leaves Southampton for Gibraltar, Las Palmas, Madeira and oh, I can't remember the others. What do you think to that then? Oh, and all your travelling expenses will be paid by these two gentlemen."

"Yes, and we'll arrange your cabin accommodation, things like that," the fair-haired man chimed in, "leave everything to us at Sea Stars."

"I haven't got a passport," was all I could muster, "never had one."

"Plenty of time for that, my dear," Jimmy lit a cigar. "The ship doesn't sail till the second Saturday in November ... that'll give you heaps of time to get cracking."

"But what about all the bookings we've got in November and December?" Sylvia didn't look as though she was really worried but continued, "we're booked up pretty solid right up until Christmas."

"Leave all that to me, I've just told you." Jimmy sipped at a large brandy. "I've had a word with Dave McGuire and he says it's O.K. with him as long as I get good replacements for his venues. Of course," he pulled at the lobe of his ear again, "my commission will be twelve and a half per cent ... to cover all the extra work I've had to do on your behalf."

"How much will we be earning a week?" Sylvia, always practical.

Jimmy glanced across at the entrepreneurs before answering. He blew cigar smoke from puffed out cheeks and said, "Well, I've worked it out roughly and by my reckoning you should, with the commission off of course, be each getting thirty five pounds a week clear. How about that for pocket-money ... for your cruise, eh?"

Sylvia and I were delighted with the sum — it was very good pay. I still couldn't believe it was true. Six weeks cruising on a ship, meals provided and accommodation. And who knows who might hear us singing? It could lead to all sorts of things, I thought happily, only the very rich could afford holidays on cruise ships, perhaps we would meet a television producer!

"Would you like to come to lunch with us, ladies?" Sexy lips brought me down to earth. "We're staying over till tomorrow ... perhaps you could tell us where we can get a nice meal?"

I looked down at my evening gown and grimaced at Sylvia. "We shall have to nip home and get changed. Can't go to lunch in these," I gesticulated at my gown.

"No problem there," the fair-haired man said, "we travelled up from Southampton in Paul's car. We'll give you a lift to your houses and then you can get changed."

I memorised his name. Paul. Although Jimmy had introduced us I had been too nervous to listen to anything properly.

"Yes, all right then, Barry." Paul stood up. "Shall we get going then ... I'm starving?" He walked over to where Jimmy was sitting and held out his hand. "Thanks very much, Jimmy ... glad we could do business. And don't forget, as soon as you get the information on that comedian, give us a ring."

Ah yes, his name was Barry — I remembered now — Barry Greenburg. It would be nice going to lunch with two good looking, interesting men. As usual, now that my awful nerves had calmed down, I was dying of hunger.

Sylvia and I signed the contracts and Jimmy put his signature on them and then Barry and Paul added theirs.

It was really happening! I finished my drink and stood up.

We had actually signed a contract for a six week's cruise.

For some strange reason I kept thinking about Rita. How she would have loved an opportunity like this. It was just what she needed too, I thought, plenty of sunshine, pure sea air and lots of good food. Still, there was always next year, a lot of things could have happened to us all by then.

Once again I experienced the old familiar tingling feeling rippling up and down my spine. Perhaps this would be the turning point in my career? The door was slowly opening and who knows what would be on the other side. Maybe Vera would get her gallon of French perfume yet!

Madeira and Casablanca here we come.

CHAPTER SEVENTEEN

Bodies pumped full of germs ready to combat any amount of frightening foreign diseases. Evening gowns pressed and packed carefully in between tissue paper. Six weeks rent paid in advance and a few pounds for Sylvia's dad although he had insisted she didn't have to pay any board whilst she was away.

Here we were at last. So this was Southampton? I felt dizzy again from all the excitement of the preparation and travelling.

A friendly man in a sentry-box directed us to our ship and Sylvia and I staggered towards a huge ship which was, of course, the furthest away.

I staggered up the gang-plank closely followed by Sylvia. Leaning against the rails of the ship were lots of handsome uniformed men smiling suntanned welcomes to all the passengers.

We finally made it to the top of the gang-plank, a man dressed in dark blue sweater, pale blue trousers and white plimsolls stepped forward.

"Leave your suitcases there, ladies. That's right, just down there." He pointed to an empty space. "I'll see to it they're delivered safely to your cabin, lovies."

We put the suitcases where he had indicated and a few seconds later they had been whisked away.

Two men in officers' uniforms stepped forward. One of the men was holding a large sheet of paper which was balanced on a piece of cardboard.

"May I have your names please, ladies?"

Oh, my Lord, I thought, really gorgeous. I simply go all peculiar over a man in a uniform.

"We're Miss Linsey and Miss Clifford." Sylvia gave him a radiant smile. "But you may have us down as the Dumonte Sisters. We are entertainers ... singers."

"Ah yes," his suntanned smile made him look like coffee and cream, "here we are ... the Dumonte Sisters. Welcome aboard, ladies."

The men leaning against the rails were eyeing us with enthusiasm. I was glad I had put my rabbit coat on, it made me feel like a film star.

The officer spoke again, "You are on 'E' deck ... cabin number two hundred and seven. You should be able to find it O.K. Just keep going down and you'll get there eventually." He smiled at us again and added, "Perhaps you'd permit me to buy you both drinks later this evening?"

Talk about a fast worker, I thought, we had only just stepped aboard and he was at it.

"May I buy you both drinks," mimicked Sylvia as we went down the steps into the lower decks, "oh, Helen, isn't it all exciting? Did you see all that talent leaning against the rails?"

"Now Sylvia," I laughed at her, "control yourself ... you're here to work remember."

"Yes," she replied, "we're here to get to work on that gorgeous lot." Goodbye Tony, I thought, and knew that she had forgotten him the minute he had kissed her goodbye as our train had started to move out of the station.

We arrived at 'E' deck and learned that we were to be accommodated in the bowels of the ship. But there was one good thing in our favour and that was the siting of the restaurant which we discovered was on 'D' deck not far away.

We opened the door to our cabin and found our suitcases already there. The cabin was very small, I wondered how on earth we were going to manage. Two bunks, one wardrobe with three small drawers either side, two chairs and a sink with mirror above. There was also a two channel radio fixed in the ceiling next to an air-vent.

We squeezed our evening gowns into the wardrobe and after a great deal of arranging and rearranging managed to get the rest of our clothes into the drawers.

"Can I have the top bunk?" Sylvia nodded towards the bunks.

"Yes," I agreed, "but you'll have to wear a nightie. I don't want to see your naked form looming over me every night. You'll give me nightmares!"

Each bunk had a tiny night-light above it and a neat tray which pulled out to rest the breakfast trays on, I guessed.

We decided to go back to the main deck and have a look at the rest of the passengers embarking. We were ready to leave the cabin when there was a knock at the door. I opened the door and a man in steward's uniform stood grinning at me. "Good evening." He took a step nearer and peeped inside the cabin. He grinned at Sylvia and said, "I'm your steward, ladies. Anything you'd like or want to know, just press that bell there." He nodded towards a bell which was near the door.

"Oh, thank you very much," I replied and then added, "could you tell us where we have to go to have a word with the entertainment officer? We're artists and we've never sung on a ship before," I confessed, "we don't know how to go on."

"You're the Dumonte Sisters, aren't you?" He tapped his finger-nails on the side of his tray. "No need to get in a panic ... you've got lots of time to get settled in. Go up to the information desk when you're ready. They'll get the entertainment chap for you. He's a good bloke ... look after you all right he will." He turned to go and then added in rather an embarrassed way, "I do a spot of singing myself."

"Oh and what sort do you sing?" I asked.

"Some modern ... few standards ... anything really."

"Where do you sing?" Sylvia asked.

"Anywhere they've got a piano," he answered. "When the ship berths in all those exotic places I go ashore and sing to the locals. If you go ashore, I'll tell you all the best places to visit. I'll sing for you in one of the bars in Madeira if you like. They love me there ... I sing with a bloke who plays a guitar."

"It sounds smashing," I told him, "we'd love to come and hear you sing." My stomach started to flutter about as I thought of the places we would have the opportunity to visit. Madeira! Casablanca where Humphrey Bogart had made love to Ingrid Bergman. The mysterious places all waiting for us to explore them. I said a secret thank you to God. The steward moved from the door. "My name's Lucky, by the way." He stepped to one side and let us pass. "See you later, lovies ... and don't forget to ring if you want anything. Oh, I know what I wanted to ask you?" He called after us. "Would you like to sleep in late in the mornings? 'Cause if you would I'll bring you both a tray to your cabin. Nice pots of coffee and few hot rolls and butter do you all right?"

"You bet," we chorussed.

★ ★ ★ ★ ★ ★ ★ ★ ★ ★ ★ ★ ★ ★ ★ ★

Sunday morning Sylvia and I got acquainted with the fellas in the band and the other artists which included Carmella and Karl a man and wife duo who, they informed us, sang country and western music. Then there was the Reg Cane Combo — a drummer and two guitarists who told us it was their first booking for 'Sea Stars' too.

There were also two dancing teachers on board and the entertainment officer told us that they too were a married couple. They made a lovely couple, I thought, the wife was really beautiful. She was in the full bloom of femininity just before going into middle-age. The age when a woman, if she has taken care of herself and discovered the right type of clothes and cosmetics, is at her loveliest. I couldn't tell whether or not her husband was handsome because he had a large bushy brown beard. I imagined being at sea for a long time had gone to his head — he wanted to look nautical, look the part.

Sylvia said she fancied him but I've always felt a bit dubious about a beard, imagined they must be full of crumbs and dust. But I expect they would be all right if you ran a vacuum cleaner over them once a day.

As there was no rehearsal until Monday morning I gave our music to the pianist so that he would have a rough idea of the kind of songs we used in our act.

After lunch Sylvia and I decided to have a good look round the ship. We tied headscarves around our heads to protect our hair from the strong sea-breezes and went to the top-deck. Nearly everyone we passed said hello, it was smiles all the way. The officers flirted with us and Sylvia was like a judge at a cake contest — eager to sample a bit out of each.

We finally went to sit in a huge lounge which had windows all the way down one side of the room which gave us a splendid view of the sea.

The waves were pale grey and the ones nearest the ship licked at the sides of the ship like demons' tongues — I began to feel scared. Suppose something went wrong with the ship's engines? There could be a fire on board, the engines could blow up? I could only swim a length so I prayed that if the worst happened we would be in sight of land. Maybe if I was scared enough I'd be able to manage a bit more than a length!

The fellas from the band came to sit with us and we exchanged stories about ourselves. They told us they had been playing for 'Sea Stars' for quite a long time and that it had become rather boring. They had lost the wonderment of it all — it was just like any other job now.

I couldn't imagine myself becoming bored with the life — not ever.

"But you all have a marvellous free holiday," I argued, "all the lovely food and use of the facilities on board."

"It still gets boring after a while." The drummer shrugged his shoulders. "You can have enough of a good thing you know."

"But what about all the new exciting places you visit?" I persisted. "Casablanca ... Madeira ... and Las Palmas?"

"Can't stand hot weather," answered the trumpet-player, "I'd sooner work Blackpool anytime. But the money's good on the boats. Can't earn money like this on

120

shore."

I looked out of the window at the sea again and could not think of anything I would rather be doing.

★ ★ ★ ★ ★ ★ ★ ★ ★ ★ ★ ★ ★ ★ ★ ★ ★

The time rushed by and Monday evening appeared from nowhere — cabaret time. Carmella and Karl warmed up the audience a little and then it was our turn. We had each downed two Guiness and ports in quick succession so our nerves were settling a little but my throat still felt dry and the palms of my hands were very moist.

We had chosen to wear the tight-fitting pale blue velvet gowns, so that we would make a good impact on our audience. We opened with 'Sentimental Journey' and the boys in the band played faultlessly, they sounded even better than they had at rehearsal earlier that day. The audience applauded enthusiastically and as I bowed before them I suddenly thought of Rita. Oh, how she would have enjoyed this moment. She would have been thrilled with the professionalism of the musicians and the glamour of actually singing to rich holidaymakers. Her renderings of 'Body and Soul' and 'How deep is the ocean' would have sounded beautiful with such first class backing, I thought sadly.

After we had sung our final number Sylvia and I made our way, like homing pigeons, to the bar. The officers surrounded us, vied with one another for the chance to buy our drinks. They made a circle around us as though they were playing ring-a-ring-a-roses. If we had accepted all the drinks offered we would have fallen down for sure, without the atishoo.

After the band had played the last waltz I decided to go for a stroll round the top deck. There was no moon and I felt cheated. You always had a moon, when you were cruising. In all those romantic films they always provided a moon nestling in a dark blue satin sky. But this sky was lead grey and ominous. As I leaned over the side of the rail a powerful, frightening feeling of terror surged through my body. One slip — lean over just a bit too far — and I would be gone forever, without making any difference at all to the perpetual dance of the waves. How unimportant we all are, I thought, how small.

I shuddered and moved back from the rail and decided to go to bed, relax and try to switch off with a good book. Sylvia was already ripping-it-up at the late night dance and would not miss me at all.

I returned to the cabin, prepared for bed and snuggled down into the bedclothes. The soft chug-chugging of the ship's engines soon lullabied me to sleep.

Sylvia came home to roost at three thirty and as I looked at her through sleep drenched eyes I could see she had plenty to crow about. She was still smiling as she climbed the ladder up to her bunk.

★ ★ ★ ★ ★ ★ ★ ★ ★ ★ ★ ★ ★ ★ ★ ★ ★

Tuesday morning after we had been awakened by the sound of Lucky singing 'Some enchanted evening' I felt that something was different. My brain slowly came to life and I realised that the ship's engines had stopped. The ship was no longer swaying from side to side.

Tap, tap, tap, on the cabin door.

"Good morning, my little prairie flowers ... and a beautiful morning it is too." Lucky's smiling face appeared round the door.

"Ooooh ... what time is it, Lucky?" Sylvia moaned from the top bunk.

"Time for breakfast," answered Lucky, "and we're at Madeira, me dears. Come along ... wakey, wakey. I'll just pour your coffee."

His eyes opened wider and a cheeky grin spread across his face. I knew that meant Sylvia had sat up and that Lucky was getting a bird's eye view of her scantily clad bosom. He certainly enjoyed his early morning peep-show.

We ate our rolls and sipped at the 'bring-you-back-to-life' coffee. I had a quick look at the ship's paper to see what was on the entertainment agenda for that day. As usual there was plenty to do if you weren't content to lounge about all day. Dancing lessons, bingo, latest film on at the cinema, fashion-show in the main ballroom, deck-quoits, table tennis, swimming, the list went on. But Sylvia and I had decided to explore the island. Maybe we won't get another chance I had told her, we ought to see as much as possible.

After band call we hurried down the gang-plank out into the strange new world which was there waiting for us to explore. Madeira — a beautiful flower-laden island. I stood on the quay side and gazed at the panoramic view. The island reminded me of a three dimensional film — a technicolor film of a lush garden of Eden. It stretched out before us, a garden of paradise shimmering beneath the morning sun. A taxi whisked us off to a little fishing village, called Camara de Lobos. We strolled round the village, our bodies drinking in the glorious sunshine and our eyes drinking in the breathtaking scenery. The locals were friendly people and left off mending their fishing nets or painting their boats to smile a greeting. There were also quite a few artists seated at their easels, hopefully trying to get down on canvas a little of the island's magic and charm.

We found a place to eat our lunch and enjoyed salad and chicken and drank coffee underneath the shade of a large umbrella outside the cafe. After lunch we then caught another taxi, this time to a very ancient looking part of the island. Narrow streets, crowded market and numerous inns, or pousadas as they were called. Sylvia and I tasted a variety of wines in a large warehouse — Madeira's equivalent of a wine lodge, which was crammed full with wine bottles, huge wine casks and shelves stacked with souvenirs.

"Taste this ... and this ... how about thees one?" A handsome dark skinned man thrust glass after glass of wine at us.

After about six samples it all tasted delicious. We escaped before we fell down unconscious.

We roamed round the market and then made our way to the beach once more where we lay down on the sand and cat-napped.

Lucky had given us the name of a good restaurant where the food was good but quite cheap. And they also had dancing and entertainment by local artists.

We found the restaurant and tucked into a first class meal, washed down with plenty of local wine. A handsome guitarist played softly in the background and it was all very romantic.

At half-past seven Lucky, accompanied by three more stewards, walked into the restaurant. They sat at a table, ordered drinks and lit huge cigars looking more like wealthy tourists than stewards.

Lucky spotted us and came over to our table. He beamed a smile at us and said, "You found it all right then? This is one of the places where I sing." He blew cigar smoke our way and added, "I'll give you a couple of songs if you'd like."

"We'd love to hear you, Lucky," enthused Sylvia, "we really would." Lucky walked over to the microphone and then said something to the guitarist. His three companions started whistling and cheering, giving him a fabulous build up. I hoped he was going to be worthy of such a build up.

I was not disappointed. Lucky started with 'Some enchanted evening'. He received loud applause before commencing with 'I'm forever blowing bubbles' and finally ending with 'Ramona'.

Everyone applauded enthusiastically and the three stewards and Lucky then came to sit at our table. One of the stewards told me that Lucky always sang in the same places. He had worked the ships for a long time and was very well known to the islanders. "He visits the same places trip after trip," the steward told me, "like a sailor visits the same woman," he whispered.

Next, a young man played his guitar for us and then a girl and her boyfriend did a dance which entailed a lot of frantic stamping of the feet. Perhaps it's the wine, I thought, but everybody looks and sounds like they were stars from the London Palladium. I had certainly seen worse on television. I applauded the local talent until my hands ached.

Daylight had faded now, it was time to return to the ship. As the taxi turned the corner of a steep hill we could see our ship silhouetted against the pale blue, gold speckled sky. The lights from the ship looked welcoming, I felt as though I was returning home.

★ ★ ★ ★ ★ ★ ★ ★ ★ ★ ★ ★ ★ ★ ★ ★

Later that evening the officers exchanged dark navy uniforms for white ones. It was enough to give a girl a high temperature. Neatly pressed white uniforms, sunburnt handsome faces and lithe taut-muscled young bodies. The attraction and appeal of these young men was phenomenal.

Sylvia and I were as usual near our favourite position at the bar when a young officer approached and said, "A few of us are having a little celebration in the library later on this evening ... we'd like you to join us." More white uniforms moved in on us — I could almost feel the body heat seeping through the cloth. Try and keep me away, I said to myself and then said out aloud, "We'd be delighted, thank you. We'll be there straight after the show."

There were eight officers at the party and seven other young women passengers, besides Sylvia and myself. There were a greaty variety of drinks to choose from and some I had never even heard of. Not even Ray Bowler had had some of these drinks at his club. I tried a drink which was called Curacuo which sounded more like a Spanish dance than a drink and it had a kick like one too. It was a delightful party, everyone on their best behaviour, and the officers had impeccable manners. We were all young, attractive and healthy. I looked round the room at everyone and once again could hardly believe I was really there — me, the nobody waitress from Carlin and Priestley's restaurant! Here I was, dressed in a lovely evening gown, sipping Curacuo and hobnobbing with wealthy cruise passengers and handsome ship's officers. And all because I had wanted to sing, I thought, fate sure has a peculiar way of taking care of your dreams and aspirations. A young officer held out a dish filled with a variety of nuts and said, "Perhaps you'd like to go to the dance afterwards, Helen?"

I smiled at him and nodded and thought that I could think of nothing nicer on earth than to put my arms around his neck and feel the desire and warmth from his body reaching out and mingling with my own passionate feelings. Being on board the ship had done something to my self-control. It was as though someone else had taken over my body — a reckless, sexy woman who was full of yearning for love and romance, a woman who longed to give herself without any of the usual feelings of doubt and misgivings. Maybe tonight I would let that woman take over for a while. The officer smiled down at me and said, "I'm Terry, by the way." "I'm a gonner," replied my secret self, silently.

Terry and I danced for a while and then he invited me to go back to his cabin for a nightcap. We made our way down into the lower half of the ship and finally arrived at 'D' deck.

We each had a brandy and then somehow, without my hardly realising it, I was stretched out on his bed.

He kissed my face and then reached down and took off my gold dance shoes. He stroked my hair and whispered endearments — all the usual things a girl likes to hear whether or not they're true. He told me I was beautiful, said that my figure was perfection and that my eyes were the most lovely he had ever looked into. I knew I wasn't beautiful and Jimmy Cook had put me right about my skinny frame, but I thought maybe my amorous escort was telling the truth about my eyes because I had often heard that line before.

Terry reached for the fastener at the back of my gown and as he did so said that he had never desired a woman more than he now desired me. He mumbled something about seeing me when the ship docked at Southampton again and at that moment the warning bells started clanging, loudly. What was I doing? How many women had lain on this same bunk and listened to these same words? There could never be anything permanent between us — a seaman goes to sea and that was that. I was his latest conquest — another woman to practice his latest Romeo act on. My thoughts flitted from here-to-there as I thought about what I would look like after we had made love. My make-up would be in ruins, my hair would look like one of the three witches' hair out of Macbeth and he would also see that I had strips of nylon shoved inside my bra. I didn't want him to see all that. I wanted to remain the woman in the lovely evening gown, with the beautifully arranged auburn curls and the thrusting bosom that heaved voluptuously. And besides, what if I got pregnant? That thought got rid of completely any romantic feelings of love I may have had earlier. I pushed him away and sat up.

"I think I'll be going now, Terry." My zip was only half-way down, I struggled to pull it back up. "Thank you for a lovely evening."

He looked angry, and said, "Oh, you're not one of those cold, teasing sort of women, are you? Leading me on and then clearing off?" His cultured voice suddenly had an east-end accent. "Bloody well giving it out all evening and then boggering off."

"It's my choice," I answered, "and just who do you think you are ... God's gift to women? I came back here for a drink and that's all."

His elegant officer's manner slipped out of the port-hole somewhere as he replied,

"Bloody whore ... you stage people are all the same. You like to play-act ... but you're all a load of whores ... I've noticed the way you and that Sylvia throw yourselves at the men. I've had dozens like you ... you're ten-a-penny."

His accent became more pronounced as he got angrier and his face looked ugly. "Go on ... clear out ... you whore."

I needed to have the last word. "No I'm not ... I'm a fellow in drag."

I felt really elated as I made my way back to our cabin. What a lucky escape I'd had — that should teach me to be more careful. I simply must keep reminding myself what liars and cheats most men are, I thought, as I creamed the make-up off my face and got ready for bed. It was like tiptoeing through a minefield — every relationship was liable to blow up in your face if you didn't tread carefully.

★ ★ ★ ★ ★ ★ ★ ★ ★ ★ ★ ★ ★ ★ ★ ★

How the days hurried by, they gathered momentum like a piece of speeded up film.

Sylvia and I had made friends with two of the passengers. They were bachelors, or so they insisted, and were travelling together. Both men lived in Manchester. Jeff was a jeweller by trade and Ron a rep. for a silverware company. Ron was more handsome than Jeff and Sylvia made a play for his attentions but he seemed to prefer my company so she settled for Jeff although still flirting like mad with Ron whenever she had the opportunity.

The ship docked at Casablanca and Jeff and Ron asked if we would like to go ashore with them.

"Better not go ashore alone," Jeff warned, "bit dodgy for young women on their own. You're likely to disappear without a trace if one of those arabs takes a fancy to you."

I could imagine it all. Sylvia and I would vanish forever after walking through a beaded curtain, in a cafè teaming with opium smoke and belly-dance music.

We arrived at a market place which was flanked by large ornate buildings on the left and lots of stalls on the right. We alighted from the taxi and were immediately surrounded by lots of small children. The poor little mites were shabbily dressed and bare footed. A girl with uncombed hair and dirty ragged dress stared at us with the look of a hurt animal. She sucked at her thumb, her upper lip was covered in sores, and flies buzzed round her face. One boy who looked quite a bit older than the rest of the children said something in French which I didn't understand. Ron made a gesture with his hand and tried to shoo them away but the children still followed us.

We started to walk towards the entrance of the market and they still followed. The boy then said something in German. It was incredible, I thought, very impressed, the little kid was a multi-linguist.

"No! ... go away! ... go away!" Ron tried to be firm.

"Aaah," the boy's face lit up with a broad smile, "you ... you are de Eengaleesh. You want market? ... you want guide market?" The boy persisted, "You buy plenty souvenirs, yes? I help ... get best price for you. Me plenty good boy ... help de Eengaleesh. Me good guide, yes?"

"Oh, let's give them some money." I stared miserably at the little ones and reached into my handbag. "Would you like some money for some sweeties, darlings?"

"Yes, here you are," Sylvia too dipped into her handbag, "then be good children and go home to your mammy."

The children made no sign that they could comprehend but continued to stare with those big mournful dark eyes — the flies buzzed round their faces and settled on the sores — the children did not bother to shoo them away.

The older boy ignored our offer of money for sweets and persisted with his patter, "I guide round market ... plenty good price ... you hire me, yes? I plenty good boy."

Ron intervened, "Don't bother to give the little ones any money, girls. This one here's in charge. Anything you give to the young ones will be taken from them. This one here uses them to win our sympathy."

The boy smiled warmly at Ron obviously not understanding what he had said. He held out his hand for money and continued, "You pay me plenty Eengaleesh money ... I your guide."

"Come on then ... you persistent little bogger," Jeff nodded towards the market, "let's have you then. And we want plenty good bargains."

As soon as the men had agreed to hire him the boy then said something in Arabic to the little ones, they scurried back to the shade of one of the large buildings and sat on the pavement cross-legged and motionless. I could not imagine any of the children smiling, they did not seem to know how. It broke my heart to see their sad, expressionless faces and it quite spoilt my trip around the market because I couldn't stop thinking and worrying about them.

We sauntered round the market and went deeper and deeper into the fascinating labyrinth of stalls brimming over with exquisite silks, brocades and silverware; spices, furs, leatherware, brass, carpets — everything was how I had always imagined it would be.

Sylvia and I each bought a brocade and silk kaftan to use in our act back in England, to knock the mens' eyes out, we agreed. They were a beautiful shade of blue with slits up each side and silk braiding all round the hems. I also bought a kaftan for Vera which was a lovely pale lemon colour. I didn't know where on earth she could wear her kaftan but I did know that she would be thrilled to receive it.

We soon got the hang of bartering but it all seemed such a waste of time and energy to me — why couldn't they just put a price on the goods and leave it at that? Still, I enjoyed taking part all the same and I felt quite triumphant when I brought the price down and the stallholder put his hand to his head, rolled his eyes and pretended to look distressed.

All four of us came out of the market heavily laden with goods. Our guide moved in closer.

"You give two pounds," he held up two fingers and jiggled some money which he had in his pocket. "Plenty good bargains ... I good boy ... you give boy two pounds."

"One pound," Ron held out the money, "one pound, English money." The boy edged away and replied, "two pounds ... you give two pounds."

"Come on you little sod," Ron looked annoyed, "one pound and that's all you're getting."

The boy would not take the money but still held up two fingers and jiggled the coins in his pocket. His obsequious smile was quickly fading.

"Oh well then ... if you don't want it." Ron put the money back into his wallet and started to walk away from the boy.

We all followed behind Ron. I was very embarrassed and tried to look as though I wasn't with the rest of the party. I would have gladly given the poor kid another pound but I decided to stay out of things because after all, I thought, they did seem to barter over everything.

The boy followed behind us calling something out in Arabic. Ron turned to face the boy and offered the pound note once again. This time the boy snatched at the money and then to my amazement spat at us and shouted, "You bastards! ... filthy bastards! ... Eengaleesh pigs and swine!"

Don't know who his language teacher is, I thought, but he certainly had quite a good command of the English language. Despite his outburst I still felt sorry for him. What a way to earn a living — grovelling to foreigners — using his brothers and sisters as bait. Once again I realised how very lucky I was and felt terribly humble.

★ ★ ★ ★ ★ ★ ★ ★ ★ ★ ★ ★ ★ ★ ★

We arrived back at the ship in time for afternoon tea. Freshly baked cream cakes, warm scones straight from the oven, white and brown bread and a variety of jams.

I sank into a comfortable chair and slipped my feet out of my sandals. The hot strong tea revived me and I smiled across at my three companions and said, "What a day, eh? I've enjoyed myself very much ... especially round the market. The market was thrilling, thank you both for taking us."

"Yes, thank you," Sylvia joined in, "it was smashing." She reached for a chocolate eclair. "They've arranged for some of the locals to entertain the passengers this evening. We've got the night off, haven't we, Helen? You'll be all right," she nodded at Jeff and Ron, "they've got some belly-dancers coming aboard."

"Oh, I don't know," Jeff leaned towards her, "I'd sooner look at your belly."

★ ★ ★ ★ ★ ★ ★ ★ ★ ★ ★ ★ ★ ★ ★

Later that evening Jeff and Ron nearly lost their eyeballs watching the belly-dancers. The dancing-girls writhed about to passionate, blood-stirring music which brought lustful looks to every man's face. It seemed to me to be a much sexier performance than that of the strippers at the air-base. The movements of the dancers seemed far more suggestive and the eastern music added to the sensuousness of the dancing.

We women got our own back because after the girls had finished their performance we were then treated to some dancing by male belly-dancers. And oh — how their bellies danced. Their lithe, undulating bodies moved sensuously in time to the music. Their movements were very suggestive and each dancer looked as though he was taking part in a collective love act. Faster and faster they danced — trance-like as though under the influence of some magic spell.

Sylvia gazed at them with her lips slightly open and a lustful expression on her face. I knew how she felt — the dancers had stirred something in my body — I felt very sexy indeed.

Sylvia leaned towards me when the music stopped and whispered, "I'll bet they make wonderful lovers. Did you clock their movements? I wouldn't mind a basinful of that one nearest the band. Ooooh ... blimey ... did you notice his hips?"

"I noticed more than his hips," I replied, "a night with him and you'd know about

127

it."

Sylvia closed her eyes and let out a deep sigh, "Oooh, Helen, don't!"

After the cabaret Sylvia and I went to the open air dance with Jeff and Ron in tow. There was to be a late night supper served on deck, weather permitting, and some of the officers were going to serve the food to the passengers.

The weather was perfect for a deck party and everything went well. The food was delicious and there were lots of iced drinks to help cool everybody down.

I danced and danced — no sooner had one man escorted me back to my seat than another was bending over me, smiling and pointing towards the dance-floor. Although Sylvia and I had sort of, teamed up with Jeff and Ron, neither man seemed to mind our popularity with other men, they danced with us when they had the chance and in between times stood at the bar or helped themselves to more of the delicious food.

I noticed to my amusement, that Terry steered well clear of me but now and then, as he danced by in the arms of yet another unsuspecting female I caught snatches of his cultured best behaviour voice as he acted out the part of an officer and a gentleman. What games we all play, I thought, as I caught sight of one of the loveliest skies I had ever seen. The moon was almost full and it was surrounded by a sky crammed full with stars — the moon was like the star-of-the-show and the stars were the supporting cast. It made me feel very romantic and once again I thought of a song. 'Blue Moon'. I refused to feel blue and gave a dazzling smile to an elderly gentleman who asked me to dance. It was all so romantic dancing on board ship, underneath the beautiful sky, surrounded by elegant beautiful people.

I felt a tiny pull at my heart and thought I knew the reason for my sudden melancholia. I needed someone to love. But how did I find that someone?

I looked at the smiling face of my partner. He seemed to be managing all right without love — and so was Sylvia. You'll have to stop being so soft, I told myself, enjoy what you've got — and what you've got some girls would give anything to have.

Later that night, as I lay in my bunk, my legs and feet felt as though they were still dancing. The dancing had worn me out completely. I fell asleep as soon as I had said my prayers and didn't even hear Sylvia when she arrived back from the dance or wherever she had come back from.

★ ★ ★ ★ ★ ★ ★ ★ ★ ★ ★ ★ ★ ★ ★

The mornings, afternoons and evenings fused together into one long round of excitement and fun. The ship stopped at Las Palmas and Gibraltar. Ron and Jeff escorted us ashore and unbelievably, one night, we once again came across Lucky in a bar singing 'I'm forever blowing bubbles'.

Sylvia and I both agreed that on this cruise we had laughed enough to last us a lifetime. And when you're young and healthy there does seem to be a lot of humour in things, I thought, and also having plenty of money to spend gives you lots to smile about.

We arrived back at Southampton and said our goodbyes to Ron and Jeff, and all the other lovely people we had become acquainted with during the cruise.

We agreed to meet Ron and Jeff for a meal when we came back from the second trip and Ron invited us to stay at his place over Christmas but of course we couldn't accept due to all our commitments.

The ship was due to leave again on the same day, it stayed in port just long enough to load up with food and pick up the new passengers. Sylvia and I went ashore for a couple of hours to have a look round the shops.

I liked Southampton very much. It was clean and tidy and the locals were friendly and helpful.

The ship set sail once again and as I watched the shores of Southampton disappearing for the second time I still felt excited but not as much as the first time. The first thrill that could never be recaptured. Maybe that's how rich people feel about things, I thought, bored with cruising on luxury ships, flying in aeroplanes, riding in expensive cars. I supposed it must get rather monotonous having everything.

Much better to have just one cruise in your lifetime, one expensive diamond ring and one haute coutùre outfit you felt a million dollars wearing.

I remembered once again how I had felt when Sylvia and I had rehearsed for the first time — nothing as thrilling as it had been with Rita. Still, who knows that might happen in the next three weeks — a lot of new things could happen for the first time, I thought excitedly.

CHAPTER EIGHTEEN

Sylvia came rushing into the cabin, her eyes were shining and she looked very excited about something.

"I've got a surprise for you ... come on ... come with me to the top deck."

"Why? ... tell me why," I tried to slow her enthusiasm down. We had just eaten dinner, the first dinner of our second cruise and I had gone back to our cabin to clean my teeth before going up to the ballroom for a look at the new set of passengers.

"There's somebody on board I want you to see." Sylvia started to laugh, "you won't believe your eyes ... come on, Helen, hurry up."

I followed Sylvia up to the top deck and she led the way towards the bar which was situated at the side of the ballroom.

It can't be! It can't be! I looked at the group of people standing round the bar. The hat was unmistakeable. It was 'George the Hat'. He was actually on board.

"He was just as surprised as I was when we saw each other," Sylvia giggled, "I recognised him immediately because of his hat. He brought us a drink remember ... when we sang at Jack Sargent's club the other week."

"Is Jack Sargent on board?" I looked round to see if I could see him.

"Yes, but George says he's ill. As soon as the ship started to move poor old Jack was sea-sick. He's in his cabin having a lie down."

"Well, they say truth's stranger than fiction." I felt pleased knowing that Jack was on board. I hoped he wouldn't have to stay too long in bed. The ship's doctor would probably fix him up with something.

"Hello there, girls." George grinned at us. "Can't get away from us nohow, can you? What'll you have to drink?"

Sylvia and I accepted his offer of a drink and chatted to him for a while.

"I agreed to come with some of my golfing pals," George explained. "This is Bill ... and Arthur ... and Cyril. Meet the Dumonte Sisters, lads. Helen ... and Sylvia." George introduced us to each other. "You can take your pick, girls. We're all bachelors and all willing-and-able." His three companions moved closer and Cyril piped up, "I'm willing, girls, but I don't know whether I'd be able or not." All the men roared with laughter.

The walk around the Southampton shops had tired me so I decided to retire early. Sylvia, always brimming over with energy said she would have a wander into the ballroom, see the latest talent. I told her to be quiet when she came back to the cabin and then meandered back to 'E' deck to the luxury of an early night and a good book. I poured myself a large gin from the stock Sylvia and I had built up from our various trips ashore and snuggled down into my bunk.

★ ★ ★ ★ ★ ★ ★ ★ ★ ★ ★ ★ ★ ★ ★ ★ ★

The next morning Sylvia and I were introduced to Frank Winters by the entertainments' officer. Frank was handsome in a skinny sort of way, with hair cut very short which showed off the delicate lines of his cheek bones. He had a very pale complexion which accentuated the dark blue of his eyes and a low, infectious laugh which I found very sexy.

Frank had a baritone voice, he told us, and sang ballads and songs from the shows. It was his first engagement on a ship and he showed the same enthusiasm as Sylvia and I had first experienced.

"We'll show you round," Sylvia smiled at him and practised her feminine wiles. "We'll look after you won't we, Helen? And if you want to go ashore we know all the best places. Casablanca's got a fabulous market hasn't it, Helen?" She linked her arm through his as we walked round the deck, indicating 'hands off' to any other woman on board who might be interested in Frank.

Frank told us a little about himself as we showed him around the ship. "I'm divorced ... the wife got custody of our little girl."

"Oh, I am sorry," said Sylvia, looking exceptionally happy.

"They live in London, with the wife's new boyfriend." Frank went on. "He's got plenty of money so I know my little girl's looked after O.K." He shrugged his shoulders and added, "So I'm perfectly free you see, to take engagements like these. I auditioned for 'Sea Stars' when they held a talent night in Barnsley where I live."

"Oh, have you got a house in Barnsley?" Sylvia looked very interested.

"I share a terraced house with a friend of mine who's in the same boat. He's divorced ... he's an old school pal of mine. He's a driving instructor, does very well."

Sylvia looked less enthusiastic when she heard about the house sharing arrangement, I thought, but who knows what was going on in her scheming, female mind?

I decided to leave them together because I felt the odd man out. I went back to the cabin and put on my fur coat because the wind had a cool bite; the sea threw itself at the side of the ship and blue skies remained hidden beneath a steel grey curtain. It was Bay of Biscay weather. Poor old Jack, I thought, as the ship roller-coasted over the gigantic waves.

★ ★ ★ ★ ★ ★ ★ ★ ★ ★ ★ ★ ★ ★ ★

The days of our second cruise seemed to be shorter than those of our first one. Always plenty of things to occupy the time, that's if you didn't want to laze around in the sunshine which I often did.

Jack Sargent surfaced from his cabin on the day the ship rounded Cape Torinana — left the Bay of Biscay behind. I was walking round the top deck getting some fresh air when I spotted Jack sitting in a deck-chair in a corner sheltered from the wind.

"Hello there, Helen," he greeted me enthusiastically, "George told me you were on board." He pointed to a deck-chair at the side of him. "Come and sit down ... I'll order coffee." He winced and added, "I'm just getting back to normal. Couldn't face anything to eat or drink. I wouldn't have come on the cruise if I'd known I was such a rotten sailor."

"You look O.K. now though, Jack. You'll be all right now we've left the Bay of Biscay behind."

"Yes, but I've got to face the blighter when we go back round it again." Jack signalled to a waiter and ordered coffee.

"It's a marvellous ship, Jack. They've thought of everything. I never realised there was so much going on aboard these ships."

"You've landed yourselves a nice little number, haven't you! Free holiday and plenty of sunshine." He nodded towards the cloudless blue sky. "I'm going to do a spot of swimming this afternoon."

We sipped our coffees and then I had a thought, a curious thought.

"Jack?"

"Uum?"

"Jack ... why does George always wear his hat everywhere?" Jack laughed at the question and replied, "Some woman once told him he looked like Humphrey Bogart, when he had his hat on. He's worn it ever since."

"Oh, I thought it was because he was bald." I had another thought and laughed, "He'll have to take it off when he goes swimming."

"Don't you believe it." Jack grinned and added, "Talking of swimming ... would you like to join me this afternoon ... when I go for a swim?"

"Yes, all right. If we swim about half-past three that'll give us plenty of time before afternoon tea. They do lovely afternoon tea, Jack. Plenty of fresh-cream cakes and home-made scones fresh out the oven."

"Oh don't!" Jack pulled a face. "Have a heart, Helen ... don't mention fresh-cream to me, not just yet."

I arranged to meet him near the pool. We couldn't have lunch together because he and his friends were allocated seats in the 'B' deck restaurant. And anyway, I thought, I expect he wouldn't want very much to eat, not at the moment.

After we had drunk our coffees Jack and I closed our eyes and lazily basked in the warm sunshine. It was a lovely feeling, lying there with the sun caressing my face and the gentle sway of the ship lulling me to sleep. And it was nice being with Jack, I thought, I liked him very much. I fell asleep thinking nice thoughts about Jack.

★ ★ ★ ★ ★ ★ ★ ★ ★ ★ ★ ★ ★ ★ ★

On the evening before the ship docked at Las Palmas, an Old Tyme Music Hall had been arranged by the ship's officers. Everyone on board was invited to take part and there was to be a prize for the best outfits.

Frank, Sylvia and I decided to perform a combined Old Tyme act. Frank could sing in our key quite easily so I harmonised and he sang straight with Sylvia. We practised some old songs and they sounded rather good, I thought.

Lucky made a boater out of cardboard and crepe paper for Frank, and for Sylvia and me, two of the loveliest hats I had ever seen. Mine was deep pink with a huge brim and covered with large paper roses and Sylvia's was a boater in purple with a silver rose at the front and purple crepe streamers floating down behind. He was a genius — it must have taken him ages to make our hats.

To complete my outfit I wore a high necked white lace blouse and a full length pink velvet skirt — I looked like a real Edwardian lady. Sylvia chose to wear a bright purple dress which was trimmed with silver lace.

Frank pencilled a moustache on himself and put a crepe paper flower in his buttonhole. The band-leader announced our act as 'Berlington Bertie and his Ladies'.

"We sounded very good, didn't we?" Frank looked pleased, "did you hear the applause we got? I reckon we ought to be on television with our talent."

Sylvia's imagination got cracking. "Yes, perhaps we could team up now and then. Jimmy Cook and Dave McGuire could get work for a threesome. Hey ... we could work the boats if we got some dance routines worked out. Can you do a soft-shoe-shuffle, Frank?"

"I can learn to do anything, love ... if the money's right."

"Might take you up on it, Frank." I stored the idea away at the back of my mind. After all, I thought, he didn't live too far away.

I didn't see very much of 'George the Hat' because he and his friends had got themselves fixed up with some landladies from Birmingham, but Jack seemed to seek out my company more and more. We swam together, relaxed in the sunshine, and danced together, the latter being most enjoyable because he was a very accomplished ballroom dancer.

On the day the ship docked at Casablanca, Jack asked if I would like to accompany him on one of the special trips organised by the cruise operators. As it was my night off — the belly dancers were coming on board once again — I was delighted to accept his invitation.

The evening went well. A taxi escorted us to a magnificent hotel which nestled high up in the hillside. The opulence inside the hotel was breathtaking. Elegant furniture; tastefully decorated; huge twinkling glass chandeliers; and first class service from the waiters and bar staff.

After the meal, Jack and I danced to soft romantic guitar music. He held me closer than he had done previously when we were dancing and I found myself responding to the obvious sexual advances.

"Helen ... I've been thinking."

"Thinking what?"

"My two clubs are doing very well and I've been thinking of expanding my interests. I've been to look at two more clubs that have come on the market. I'm going to buy one of them ... and that's for definite. And the other one ... well maybe."

"You'll be a very rich man then, Jack?"

"One day I hope. But I've got a lot of planning to do. The money's in nightclubs. I want to open a couple of nightclubs. Late night drinking's the thing nowadays, Helen. There's plenty of money about. These are the golden years, Helen. You mark my words. You'll look back on the fifties and sixties as the best years of your life."

"Well they will be, Jack. These are the years of my youth. You can't buy time, can you?"

"No ... I mean everybody. There's plenty of good jobs going. Look how many people have got cars. Only doctors and people with loads of dough could afford cars before the war. Now look at the roads. Everybody's got a car."

"I haven't." I was flippant.

"You know what I'm on about, Helen. Anyway, as I was telling you ... I'm going to expand. How would you like to have a resident booking at my new club?. I'm going to have strippers on every Sunday lunchtime. You can be my resident singer. I'll pay well.".

"I'll bear it in mind." I wanted time to think. Appearing with strippers every Sunday lunchtime was not my idea of the bigtime. Still, it was money and I wouldn't have far to travel. Jack read my mind.

"You could have a taxi out to the club and charge it up to me. I'll run you home after the show," he smiled shyly and added, "or perhaps you could come and have lunch at my place afterwards? You could come and sample some of my cooking. Or perhaps you could do a spot of cooking?"

I thought about his nice home and the more I thought about his idea the more I liked the sound of it.

"I'd certainly be able to work Sunday lunchtime. Yes, I'd like to accept, Jack."

We returned to our table and Jack ordered more drinks. He smiled at me over the rim of his glass and there was romance in his look. And then — suddenly — I knew I had found the answer. I needed someone like Jack! A man with character and charisma. An older man I could depend on — trust with my problems.

It had taken me a long, long time to find out what I needed from a relationship and I had had to travel all the way to Casablanca before I found the answer. Now what was it Humphrey Bogart had said in that marvellous film? Oh, I couldn't remember, but I reckoned that at this moment I knew how Ingrid Bergman had felt.

★ ★ ★ ★ ★ ★ ★ ★ ★ ★ ★ ★ ★ ★ ★

Our second trip was over and we were plunged back into the cacophony of roaring traffic, throngs of people frantically shopping for Christmas presents, and worst of all, a bitterly cold December complete with fog.

Frank and Sylvia had promised to keep in touch, and Jack and I had made a date for the following Monday evening when I was free from any singing commitments.

Sunday evening, Sylvia and I had accepted another booking at the Glass Bowl. It was rather a comedown from a cruise ship but I quite looked forward to the booking because I knew the audience were enthusiastic about the act.

We had done our first spot and were sitting at a table near to the huge coal-fire. The usual ribald remarks were coming our way from the old men and some of the youths. I parried the sexy innuendoes with a few witticisms of my own and Sylvia joined in the fun. Suddenly, she said, "Oh by the way, Helen ... I'm going to team up with Frank. I hope you don't mind, but we've got some really terrific ideas for a new act."

I stared at her open-mouthed and then answered. "Thanks for letting me know. And when did this top-level decision occur then?"

"It all came about from when we sang those music hall songs. Frank thought it'd be a smashing idea to team up as a duo."

"You planned this aboard the ship then?" I felt angry now.

"Sort of," she looked down at her feet, "and we've got a thing going between us you know."

"Oh, really!"

"He's asked me to go and live with him."

"He's not mentioned marriage then?" I was sarcastic and couldn't help myself. "And what about the driving instructor?"

"He'll have to find himself another garage." Sylvia laughed at her own joke. "Frank and me are going to dress up like Fred Astaire and Ginger Rogers. People love to see you dress up. And we're going to sing love duets ... from the shows. We've been

134

actising holding hands and gazing into one another's eyes. I burst out laughing, but I ppose I'll be all right in front of an audience."

"I'm sure whatever you do you'll be all right," I answered. "And what have you told Tony? I suppose you have mentioned it to him?"

"Oh, there was never anything much between me and Tony. He's nice enough, but he's got no 'go' in him. I only wanted him as a friend. And he came in handy for lifts, didn't he?"

I was disgusted with her last remark and said, "I'd better start looking for another partner then ... let Jimmy Cook and Dave McGuire know."

"Oh thanks, Helen. You'll let them know then?" She looked relieved. "You see, i'm going next Friday." The last bomb-shell landed on my head. "Isn't it all exciting?"

For the rest of the evening I could hardly bear to speak to her.

After all the hard work I had put into our act. It seemed as though I was fated not to have a steady partner. I would have to face up to going solo again. The trouble with my nerves would get better, I told myself, it was all a matter of experience. Perhaps I could get another booking on a cruise!

That night the telephone rang, it was Jack. I told him the news about Sylvià and Frank.

"What about Rita?" he suggested, "I thought you said Rita wanted to get back to singing again?"

"Yes, she did say that, but I'm not sure she meant what she said."

"There's only one way to find out, Helen. Give her a ring tomorrow."

"You always fancied Rita didn't you, Jack?" I felt jealous. There was silence for a while before Jack answered, "But it was you I wanted." His voice sounded husky and full of emotion. "It was always you, but I thought I didn't stand a chance with you."

"Goodnight, darling."

"Goodnight, Helen. See you Monday."

I replaced the receiver and looked forward to Monday so much.

★ ★ ★ ★ ★ ★ ★ ★ ★ ★ ★ ★ ★ ★ ★ ★

"So that's it then, Rita ... you'll have your big come-back next Friday." I ordered two large gin and tonics and grinned at my friend. "Hey, the gin brings back memories, Rita. Can you remember how we used to pinch old Ray Bowler's gin?"

"Yes, and can you remember how he used to pinch our behinds?" We giggled and sucked on the slices of lemon peel impaled on cocktail-sticks.

A large figure loomed in the doorway of the pub lounge, then it wobbled across the room towards us.

"There you are, my dears," Jimmy Cook's familiar voice boomed out at us, "and how are you, Rita?" He looked her up and down appreciatively. "Still a lovely girl ... plenty of meat on you I see." He ordered a large brandy for himself and two refills for us. "Back together again then? Oh ... by the way," his eyes sparkled with mischief as he looked across at the bar, "do you like cocktails, girls?"

"Yes," we chorussed.

He leaned closer and replied, "Have you heard this one?" His belly bounced up and down as he roared with laughter.

Like old times, I thought happily, as I looked at Rita and Jimmy. There was nothing

on earth as exciting as showbusiness. It had become my whole life — I wanted nothi[ng]
more. Well, perhaps someone to love, and I think I had found that someone. I sipp[ed]
my drink and thought how lucky I was.

I SANG FOR MY SUPPER AND OH ... WHAT A FEAST!